Painted Ghosts

Neil Beardmore

PNEUMA SPRINGS PUBLISHING UK

First Published in 2021 by:
Pneuma Springs Publishing

Painted Ghosts
Copyright © 2021Neil Beardmore
ISBN13: 9781782284796

Neil Beardmore has asserted his right under the Copyright, Designs and Patents Act, 1988, to be identified as Author of this Work

British Library Cataloguing in Publication Data. A catalogue record for this book is available from the British Library.

Pneuma Springs Publishing
A Subsidiary of Pneuma Springs Ltd.
7 Groveherst Road, Dartford Kent, DA1 5JD.
E: admin@pneumasprings.co.uk
W: www.pneumasprings.co.uk

Cover illustration from an original painting by Neil Beardmore

For Ashra

I wander through life,
With the searching mind,
That is never at rest,
Till I reach the shade
Of my lover's door.

Sappho

ACKNOWLEDGEMENTS

Many thanks go to my wife Ashra for editorial help, her invaluable reading for detail and authenticity and guiding me through difficult patches. Long term friend and astute novelist Guy Russell's input went beyond the editorial, being a mentor helping me fully realise and develop themes and ideas. Catherine Rubin Kermorgant consistently helped with detail about Devadasi temple prostitutes and her remarkable page-turner of a book *Servants of the Goddess* (ISBN 978 81 8400 462 5) about her work with Devadasi women in Karnataka was my bible. Michael Yorke whose documentary *Eunuchs: India's Third Gender* on hijra transgender peoples was an inspiration; I'm grateful for all his support and being there to answer my questions. My thanks go out to the hijra community, to those I saw at weddings in India, and in particular to the one who danced a blessing for my nephew — then a baby — in the Himalayas, who was an inspiration for *A View of Glass Mountains*. Jananne Rahman, Anil Goutam, Sukhi Kaur, Kaiyden Hinds and Neetu Nair of Questors Theatre, London and their support workers all contributed to the stage play version of *A View of Glass Mountains* and thus helped shape the final piece. I'm fortunate to enjoy the life long unconditional support of my brother Alan, his partner Jane and cousin Sue. Rupesh in Palolem, Goa has been a great friend and helpful source of accurate information. Leslie Tate and Sue Hampton consistently promote my work on radio and other live events. Other people who have given continuous support and encouragement include Paul Fitzgerald and his wife Linda, Mick and Guler, John Marshall, Carol Barac, Dick Hancock and Bedford Poetry Cafe, Toddington Poetry Society, Ouse Muse, Bob Devereux and all at the Frug in St Ives, and New Bradwell Writing group. Hilda Morley and Pam Weaving-Hadad travelled miles to Questors Theatre in support. Apu and Cynthia Bagchi have guided me with readings and pointers. Anil Goutam, Patricia Cunningham, Debbie Murray, Guy Russell all helped in the stage version of *The Garden of Izzat Baig* which went out as a fund raiser for the Globe Theatre. Many others consistently offer support: Viki, Shi, Kush, Gil, Frankie and Rod. Matt Goulden is remembered for his friendship and encouragement along with other supporters who are no longer with us: Ashan, Sabiha, Lance, Andy, Michael and Didier. And of course Mum and Dad.

CONTENTS

PAINTED GHOSTS

Neil Beardmore

1

'This is the book I wanted you to have.' Tommy pushed strands of brown hair away from his forehead. 'This is what I wanted to show you.'

'Wow.' She threw the gold wrapping aside.

'You only get one sixteenth birthday.' He was tall, always wore jeans in the studio, tight fitting round the waist but widely flared at the ankles. His dark green shirt with rounded collar had smudges of paint across the front. 'I signed it, look — ' He flipped open the front and she could just make out his scrawl: *'To Daphne from Tommy. Enjoy. My best student. And paint loads more. June 73.'*

'Indian Art. It's wonderful, Tommy.'

Daphne watched his grey eyes as he enthusiastically flicked through. He was more of a friend than someone her father had selected to teach her how to paint; he had talents she wanted for herself.

His little studio was a rickety conservatory which he constantly apologised about, saying when he sold more work he would get somewhere much more flashy. Sitting together on the divan with worn purple covering near a couple of easels, they laughed about him becoming famous and he joked about being too old. A small table was overflowing with brushes, tubes of paint, pallets and bottles of Turps. The abstract shapes of used paint on old pallets fascinated her — how the colours had come together randomly to form images to explore.

'You're only in your thirties,' she said and he laughed louder. 'It's still young enough.' She had on her new blue flower patterned skirt and cream coloured cotton top.

'Even you think I'm ancient, Daph.' He was still laughing, his grey eyes searching her face. His nose was long and straight and his shoulder length light brown hair hung in straggly waves. His smile seemed genuine to her, lit up his eyes, and it was that that drew her to him. 'But it's this, look at this.' He took the book gently from her and flicked the pages. 'This—' He opened out a page to reveal a photograph of a wall painting of two Indian women. 'Indian princesses. Just look at their eyes, so sensuously done.'

Each was adorned with gold necklaces, intricate tiaras with diamonds and pearls, and lotus flowers seemed to flutter round the younger one like butterflies. They had been posed naturally, both with hair tightly wound in a bun with flowers at the back of the head. The woman to the left, who seemed to Daphne to be the younger, was staring over to the right passed her sister who was looking downwards coyly, her breasts uncovered.

'But the eyes don't follow you as you move around.' Daphne was excited. 'They are both looking outwardly,' she paused, 'but strangely, mysteriously, looking inwardly as well.'

'Yes, you've got it,' he said, 'you've seen the melancholy in the elder girl's expression.'

'Is it melancholy? Or is she looking down respectfully, with a kind of reverence or something.'

'Or doesn't she really fancy that prince that's lined up for her.'

They laughed.

'There's more to it than that though,' she said, studying them. 'Their eyes do tell a story. They have seen a lot and know many things. Things they cannot talk about — not in their society anyway.'

'That's what I like about you, you see art how it should be seen. This is Ajanta, Daph. We've got to go. The only known Buddhist cave paintings, before they got into sculpture big time. Some of the caves were temples, others monasteries. It says look, they were created over a long period: around 200 BC to 650 AD. Can you imagine them preparing the surface with a thick layer of clay and then a lime coating. Then painting in fresco on the wet surface. Aren't they just, I mean — the images of animals and plants on the ceilings. And there, the images of the Buddha, youthful and slim, with fantastic head dresses. They used a limited pallet: red and yellow from ochres; green from volcanic rocks; white was kaolin or gypsum based; lapis lazuli blue from central Asia. And lamp-black. How they could make such beautiful images. Not just of stories of the young Buddha, but pictures of the courts of the time. The two princesses: the detail, the gold earrings, bracelets, anklets—'

'That's how we want to paint, isn't it?' She laughed looking in his eyes a moment. 'Can we go there? Can we see it? Together?'

He quietened, letting a finger slide through the hair hanging over her cheek and drew it back. 'That little nose of yours. Those large meaningful pupils of yours, dark brown to almost black — just like the young princesses. Perfectly aligned eyebrows. Silky light brown hair, almost blond. That's why I wanted to paint you. Yes, that was it. Like the younger princess in the photo.'

She liked the gentle way he played with her hair. She was growing to know life, to know her body and its attractions to him; he already knew the world and could take her places and she was glad.

'I'm nothing like them,' she laughed. 'I can't compare to them.'

He leaned closer to her. 'What I see in you is as special as those princesses.' He brought her chin to him with a delicate touch and pecked her lips.

Trembling, she fell away chattering. 'This is the inside of the temple?'

'Buddhist temples cut in caves in the cliff face along a river.'

'Look at this figure.' She was confused, pushing back a longing for him and frightened and embarrassed by it. 'At the

11

back, as though she is actually part of the tree.' A young woman with full breasts had coiled her left leg and left arm around a sturdy sapling, while her right hand reached overhead holding a branch. Her long black hair hung in a single braid below her waist and she wore a wide gold necklace and strips of bangles above her wrists and her ankles. Like the princesses, she gazed aside, although to Daphne she appeared more deliberately sensual than them. 'It's like she reminds me of somebody. Like—'

'Beautiful,' he almost whispered now. 'Like you. Maybe.' He laughed then. 'A past life.' She watched him without smiling. 'You were a courtesan in the court of a great king, a Raja,' he went on, gesticulating, 'or you were a model for a painter so he could make a depiction on the wall.' He paused deliberately. 'Perhaps you were his lover.'

'You—' she pushed him playfully, keeping her eyes on the young woman caught erotically around the tree with a faint alluring smile. 'She's got a smile like the Mona Lisa. You know, the high cheek bones. I'm sure I've seen her before.'

'And you know, like the smile of Hendrickje Stoffels in Rembrandt's *A Woman Bathing*. Yes, just like that. It's in the National, I will take you. It's a place we can always meet, by the woman bathing.' Tommy drew her into a kiss, pressing his tongue inside her mouth. She leaned back slightly, taking him in, enjoying the sensation. An artist, he would be in demand from many women, but he wanted her and she was ready to go further.

The muffled sounds of children's laughter and yells echoed through the place, followed by the richer tones of a female voice.

He ended the kiss abruptly and she was shocked by the break, trying to control her emotions, wanting more. Looking down at the picture she wondered whether the young woman would leap from the tree and sing and dance. Or, would she bring a warning of some kind? She was a ghost, this figure on the tree, some sort of painted ghost.

'Jenny's home with the kids,' he smiled as though nothing had happened. 'Lesson is over —'

*****

The long divan they made love on was covered in a purple fabric dominated by rich paisley patterns that swirled like constellations. He showed her moves, made her shine, but first he would arrange her naked in pose, paint until he could not resist touch, then he would come to her slowly, embracing her and kissing her face, her neck, her breasts, her body and as she gasped for him, he came to her, flowing into her and through her. So she rode on in wave after wave, finding herself rising to a plateau of completion, and yelling and gasping, and laughing with the joy of it.

'We can run together,' he told her as they lay close under a blanket. Their easels stood ahead of them, their tripod legs spread so they appeared like strangers watching them. 'Off to the south of France. See Arles where Van Gogh painted, and Collioure where Matisse went while the First World War raged —'

'But India, the painted ghosts —' Daphne stroked his cheek. 'Like in the book. Those strange and beautiful men and women, the gods. It's so different from anything we know in the west.'

'Painted Ghosts.' He turned the expression over. 'I like that.'

She watched his lips as he mouthed the words, his chin rising and falling, questioning to herself whether he would leave his wife and daughters.

'We'll run, Daphne.' He seemed not to notice the worries in her expression. 'We won't take anything. We can buy paints and canvases wherever we go.'

'Run, run,' she laughed. 'Run, and run, and run —'

'Yes —'

The world would open out for her, she would paint and

draw with him and travel. She would meet her ghosts and pay homage. One day she would paint like the ancient craftsmen at Ajanta over a millennium and a half ago, she would have skills others would covet. She would learn and so would become known and valued. Tommy would guide her.

'Enjoy this moment,' Tommy told her. 'Enjoy every sensation. We can be whoever we want to be.'

She laughed. They kissed. In him, his body and mind, she had everything. She laughed again.

'You should be grateful to your father,' he laughed with her. 'He sent you to me. He thinks he's a good painter, but he's not that special you know.'

'He is.' Riled, she pulled the blanket to her chin. 'I know all his work: landscapes and figures. He's famous for his Life studies — and he's starting to sell some. He tells my mum he's going to make it. My mum's aunt left her a lot of money so she lets him get on with it while they can afford it. And she says she'll carry on working in the office until he's got there. There's no need to be jealous of him—'

Tommy ignored her challenge. 'Why doesn't he teach you himself?'

'He's busy, he hasn't got the time,' she defended him. 'Anyway, he knows you're a good painter and you're a teacher. He's got no patience, he would be shouting at me all the time.'

'Or maybe you'd get in the way of all his glamorous models.' Tommy leaned back and she loathed his arrogant manner. 'There's lots of things you don't know about your sweet daddy. Are you spoiled by him? Is he the bestest daddy in the world?' He smirked at her, his breath on her cheek.

'Stop it, you.'

'It gets around, you know.'

She was aware again of the easels around them. Beyond, the little table overflowed with paints and pots.

'I don't think you're so innocent as you look, Daphne. You

surely can't be completely ignorant of what your sweet daddy gets up to with his models.'

'Like you?' She poked his nose. She defended her father because she thought she had to but they weren't close. He was a figure who appeared at meal times, talked incessantly about his achievements, showing little interest in her art, and when cornered by her mum turned on the charm.

'He's not as good as you,' he said.

'What on canvas, or in bed?' Laughing nervously, she hid her feelings of anger and confusion as she tried to work out why Tommy was attacking her father.

'Now you're being sordid,' he laughed.

'How do you know all this anyway?'

'Samantha told me.'

'She's one of yours, is she?' she said, still on edge.

'Daphne. Now you're showing your age. It's all round the local Arts Society, everyone knows.'

'Samantha comes round here and takes her clothes off for you, and you tell me I'm special?'

'I've told you, we'll run.' He smiled. 'That makes you very special indeed.' He paused, took up a packet of cigarettes, eased one out and lit it. 'But your daddy is a very naughty man—'

'And you're different?' She concluded it was a clash of male egos.

'My wife and I don't see eye to eye. Never did really. We met too young and bang, suddenly you've got a kid. It's not like I'm cheating on her, like your dad's cheating on your mum. I'm going to be honest, tell Jenny we're together, and off we go—'

'You make it sound like she won't mind.'

'She knows it's over. We just don't connect anymore. For your dad, it's different, he's not going to give up your mum — not with that big inheritance — he depends on her.'

She played out a scene at home, mum doing everything for

dad. He painted and did nothing else and Daphne wondered whether her mother had the strength to stand up to him. Daphne had not made a secret of that to Tommy. But she felt the conflict of loving a father with flaws.

The unfinished painting Tommy had done of her was sketchy, but accurate. She liked how he had used white to make the outlines blurred and misty, and to mellow the harsh tones to pastel pinks and blues and greens. It made her shiver to reflect on his talent, and how much she loved him.

When she got back home from college several days later Daphne's mum and dad were sitting at the kitchen table looking up at her silently.

'Sit down, Daphne.' Her mother gestured. A tall woman with her hair in short curls, her skin was always pale, as though she never went outside. Daphne often tried to get her to put on more make up, to rouge her cheeks, make herself less ghost-like.

'What's happened? Has somebody died?'

Her father sat motionless, his shoulders hunched. Today he did not seem to have that sparkle about him that charmed her. Whereas her mother sat upright, her body stiff, his shoulders slouched forward. She wore tight fitting blouses and skirts to the office; he had on jeans and a paint-flecked T-shirt.

Daphne had often wondered how such opposites had come together. And beyond that, how they had rubbed their bodies together and created her. Perhaps they had only ever done it once.

Perhaps too, what Tommy had said about her dad was right, that he could find nothing in Daphne's mother's arms, and looked for love and acceptance in other places.

'No, don't be silly now,' mum continued. 'This is good news. Your father is starting up a business.'

'But he's an artist, and he's getting a name.' Daphne looked at her father expecting him to resist her mother, but as she stared at him he turned his eyes away. Daphne had a sinking feeling of sadness filled with anger. She knew the artist in her father, felt the meaning of every brushstroke he made. They were the same. She took in the contrasting body language of both. Then she looked at her mother. It was obvious to Daphne now: her mum had found out about his affairs with models. That was it.

'Tell her, Arnold.' Mum tapped the table impatiently. He would not look up. She was distant and unknown to Daphne, her façade solid and impenetrable; you had to work out what she thought and felt, and the sound her words made was sometimes hard and brittle. 'Dad and I have decided it would be better and more financially viable to run a shop selling art materials. You know I've had this dream for ages, Daphne and I've been looking into it. There's lots of opportunities in the High Street — I've found an empty shop that's just right. Behind the scenes I've had help and advice and looked at the viability. Now that my mum and dad have gone and I have some money to invest, it makes sense and will be better all round.'

Daphne was speechless for a moment, looking to her father for a response, but he showed no emotion and said nothing. 'You can't give up now, dad.'

Mum cut in, 'Once one shop is successful we can open more.'

'You can't sell dad out, not now.' Daphne found herself screeching, but he kept looking down.

'My money will not last forever, Daphne. Your father can't live on one painting sold a month, we need something else. I'll keep on at the office until things are up and running. We'll see how well it all goes, then think of broadening the business. Tell her the rest, Arnold. Arnold—'

Her father brought his hands together and rubbed them a little. He always had cold hands, had to warm them over a candle or even the gas ring in the mornings to get them going ready for painting. 'For me to open and run a business and concentrate on a bit of landscape painting on the side — which we can sell there, I'm going to need some help.'

Daphne let the words sink in for a moment. 'I'm going to be an artist, dad. You always said.'

Her mother faced her again. 'You are going to be needed in the business and running the shop. There'll be time after work for you to dabble—'

'Dabble? I have to give up because of *him*?' Daphne left the question rhetorical as she glared at her father.

'Tell her the rest Arnold. And mean it.' Daphne's mother said with quiet urgency.

'You have to give up lessons—' he started, and for a long moment she felt her own grief at the coming loss, followed by pity for her father and anger at his weakness.

'You can't make me.'

'You can't go back to him, Daphne,' her dad said.

'You've got no conviction,' her mother scoffed at her father. 'None at all. You two were always as thick as thieves.' Mum drew breath. 'You think, Daphne, I don't know what goes on. Tommy's wife Jenny has just joined my office. She knows all about what you artists get up to when you're not painting masterpieces. You can forget ideas of running away with your fancy man. You're a business woman now.'

'You can't stop me.'

'I already have. Your father and your uncle went round to warn him off. And you know what he said, the cheeky bugger. How much was it worth? He'd stay away for cash. That's what you were worth to him, Daphne. No galavanting in the south of France, he'd rather have the money.'

'He wouldn't do that.' Daphne stood up and stormed out.

'Grow up, Daphne,' her mother called after her.

2

'These are the caves, Ben. This is Ajanta,' Daphne yelled to Ben with delight. 'Come on.' It was early morning and the caves were in shadow, but the cliffs on the other side of the valley were lit bright ochre by sun beams. Daphne looked down at the dusty river bed winding its way in a great crescent, as though some great god like Shiva had carved the valley from above with his sword out of parched land. 'The only known Buddhist paintings.'

She urged her slower photo-taking partner on. Of slender build and in his mid twenties, he had long dark hair and dark eyes. The family's art shop — *Paint Clever* — was doing well and she had met him while he was working in a company supplying art materials to them. She liked it that his eyes lit up when he smiled. And mum knew him well, had introduced them to each other, and liked him. The match was a good one. She was happy.

It seemed an age ago that she had run round to Tommy's place and found that he and his family had left. And although she disbelieved Tommy thought so little of her he would demand payment not to see her again, feelings of unease about him and the quality of her relationship remained. But she could not dismiss memories of the fondness she had for him.

Daphne was arrested a moment by the view of the carved ravine of Ajanta, the cliff face on her side of the valley dotted with cave-temple entrances linked by a precarious path.

The flight had been arduous so they had stayed overnight in Delhi before heading for the railway station. The train to Bombay had been packed to the rooftops with travellers. Before she got on board she had watched numbers of men, some with their heads in loosely wrapped turbans and carrying belongings in cloth bags, climbing up on the roof of the train. When they got going the black old engine ahead blasted out heaps of steam that filtered into the carriage through open barred windows where children gathered, boys in white kurta and girls in shalwar kameez, while parents talked, shared food in tiffin carriers and admired the world passing outside. Laughing youths gathered around open carriage doorways joking as the world passed them. The married women wore their best brightest saris, the range of colours and designs fascinating Daphne, while the unmarried wore plain but bright shalwar kameez.

Life on board was full of noise and joy. Excitement rose when the train chugged slowly past a Mandir — a Hindu temple — people pointing at the pastel colours of the Gopuram, the central tower painted in bright ochre. A family man told Daphne and Ben it was a temple to Shiva, a god in charge of death and rebirth. He introduced his wife and they chatted, Daphne and Ben answering questions about where they were from, what work they did, how much they earned. And when the family discovered they had just got married and they were celebrating Daphne's birthday, the whole carriage got to know with many people clinging to the door of their compartment, smiling, giving sweets and titbits. Sometimes Daphne managed to doze off, but each time she shook herself, not wanting to miss anything: the noise, the bustle, the movement of the bright colours of the saris and shalwar kameez.

They spent two nights in a hotel in Aurangabad, a busy city in the state of Maharashtra and the following afternoon toured the Taj of the Deccan, a small version of the Taj Mahal constructed mainly of white marble. Only two or three other people were wandering around the grounds baked by the merciless sun. The Mughal Emperor Shah Jahan had built the Taj Mahal for his wife Mumtaz, mother of Aurangzeb who had built his own version here in the town named after him for his wife who had died in childbirth. A brilliant white mausoleum, its onion domes shimmered in the morning heat as they traipsed taking photos around the gardens and mirror lakes.

The following day they had been introduced to a taxi driver by a hotel receptionist, who drove them for nearly three hours over bumpy roads and tracks to Ajanta. They had little option but to stay in the only hotel they could find there, it was a small building with fans but no mosquito nets.

With mixed emotions, still looking along the dry river bed of Ajanta, Daphne was in reach of the place she had yearned to see for years. Half a kilometre ahead a group of women in saris and shalwar kameez bright against the dark rock caught her eye as they glided along the track and disappeared in a cave entrance. A family were sitting on a blanket outside around tins and plates, about to eat. The rock face varied from dark ochre to umber.

She pulled Ben along, jerking him away from the scenes he was photographing. 'Inside,' she said, pulling him to the first cave, its archway covered with carvings of the young Buddha and his devotees.

The darkness enthralled her. It was clear from Ben's whispering that he was awed by the sanctity of the place as well. 'Carved out of solid rock.'

She whispered back, 'Can you imagine the dedication, the sheer work.'

As their eyes became accustomed to the dark and images began to appear on the walls and ceiling, Ben pulled a torch from his pocket and switched it on.

'This is it.' Ben gestured. 'What you wanted. Not bad for a twentieth birthday present, not bad eh?' He searched her face through the gloom for praise.

'It's wonderful, Ben, so wonderful.' She hugged him and they embraced under the eyes of two painted Buddhas, one on either side of a gateway.

'You're not sorry then?'

'Sorry?'

'You married me?' He laughed, but she picked up the sense of insecurity in his tone. She kissed him again for reassurance, but couldn't keep thoughts of Tommy at bay.

'Hah,' he laughed. 'I managed to pry you away from your mother's business for long enough.'

'She's always fallen for your charms,' Daphne said. 'All that stuff about my birthday and an amazing honeymoon. Who knows? Maybe she thought she owed me something. Anyway, she wants me back before you — jammy sod.'

'Your mum owed you something — What do you mean?' He was distracted from the wall paintings by her words.

Mum had reassured Daphne and her dad that they could paint in their free time — evenings, weekends and holidays — and that when the business was thriving Daphne would have lots of free time. But it had not worked out that way. *Paint Clever* took off. It was a full time head on business. They had offered framing which they had started at a small level. Mum had sent Daphne on training courses so she could do framing while the shop was empty. This side of the business was so profitable it enabled them to open another two shops in north London and they had set up a framing business of their own to supply all three. There was little time to paint — she did a few sketches sometimes, but there was never enough opportunity to develop her skills and push herself, so with Ben joining the business and the plans he had, her artistic drive evaporated.

It had been worse for her father. Not only was he involved in the framing too, in one of the bigger shops they had set up a small gallery selling local art as well as visiting national artists. He had more time off than Daphne, but the spark had gone for him and disillusioned he found solace in alcohol. Never that worse for wear that he could not turn up for work every day, he sucked peppermints to hide the smell on his breath, and left more and more of the work to Daphne.

'Nothing. Just stuff in the past.' She shrugged. 'Anyway, she likes you all right — you get extra time to go off to see your mate in Goa while poor old me has to go home and bail out my dad.'

'My mate Jagar'll take me to his cousin's gallery in Kerala — it's a link, Daphne. You never know what'll come out of it.'

Ben had enterprising ideas and was always on the lookout for new areas for expansion, so she went along with his ventures. His old friend Jagar from school was visiting family in the south of India and Ben had assured her that if he went down to see him they might link up ideas on art materials, framing, galleries. Ben could go and check out what the art scene was in India.

She took his hand and led him to the two young Buddhas. The one to the left, his shapely androgynous torso bared to the waist, held a lotus flower in his right hand. He wore a tall pointed ceremonial hat, necklace, a ring on his little finger and a bracelet. Casting his view downwards, his head leaning to his left, he exuded an aura of contentment. His half smiling lips in particular were finely drawn reflecting something of his confidence in his inner knowledge.

The other Buddha was scowling, his mouth open in rebuke it seemed, or as if he were singing, or shouting even. Although this Buddha clutched a lotus flower it was not a portrayal of inner calm; this was a Buddha of fury. He held a thunderbolt in his hand, frowning downwards at some unseen force. His head was covered in an intricate gold crown with arches and curlicues linked with tiny hanging golden chains.

'The two paths,' she told Ben, 'represent the two paths in life, or the two sides: the gentle compassionate Buddha, and the Buddha angry at the injustice, cruelty, revenge and hatred he sees in the world. Amazing.'

'The two coexisting natures of human beings,' he added.

She nodded, still looking in awe at paintings that had survived over fifteen hundred years. Parts had disintegrated through time leaving blank spaces, but the faces and bodies of most figures remained intact. Some had been vandalised, but defacers could not reach the roof which also blazoned with the lives of the gods and buddhas along with animals and birds.

She stood in awe for a time as Ben eased away exploring other images and was met by a man wearing a dhoti and pink shirt who insisted on being his guide. Daphne watched them as the man turned on a small torch and pointed the beam at the painted face of the compassionate Buddha and talked.

Daphne was about to join them when she saw quick movement through ripples of light and shade to her left. A young Indian woman appeared to be beckoning her. The face and body were in darkness, but the fingers and hand fluttered like a dancer's in a flash of torchlight. Daphne stepped forward as the woman continued her gestures and shuffled ahead, her face suddenly visible for a second in a beam of light from the entrance. The figure moved with haste and was lost, her shape being dissolved in the deep shadows of the sanctum.

Daphne noticed the echoing mumbles of Ben and the guide and dismissing the phantom as an aspect of her imagination was about to join them. She noticed then a painted figure some way from the two buddhas.

Daphne tried to remember what Tommy had called this image. A lightly clad young woman was depicted entwined round a sapling, her curving shape echoing the branches, her breasts full of milk, her hips ready for childbearing, her shape enticing, drawing you in to her earthy sensuality.

Tommy would have run away with her; he would have never taken the money and run on his own. She should have pushed harder to find him. That life would have been — risky — but exciting.

She was mesmerised by the painted woman and could imagine her dancing erotically in and around the tree as though in some fertility rite.

If they had come here together — how would that have turned out? They would have followed their instincts, been true to themselves. Yakshi. That's it. Tommy called her a Yakshi tree spirit.

Ben wanted to drag her to the other cave-temples, urging her to see the one with the reclining Buddha, but she was reluctant, wanting to pay full homage to the two Indian Princesses which she had only glanced at. She gave in, telling herself she would go back to the princesses later, and they spent the next two hours touring most of the rest, ending with the cave cut temple with the huge stone-cut statue of the reclining Buddha. Some seven metres long the Buddha was lying on his right side, resting his head on a carved pillow. Portrayed with his body covered in a thin shroud, he lay relaxed, a contemplative smile on his lips and eyes half closed in meditation.

'The Buddha achieves nirvana,' Ben said. 'Look at all the disciples lined up along the plinth — in lotus position — lamenting their loss, I reckon.'

'And the spirits above, welcoming him —' she added. Each cave-temple had its own exciting secrets, but none for her as spectacular as the first painted one.

The brightness hit them as they left the cave and wandered back down the path with tired legs, exhausted minds and hot bodies to the exit of the complex. As Ben went ahead of her taking more photos of the valley, Daphne was accosted by a man selling small icons and souvenirs. She had become accustomed to giving casual vendors a polite, 'no thank you,' but this time she spied a small metal image in the bundle of bracelets, ankle chains and other jewellery he held in a bundle.

He immediately picked out a shining trinket of Shiva dancing in a circle of flame and held it up for her. 'This is good, very good,' he said. In his forties with a thin face, he had short black hair streaked with silver, lined skin and a smile under his moustache that betrayed charm. 'And here is Buddha.' He held out another small icon.

'Yes,' Daphne said. 'But who is this?' She teased out the tiny metal figure of a lone woman.'

'This is Yakshi,' he told her.

'Oh.' She could make out the small shape: a sensuous young woman only barely dressed. Branches wove under her outstretched arm, her greenery sparkling like a halo around her head. She had a charming seductive smile, so there was something earthy and present about her but something ethereal too, as though earth and air met at the borders of her halo of foliage and penetrated her glassy stare.

Daphne bargained, getting it for a price she was happy with, and explored the image with her index finger, enjoying the Yakshi's cheeky grin.

'I must see the princesses properly tomorrow,' Daphne said over the evening meal at the hotel. They shared a thali of red lentil dhal, cumin rice, plain yoghurt with a small bowl of spicy mixed vegetables. 'You've seen your reclining Buddha. It's my turn now.' She smiled at him.

He nodded. 'I'm as keen as you. They do look amazing in the book. You're right, we only did get a glimpse at them.'

'There's something that draws me back to them — and the other figures — the Yakshi.' She relived the private dream she had had while he was talking to the guide. 'Just like my little trinket.' She stopped eating and held up her dancing tree spirit on the end of a little silver chain.

He took it from her and twiddled it around. 'Yes,' he said. 'It's just you. Are you going to wear it as a bracelet.'

'Too fragile. I tried it.' She took it from him and tucked it back in her purse. 'It's safe in here.'

'First thing tomorrow — the two princesses —'

She slept with the Yakshi trinket under her pillow and woke refreshed and ready to see the painted women. Rushing through breakfast and chivvying Ben on, she got the receptionist to book a rickshaw to take them to the entrance to the cave complex.

'No more photos outside.' She laughed as she pulled him along the track to the first cave. 'You've got all you need of them now —'

He tagged on smiling.

The sudden darkness inside blinded her as she headed for the princesses, and as her eyes began to adjust she could make out the back of a young woman in a sari near them. The whites of the eyes of the two princesses on the wall shone through the gloomy light making them appear for a moment as real as the figure standing near them. To the left of the painted image the younger princess with the lotus flowers had large circular earrings, while her sister had jewels and finery adorning her large uncovered breasts. Both had tiaras of worked gold with tiny dangling links and chains also joined to other ornate gold shapes. The sister on the left was looking directly at her sibling, while she looked down. Both had full lips slightly upturned which, with the serene gaze from the pair, gave a look of calm and contentment, although Daphne could read some sadness in the downward gaze of the sister on the right. Both had several necklaces, each with one necklace with two black beads at the front on either side of a red one.

Ben concentrated on the picture for several minutes, but Daphne needed longer, allowing him to slip away looking at other images.

Daphne was distracted by the woman to her left who had also been enjoying the painting of the two princesses. Daphne surreptitiously glanced at her now and again, so as not to stare rudely. No woman could not be jealous of her figure and her long black hair woven with tiny flowers to her waist. Daphne guessed her to be about nineteen − around the age of the figures on the wall − and wondered why she was alone.

Far over to the left and in the background the Yakshi figure was poised in branches.

The young woman turned to her, staring at her with large brown-black eyes. Daphne was right about her age; her skin was young and unblemished, her face had perfect symmetry. She had a small nose and full lips like the princesses. But it was the fieriness of her aura that excited Daphne, attracting her with an alluring half-smile she stood as poised as a goddess with her princesses painted like ghosts behind her on the wall.

Daphne was off-guard and suddenly nervous, feeling as though the woman was gazing into her thoughts.

'Yakshi,' Daphne said, her words echoing through the shadows in the cave. 'The trinket I bought yesterday. Yakshi.' She searched the wall a second, finding the figure caught up in the tree. 'You're a Yakshi.'

'Some years the monsoon does not come,' the woman whispered, her voice sweet and mellow to Daphne, as though she was singing the words. 'People think all India has rain, but in many places the monsoon does not come. They wait. Trees and people. And no rain.'

Daphne found the trinket in her bag and explored it with her fingers. The two were alike, the silver figure and the woman behind the princesses.

'If the monsoon does not come,' the woman said again, 'the ground is hard.'

'Yes.'

'Nothing grows.'

Daphne wanted more from her. 'What's your name?'

'Trees die.'

Daphne compared the painted image with the figure in front of her. 'You're alike. The same.' When she turned back the young woman had disappeared in shadows and she was left with the two princesses and a figure in a tree over the back in semi darkness. 'Yakshi.'

3

'It's hot, Carl, sticky, sticky hot. I'd forgotten how it gets in Ajanta,' Daphne could not keep herself from fiddling with the painting, prodding here and there with a brush loaded with oil paint. Carmine. 'It's been so long.' She brushed aside a few strands of hair from her face. The combination of sun, sea and dust was washing out the brown and letting the real grey through. 'And this damn painting. What's wrong with me. It just won't work—'

'Put the air conditioning on, mum.' Carl went to the fridge and got some tonic water and ice to add to his gin.

Agitated, she said, 'I simply can't get used to cold air blowing all over you, it's just—'

'You can regulate it. Look — controls. You can set it how you want, whatever temperature.' He swirled the liquid in his glass. 'I said mum, before we came — the heat. How long is it? It can't be since you married dad.'

'I'm trying to concentrate here.' She did not intend to sound snappy, but she found it hard to focus on painting while people were around. They talked, they distracted, asked difficult questions, while her mind was in a different sphere, plotting, shaping, colouring, configuring.

Frustrated with her efforts, she pushed paint around the background behind the figure.

'Forty years?'

'Probably.'

'May is just too hot in India.' He fiddled with the controls until she nodded that he had got the temperature right.

She dabbed the background with Ultramarine again and tutted. She did not like Carl's drinking, it reminded her too much of her father, and of Ben — he could knock a few back too. Carl had Ben's eyes and nose, and something of Daphne's lips. He had a youthful grin, the charm of his father in his smile, but his eyes did not dart about excitedly and with curiosity about the world and people like Ben's. She must tell him to cut down, he was putting on weight, it didn't suit him, and whatever weight you put on in your late thirties and early forties you carried for the rest of your life, adding as you went along.

'I told you.' Carl flopped heavily in the little sofa. 'But do you take any notice?'

'Ajanta seems to draw me here,' she said, dabbling. The central figure would not work either, the face was all wrong, the body not slim and young enough. She struggled to get that sexy look, the eroticism, the sensual nature of the pose into the figure. Daphne cursed herself for having lost her youthful gifts, for not spending her free time after work pursuing the graft of painting. Doubting they would come back after all this time, she challenged whether she ever really did have any talents of worth.

Carl leaned back, crossed his legs and sipped his drink. 'There are plenty of other places in the world you could have spent your sixtieth birthday.' He flung up the open palm of his right hand.

'I want to see the caves again,' she said firmly, pushing aside a nostalgic memory of herself with Tommy and the book open at the two princesses. 'And Shanta.'

'They're still here. Why didn't you come before?' he said with an edge of sarcasm.

'You know why.'

'It can't just have been running the business and bringing me up. Dad came over plenty of times. Even brought me a few times.'

'You know I had a touch of malaria. I was very ill and scared. Damned mosquitoes. I wasn't up to it until now. And then I had to look after my mum before she died.'

'But May, mum — just before the monsoon.'

'I might not get another chance.'

'Of course you will.'

Daphne stepped back, sighed, tossed the brush down and looked out of the window. Ochre ridges edged towards the horizon and over to the left a cleft in the hills led down to the caves at Ajanta. The thrill of being back for the first time in forty years shook her. The trains were the same and the stations, always full of people from all walks of life, from beggars to policemen, businessmen to newly married couples. There were more cars on the road, not just old Ambassadors but new Fords and other makes. Lots of men had scooters and occasionally a motorbike would come by with a man driving, a woman sitting side saddle on the back and a child sitting in front of the driver, holding the handle bars, a big grin on its face. More houses had television aerials. In the city she had seen McDonalds, and people were drinking Coca Cola everywhere.

Ajanta was unchanged though except for a new ticket office. The caves carved in the cliff side of the ravine were the same as before, rock faces were the usual ochre and umber colours and the dark stains where the waterfall cascaded during the monsoon looked as dirty as when she first came.

This time everything had been going wrong: taxis breaking down, trains missed or late, tickets lost and found again, money lost. She was particularly frustrated by the obstacles on this trip as at last this was a time when she was free enough from ties and controls actually to start painting herself — and the picture was a mess. She hated herself.

Circles had to be completed and it was important to fulfil what Ben had requested in his Will. With the excitement came feelings of apprehension. Although she had spoken on the phone to Shanta and corresponded with her numerous times, Daphne had not met her before.

Shanta was now one of *Paint Clever's* main suppliers: from her base in Karnataka she exported hand made papers, hand made brushes, powder pigments and inks. Ben had set up the link through his friend Jagar. When Jagar had got married in India over twenty years ago, Ben had gone to the wedding. Keen to help Ben's business and that of his cousin Shanta who was running some kind of cooperative for women, Jagar introduced Ben to her and deals were struck. So successful in the shops at home were the sales of the Indian sourced goods, Ben travelled back, usually at least once a year, to develop further contacts with Shanta's *Kali Ko-op*. Shanta and her partner Vishnu were able to source brilliant fabrics, icons of Buddha and Hindu gods, carved boxes and silver trinkets, enabling *Paint Clever* to expand.

'You're thinking about me, I know you are.' She was gentle with Carl. 'But I've done the grieving for your father now.' She could not turn herself away from her view of the dusty hills.

'I'm not so sure, mum.' Carl got up, went to the fridge, found some ice and clunked it in with another top up of gin and tonic. 'Grief doesn't simply evaporate in a matter of a couple of months. Does it?'

She carried on gazing beyond her easel and canvas. Now there were several hotels in the village. Their previous one looked shabby, but The Shining Buddha Hotel where they were staying was more upmarket, consisting of about twenty cottage-like buildings scattered over a grassed garden that had seen no real rain for months. Every evening a little man came out of a back door to the restaurant, took up a hose and sprayed the grass which responded weakly by turning from yellow to a weak shade of sap.

Each little abode had a veranda facing the hills ahead of the valley of the caves. Daphne was about to open the French doors and step out into the heat, but Carl called her back with mocking laughter, 'You can't have the air con on and open the doors mum—'

'All right.' She threw up her hands. His expressions and gestures were so similar to Ben's it aggravated her. The way he sat down, the way he leaned to the left when he was sitting and talking, the way he held his glass up and waved it about as he spoke were all a reminder of her late husband. She wanted none of his righteousness now either, especially when she was trying to paint, and not from a thirty nine year old son who was also no stranger to living life to the full. 'Ben was a wonderful husband to me — entirely faultless — and a great father to you, although you won't admit it. And now because of the loss you're being over protective. Are you like that with your daughter? I hope not.'

Carl gave her a wry grin. 'We can't have that, now can we?'

'I'm serious.'

'All I'm saying is you still need time, and a trip to Karnataka just before monsoon is just, well — and I could be—'

'Yes, you could be doing lots more back home. But you know Shanta. You can introduce us while she's up in this district. And you can get us down to Karnataka and back, you've done all this before.' Daphne did not mean to stress her words so strongly.

'I don't like leaving *Paint Clever* for so long with Geoff in charge. Things go wrong when I'm not running things. We've done Goa, you've swum in the sea and enjoyed yourself, it's been five weeks — The smell of that bloody Turps in the room—'

'I wanted the door open for you, I knew you hated it—' She was about to head for the doors again but he was shaking his head.

'I'll put up with it.'

Having screwed the cap back on the Turps bottle, she sat with him on the sofa. 'I know it's been hard for you, Carl.'

'You don't have to, mum—'

'Well, it has.'

'There's so much needs doing,' Carl persisted. 'We're expanding the framing side of things, we need more storage space. But mum, there's even more important things—'

'Running a business is never ending, you don't have to tell me.' She sighed.

'If we don't get our act together we're going to get overtaken and lose our place in the market.' He was getting agitated. 'Our website is way out of date and we have to develop our online business — selling art materials and all the wonderful fabrics and icons and stuff on line. That's the future, mum.'

'I want what's best for you, but it's time for me to hand that all over to you and to do what I should have done years ago: paint.'

'All I'm saying is meet Shanta here — if I can get hold of her. She's always busy doing this and that, sourcing materials to send us and so on. And then we go back.'

'You have to get hold of her. Ben left a lot of money to Shanta out of the inheritance his family left him. Let me contact her directly—'

'That's good.' Carl shrugged. 'It'll keep *Kali Ko-op* going and make the business relationship with Shanta even stronger.'

'It seems so much to leave—'

'Dad always knew what he was doing. The links with Shanta have enabled *Paint Clever* to grow. She's essential — Leave it to me. Since you've let go of the reigns of the business I've been in constant touch with her. Let me see if I can get hold of her.'

'Which is why I must meet her. And I want to see this *Kali Ko-op* she runs.'

'It's just a cooperative for women—'

'Destitute women?'

He nodded. 'To get them working and supporting themselves.'

'It's such good work. I'd like to see it for myself.'

'A full day's drive away in Karnataka in the heat — mum —'

'I may not get another chance—' She regretted that conversations with Carl always seemed to turn into a joust.

'You're so melodramatic.' He laughed. 'You're going through your second youth — painting—'

She did not want to alert her son to the worries she had of another bout of malaria and the fact her doctor was worried about her heart.

Surveying her canvas on the easel, she decided she should radically adjust the face, make her younger, give it more symmetry with slightly higher cheek bones, more depth to the eyes and with kajal round the edges. She could see what was wrong, but doubted her ability to correct it.

Daphne looked back at him. 'I know what you're thinking. "Did she really have to bring this painting gear?" Well yes, I did as a matter of fact.' She put on the surly tones she knew he hated. 'I've been denied it all these years. Now I'm doing it, wherever I can and whenever I can. And it's not a lot: a small box of starter oils and a portable easel. It all dries much quicker in this heat —'

Picking up the brush she wiped the remaining paint away from the tip and searched for Burnt Sienna with dabs of Naples Yellow to brighten some of the skin tones. Her hand moved clumsily and she had trouble stilling a mild trembling from her wrist for a moment.

She had painted a ghost, a lost figure with no dimension to her, staring out of the picture. She could not paint anywhere near as well as the ancient artists in the Ajanta caves — perhaps never would, and perhaps would never be able to create a meaningful picture at all. Had it really all gone, that talent? She doubted it was ever there and then inwardly cursed her mother and father.

'Damn this painting.' She screwed up her face.

'Don't throw one, mum, it's too early in the morning.'

'Throw one?'

'Why do it if it never works out?'

'Why indeed.' She carried on scowling at her work, prodding here and there. Maybe it was a mistake even starting it before she had been back to the caves. She wondered if once inside she would experience again the strange dreamlike visions she had had before — the shifting images of the Yakshi she was trying vainly to paint.

'You haven't painted for years, mum.'

'"And why start now?" That's what you're saying,' she snapped. 'You wouldn't understand.' She sucked the end of her paint brush.

'I'm trying,' he said, glancing at his phone. 'I've got people to meet. I can leave you alone with your blessed painting.'

'All right, all right—' She waved her hand impatiently at him. She had wanted peace all morning to work.

'Just let go of it.' He got up and placed his empty glass carefully on the table. 'Do what you have to, then go home and get some counselling.'

'My counselling is painting.'

'Why don't we just take you back now, mum. We can get a flight back in a couple of days.'

'Not until it's done.'

He shook his head. 'Well just enjoy the scenery instead of pushing yourself. You've been doing that all your life, up early, doing this, doing that, always on the move. It's time to chill out now, mum. You can retire and relax. You've got the money and you don't have to worry about the business.'

'You're right. It's just that—'

'What?'

'I'm not sure you'd understand.'

'I'm just the ignorant son who's lived a sheltered life, what would I know?'

'I've always wanted to have a proper exhibition. You'd be so proud of me.'

'I have got to go, mum.' Carl gathered his phone, keys and wallet.

'Whatever I try creatively now just does not work and it leaves a sort of feeling of desperation.' She slammed the paint brush down, ignoring his retreat. 'It's not like when you're young and ideas just flow into you and you just run with them. In those days I could do anything. I had a wonderful teacher — Tommy. I learned everything from him. The things he could do with oil paint, it was so exhilarating and challenging and new and exciting in those days. To have that youthful belief — that anything you do is a product of genius — you just take awful risks at that age, and somehow they come off. We could have run away together — the south of France, India, anywhere. He told me to shake off all preconceptions and just get on with my vision — don't think about it, just do it, however it comes to you, that's what he said. Why can't it be like that now? It was like I could open a tap inside myself and it would all flow out. Now it's so dark in there I can't even find the tap.'

'Why didn't you? Run off with him?'

She laughed.

'I wouldn't be here if you had.' He laughed with her.

She saw the little boy in him again and was moved. 'You were loved,' she said. 'You were Ben's little man.' She came to the fridge and opening it took out a bottle of water and poured herself a glass, 'I'm forgetting, you are grieving too. You and Ben were very close.'

'You don't have to—' He jangled his keys, ready to go.

She stepped back, thinking for a moment. 'You're very patient with me. What a man Ben was, bringing me back here. And now you bringing me too.'

Carl came over slowly to the painting and leaned forward scrutinising. 'What are you trying to do?'

'A Yakshi is an ancient tree spirit that is depicted entwined round a sapling.'

He shrugged. 'I'll take you to the caves tomorrow. Your favourite one — number one — the princesses.'

'With Shanta,' she insisted. 'Your father always spoke so highly about her — that is, when he did speak about her — which only happened when I asked him about her, I have to say.'

He pecked her on the cheek, said goodbye and left.

Mixing more Ochre with touches of Zinc White and Naples Yellow, she developed earthy slips of neutral colour with which she hoped to enhance the tones of the Yakshi's body. Remembering things which Tommy had told her years ago, she relaxed her body, relaxed her arm and allowed her 'whole body' to paint, as he had instructed. In that way she could allow her torso to sway lightly with the movements of the brush, so that the act of painting became one of the whole person, not just the arm and not just the brain. 'Art,' he had told her, 'involves all parts of the body and the psyche. If you just paint with your hand, it is a hand painting. But if you paint with your whole self it becomes an impenetrable complex of consciousness, especial and unique only to you. Then you are well on the way to becoming a real artist. Many people never get there — in fact most don't. And you are close, Daphne, very close. You will get there if you persevere.'

Tommy was the only art teacher who had taken her on the path to becoming an artist. There had been others who had handed over techniques, philosophies and dogmas, but Tommy was the one who, working from his heart, had imparted the wisdom of the process.

It was still not good enough: the Yakshi would not come alive, she was two dimensional and had no life-spark to her. You must feel in a painted figure that it has a life of its own, that when it steps out of the picture it gets on with doing its washing and cleaning and surviving. Unless it is symbolic of something higher, more ethereal, cosmic, or an image of mythical or divine transcendence — so Tommy reckoned anyway.

She threw the paint-loaded brush on the pallet, crossed her arms and stared at the misshapen nymph and cursed under her breath.

Through the French doors of her hotel cottage-apartment she could see, a mile away, the main entrance to Ajanta. A small queue of Indian tourists were lining up, the bright colours of their children running in and out of them. Beyond the ridge she could just make out the top of one of the caves.

She resisted the urge to leave everything and go alone. Much better to wait and let Shanta be her guide. In the past when Daphne did have commercial contact with her rather than her partner Vishnu she was business-like with an eye for detail and a genuine interest in people, always asking after family. Ben and Carl said she was a highly educated, remarkable and enterprising woman who found time not only to source materials for *Paint Clever* but to support her local community by running her very successful co-operative, *Kali Ko-op*, which Ben had been instrumental in helping her set up both practically and with injections of cash.

She looked forward to the meeting — they could both expand their interests, friendships could flourish and Daphne could witness at first hand the achievements of her late husband. A journey to Karnataka for Daphne to see the good work that was being done and how Ben's money would be spent would soften her feelings of grief and she could at last shed old skins, face old ghosts and find a new sense of self as an artist with which to go forward in her life. She was tired of finding reasons to get out of bed in the mornings and look at herself in the mirror. And Shanta may be familiar with the Yakshi images Daphne was haunted by and help her resolve them.

She was saddened that she could not explain that all to Carl. He could be stubborn like his father sometimes, and headstrong, just getting on with his own thing without thinking about the needs of others. But Carl did stick with her and if she softened her attitude to him he would help her.

4

Carl was back mid morning the next day grinning, although when he noticed Daphne at the painting, he stiffened.

'I know what you're thinking.' Daphne waved her brush about. 'But I'm going on with it.' She noted he looked good in white trainers, white trousers and blue and red patterned shirt and should have told him so.

Heading for the fridge he said, 'Like some phantom from hell.'

Ignoring the cruelty of his remark about her work she kept to her task. 'Have you contacted Shanta?'

'I'm waiting for Raj.' He poured himself a gin and tonic, avoiding Daphne's glare.

'Shanta's son, Raj?'

'He drives me around when I'm over here. He'll be here soon.'

'Wonderful,' she smiled at him. 'I've not met Raj either, so that will be good. Everything can be arranged now — And there's our driver for the trip. So that's who you keep slipping off to see?' Then she looked excitedly towards the caves where a small queue to get onto the path that led up the valley was forming. Women in red, gold and green saris attended girls in white and pink frocks and boys with bright white shirts, while men chatted in small groups. Regarding the cheerfulness of the families made her reflect on her own. She was particularly keen on Carl's fifteen year old daughter. 'I do miss Melody not being here,' she reflected. 'It would have been good for her to meet Shanta and see the good work she's doing at *Kali Ko-op*. I have high hopes for her — she's quick, intelligent, good academically —'

'It's that age, mum.' Carl flopped on the sofa. 'She wanted to spend her fifteenth birthday with her mates. She's happy with her mum.'

'I don't get to see her much. I really would have liked my only granddaughter here with us, she has such energies, and she's open to new things. She would have liked the caves, I know she would.'

'I thought you two never really got on.'

'We've had our disagreements, and when she shows attitude and is rude I am going to tell her off — as you should do. And you don't do it often enough,' Daphne said. 'You should never have let her mother go off like that and take her.'

A tall girl with flowing blond hair, she had her father's lips and mother's blue eyes and when she made up her face with subtle pastel colours that complimented her features, she looked nineteen. Although Melody could snap sometimes there was a sensitive side to her and she could still a bad atmosphere with enchantment. Daphne felt a sense of connection with her granddaughter that Carl had missed. Melody was interested in art and painted little designs and liked to design clothes.

She would also be someone who could take over the business in time. 'I do try with Melody's mum, you know,' Daphne said.

Carl shrugged. 'Who knows what a fifteen year old girl wants?'

Daphne turned to her painting and tried to adjust the nose, layering in a touch of Cadmium Yellow and White with a touch of Burnt Sienna. The thick line of paint made the Yakshi's nose bulge; it was all wrong. 'I don't suppose you spent much time dissuading her?'

She took a cloth and folding it round the point of the index finger of her right hand applied it to the over-thick paint on the nose and scooped some away.

'She's a teenager who changes her mind like the direction of the wind. Don't take it personally.'

Daphne regarded the mess of colour on her canvas, resisting for a moment the desire to rip it apart with a pallet knife. Growling, she stormed away from it.

'You're impossible, mum.' He sipped. 'Twelve hours in Raj's beaten up old tin can in baking weather.'

Carl was looking out past her, turning over his thumbs, a habit which annoyed Daphne. A person who believed every moment should be deliberate, almost pre-planned, Daphne found his fidgeting a distraction. If it wasn't his fingers it was the rocking of one leg over another, just like his father.

'I'll be fine.'

'Paint your pictures.' He gesticulated with his hand, the motion nearly spilling his drink in the other so she picked up his frustration. 'You can talk to Raj when he gets here.' Carl downed the dregs. 'He knows his mum's movements.'

Daphne let go and turned back to her picture, a rage tossing through her. 'And now at last I have the time to paint — I can't do it. I've lost the talent.' She bunched her fists. 'I can't paint anything anymore.'

'It'll come back. It always does with you,' Carl said lightly. 'This stuff is a little drama you like to play out for my benefit.'

'It won't,' she said, pushing back tears: she was not going to cry in front of Carl. 'It's gone. If you don't fulfil these things when you're young, you become a shell, an afterthought.'

*****

Raj was a couple of inches shorter than Carl and half his age; Daphne reckoned he was around twenty. His thick black hair was pushed back on top and finely shaved around the edges and he had thin dark eyebrows, narrow lips and a smile of warmth and authority.

'Come in Raj,' Daphne beckoned to the shy young man. 'Have a drink with us — we have sparkling water, ice —' She led him into her room.

'Madam,' Raj stepped forward with a slight bow of his head and proffered his hand for shaking. 'Is it your first time in India?'

'You can call me Daphne. I'm very pleased to meet you, Carl has told me so much about you and your mother. And to answer your question, my husband Ben brought me many years ago as Carl will have told you.'

'I heard what happened,' Raj went on. 'He was a good man. I'm very sorry.'

'You knew him well?' Daphne motioned for him to sit and he obeyed. 'Through your mother?'

'Without him I would have had no school, I would be nothing. I'm driving now, but taking a degree soon.'

'Then you can take over from your mother.'

'We can work together,' he smiled, 'to build things bigger, wider —'

'It's very exciting. I'm so pleased to meet you. Get him a drink Carl. He might want water —'

'Not if I know Raj.' Carl poured Raj a small glass of whisky and another gin for himself.'

Daphne glared at her son. 'You're really too bad Carl, encouraging him. He's a driver remember. I can just imagine you two and Ben —'

Accepting the glass from Carl, Raj let out a short laugh, stopped, and smiled back at Daphne. 'It wasn't quite like that — Daphne.'

'I'm so glad we were able to help from our end,' Daphne said. 'And get your mum's business up and get you an education. Ben was always at the forefront of giving to others.'

'Mum won't have anything bad said about my dad, Raj.' Carl gave him a glance.

'He was always good to me and he had a big heart. You know that.'

'Yes, he did have a big heart.' Carl nodded, sitting on a chair near the sofa.

'You don't have to say it with so much — sarcasm and irony.'

'He did, mum. But you over praise him. He had faults just like everyone else.'

'He was always kind to me,' Raj added. 'Like a father.'

Daphne poured herself a glass of water, 'I'm talking to someone who knows what he's talking about. I can see you and I, Raj, are going to get on fine.' She waved her hand at Carl. 'You can put the air con on now it's getting stuffy.'

'The sun's getting up high,' Raj said and seeing Daphne's painting, he stood and walked over to it. 'You paint, er, Mrs — Daphne.'

'You mustn't look at that.' Daphne tried to get in between her visitor and the picture on the easel. 'It's just a work in progress, you understand. It's nothing, really.'

Despite her move to block him, he had managed to slip past her.

'A Yakshi,' he said.

'You can tell, you can see it?' Daphne let out a short gasp.

'This is a special Yakshi - a Shalabhanjika tree spirit. How did you know?'

'You can really recognise it?' Daphne fumbled in her pocket and came out with the trinket she had bought with the little Yakshi dangling from it.

'Like a ghost,' Raj laughed. 'They can haunt you.'

'Don't you start,' Carl said getting the air conditioning going.

Raj smiled at her again. 'You do not have to worry. But the Yakshi is like a spirit that lives in the mountains and the woods guarding valuable metals and jewels in the earth. Yakshi is female and Yaksha is male. Even in Buddhist times you would see the entrance to a house with a Yakshi on one door post and a Yaksha on the other. They would stop bad spirits from entering and bring prosperity to the owner.'

'If you believe that stuff,' Carl laughed.

'I can't get it right, though,' Daphne said, 'not properly.'

'Mum thinks she can do it.' Carl gesticulated with his glass.

Raj looked at her, 'I'm sure you can.'

'You'll be my friend for life, Raj.' She leaned to him and lightly touched his arm.

'Perhaps the face,' Raj went on. 'A little bit European. If you don't mind me saying.'

'I don't mind you saying at all. You're so polite.'

'My mother paints,' Raj said.

'Shanta?' Daphne scowled at her son. 'Another thing I've not been told.'

'She dabbles, like you, mum. Nothing special.'

'Thank you for that, darling.' Daphne fired at Carl, enjoying a moment of revengeful irony.

'She painted a Yakshi once.' Raj still observed Daphne's picture. 'A big canvas. A commission for a friend.'

'Then she's not a mere dabbler like me then.' Daphne sent another scowl at her son. 'She can help me.'

'I'm sure she can,' Raj said.

Carl sat forward. 'She's very busy, Raj, what with your sister. I keep telling her—'

'Yes now that my sister is ill and *Kali Ko-op* is — how do you say —rejuvenating — itself.' Raj carried on studying the Yakshi painting.

'Rejuvenating?' Daphne held her gaze on Carl. 'What do you mean? Why haven't you told me?'

'Dad told you all that, didn't he?' Carl said.

'My big sister Rani is sick.' Raj shrugged. 'There's lots of doctors' bills. My mother has had to sell things off.'

'She'll still be able to supply us?' Daphne turned to Raj.

'Of course, of course.'

'It's nothing, mum,' Carl said, giving Raj a sideways glance.

'I don't want her business ruined if we can help. What exactly is happening?'

Raj turned back to the painting. 'I'm sure she'll help you with the painting.'

'Raj. What's happening to *Kali Ko-op*?'

He turned back to her, smiling. 'The Devadasi women at *Kali Ko-op* make only purses, boxes, and things out of textiles like cushions and curtains. All the art materials we supply you, the hand made papers, the paints, inks and colours come from other sources my mother set up and runs. She knows suppliers and wholesalers. The little things the Devadasi women of *Kali Ko-op* make and supply to you is not enough to keep it going. It needs rupees it makes on art materials, fabrics and icons my mother gets from her suppliers, before selling on to *Paint Clever*.'

'So what's the problem?'

'It's nothing, mum —'

'Raj?'

'One of the suppliers of your best selling fabrics and icons is no longer selling to small businesses. It's got big emporiums in India and big retailers in England and America to serve.'

'Shanta's very resourceful,' Carl reassured her. 'She'll get new contacts — she knows her way about—'

'How long can your mother go before she can't pay the women?'

'They will have to rest soon,' Raj said.

'How long?'

'Shanta can do it,' Carl cut in before Raj could answer.

Daphne replied, 'It sounds like you need money — fast.'

'I've been saying how much they need what dad's left them.'

'My mother will sell her big house and get something smaller if she must. She will do anything to keep *Kali Ko-op* going and the women in work.'

Daphne continued to Raj, 'The women — you call them—'

'Devadasi,' Raj supplied the words for her. Daphne noticed Carl exchange a glance at Raj, then Raj said to her, 'They have other work. Devadasi never starve.'

'What exactly are they? What do they do?' Daphne carried on with Raj, noting he looked serious. 'Why the special title?'

Raj looked at her. 'Courtesans. They sing and dance,' Raj said. 'In the old time they were very well respected and very educated.'

'Prostitutes, then,' she said.

Raj intervened. 'He did everything he could for the co-op and the women.'

'That's admirable, Raj — what your mother has done for these women and how Ben has helped her in that.'

'My mother,' Raj said quietly, 'can come and tell you about it. And help you paint your picture. Everything will be fine.'

'I will be very pleased to meet her.'

'She has a degree, madam,' Raj's nod appeared more like a bow to her. 'She works very hard for everyone.'

'This afternoon then Raj, can you bring her here? I'm lunching in the hotel restaurant now. You two will join me?'

'Later maybe, mum.' Carl sipped his drink and looked over at Raj as she gathered her bag and left.

5

'I told you,' Carl waved his glass at Raj when Daphne had gone, 'what would happen.' He brought the bottle of gin over and topped himself up.

'They're going to meet sometime,' Raj replied. 'You can't stop that.'

'I said: "leave it as long as possible." And you suggest your mum come over and paint pretty pictures with her. My mother can't paint, for god's sake. Nothing is going to change that.'

Raj sloshed another splash of whisky in his glass. 'She's not going to give up until they've met.' He shrugged. 'Let them be friends, that way it will work out all right—'

'She mustn't know. No really, I don't know what it would do to her. I do worry about her, her health isn't good.' Carl softened his tone and spoke gently to him. 'It's just for a while. We've been close for a few years now, haven't we?'

'Pretending I'm a taxi driver.' Raj shook his head.

'It's for the best. Trust me. When this is all over, you'll have everything. Let's get this meeting over quickly then. And they must like each other — but not too much. We don't want my mum making regular trips over here because she's enamoured by Shanta.'

'We do what we can.'

'My dad was a saint in my mother's eyes. Help me with this and then Shanta will get the inheritance from him.'

'You will carry on?' Raj glanced at Carl. 'The business?'

'I'm persuading everyone in *Paint Clever* the need to change: streamlining everything, developing on line sales. It'll take some time, but in a few years I'm working towards having no more shops.' Carl leaned forward selling his ideas, 'I'll help you develop on line sales with your mum, so when you've both sorted out new suppliers our two businesses expand our links with each other and other organisations, selling to a wider market and making more money. And — *Kali Ko-op* can get their wares out further — globally — the business opportunities for you are endless. Everyone wins. It's all good. We don't want any of it messed up, that's what I'm saying, Raj.'

'Your company knows all this?'

Carl smiled. 'It's the sensible thing for the future: get rid of all the buildings we rent, the people we employ. Why have that when you don't need it anymore. Times are changing. We have to run with the changes, or we go down. One of our shops is already struggling — although my mum won't admit it.' He paused for a sip and anticipating Raj's apprehension added, 'Haven't I always looked after you?'

'Like a brother,' Raj nodded.

'All I'm saying is, just keep the lid on things we don't want getting out — that way your mum gets Ben's money, everyone's happy and, best of all, business booms.' Raj looked away. 'The thing with your sister will be resolved — you can then pay for all the cancer treatment Rani needs. Mate.' He patted his shoulder. 'These days Lymphoma is treatable. Your mum won't have to sell her house, I know you both love the place and don't want to let go of it. We can do this — if we play this right.'

'You really think so?'

Raj smiled with him but stayed silent for a while, then spoke enthusiastically, 'Let your mother paint and be happy — in retirement.' And carried on as though thinking out loud. 'Keep telling her she's brilliant. That way she's happy. She knows she needs a bit of help and that's where my mum comes in—'

'Change tack, you mean?' Carl leaned back thinking for a moment, 'Encourage them together as artists. Maybe you've got it.'

'There's no reason for anything to get out — they can be happy painters — my mum and your mum absorbed in their own world of art.'

Carl whacked the arm of his chair. 'You're a genius Raj. I always said you were a fixer.' They laughed together. 'All right.' Carl stood, straightening himself. 'So get Shanta here as soon as you can, and let's get this thing rolling —'

Raj stood for high fives. 'We can do it. Together. We can get there, Carl.'

*****

'Come in,' Daphne greeted Shanta as she entered her room, looking her up and down in amazement. 'You're absolutely glowing — even more than when we've done business links on video.' She gestured at Shanta's red and green silk sari. 'At last we meet properly, face to face. Come and sit down. It's been far too long.' She ushered her towards the sofa. 'And I couldn't wait to meet you.'

'How is it we've never managed to meet until now?' Shanta laughed.

She had round gold earrings which matched a simple gold necklace. In her forties, she looked much younger, Daphne reflected, still retaining a shapely body. Her eyebrows were neatly trimmed and balanced over her deep brown eyes. She held her smile, which encouraged Daphne to smile back and relax. The general feeling of geniality that flowed to Daphne from her was an assurance to Daphne that they could become friends.

'I'll get you a drink. Juice? Water?' Daphne headed for the bottles. 'When the sun is passed its peak — the heat here —'

'Water will be fine,' Shanta's tones were soft but clear.

'You've travelled so far. I can't get used to the distances in India,' Daphne laughed.

'Today?' Shanta said. 'Raj brought me from Aurangabad. He is such a good son. We came up from Karnataka several days ago. I heard there are some suppliers in this area. We visited some in Pune first, and now in Aurangabad. You have been to the Little Taj? It is so beautiful.'

'The Taj of the Deccan? Ben and I went there on my first trip — yes, its white marble just shines in the sunlight.'

'They say it is marvellous in moonlight too.'

Daphne headed for the water jug and poured a glass for her guest, dropping in a slice of lemon and some ice cubes. 'Raj is so polite and charming. He and Carl get on so well. It's been hard for Carl though, he will not admit it — losing his father.'

Shanta took the glass. 'Your husband was very good to us. Without him my livelihood would not have been possible — not in the same way.'

Daphne placed a plate of biscuits on the table for her guest, along with Bombay Mix and some sweet Ladoo. 'It's good that Indian girls are now expected to get a good education. Ben was always keen on equality.'

Shanta's tones were again soft and clear but with an edge of authority and confidence. 'For one thing, they become a good marriage prospect that way.'

'And you are an example of that with your education. It's clear you run things at *Kali Ko-op* and it's Vishnu that helps you —'

Shanta smiled. 'And of course it means that if a woman can develop her own career and earn her own money she doesn't have to get married at all and can still survive.'

'That is happening now?' Daphne showed interest and surprise.

Shanta said, 'Ben could see the need for all women in India to be educated, so they can have some control over their lives. Carl has carried on with that, and with the help of Raj, the links between both families can be strong; I want that to continue.

But we shouldn't be talking about that now — you are still in grief.'

'You make Ben an even greater hero in my eyes. What a man he was.' Daphne pushed back her emotions.

'I'm so sorry.'

'I have him in my heart, Shanta, with all his benevolence.' Daphne put her hand on her chest. 'I must sit a minute. My heart is not what it was. The doctor says I must take it easy. He was not keen on me travelling.' Daphne sat gasping a moment. 'But you know my family — headstrong.'

Shanta smiled in agreement. 'I can arrange for you to see a doctor, Daphne. You mustn't overdo it.'

'Just palpitations, nothing much really. I've just got to take it easy. A little breathless you know, it's nothing, Shanta. Just the heat and the different food. I'll be all right. Don't tell Carl.'

'I think you should, you look very pale.'

Daphne waved her hand, 'I can see Dr Brand when I get home. He's the only one I trust.'

'And you are grieving—'

'But it's even better meeting you at last. And in your finest jewellery for me. You must tell me about yourself. The few phone calls we have had and the recent video conferencing has all been about work.' Daphne revived herself with a sip of gin and tonic. 'You grew up in the south?'

'Just a little village in Karnataka, there was nothing much there. The biggest town was miles away.'

Daphne nodded. 'Brothers and sisters?'

'A brother and two sisters.'

'I like it that your father wasn't too old fashioned to insist you get your education,' Daphne smiled. 'And Vishnu helps in all your enterprises?'

Shanta turned aside to sip some water. 'We have so much in common—'

Daphne watched her a moment as she took in what she was saying. 'You lost him too? Vishnu? Recently?'

'Vishnu helps me run the co-op — my cousin.' She smiled. 'He's running things while I'm up here. He's so reliable.'

'Oh, I thought — after all this time — I —' She began, realising Vishnu wasn't her husband and pondering on her ignorance about the co-op and Shanta's suppliers in India, Daphne felt embarrassed and confused. Angry with herself for leaving everything to Ben and then to Carl for so long without getting full details of the set up, she hid her feelings from Shanta, offering her sympathy. 'Your husband must have been very young.'

'We do not have health care.'

'He was very ill?' Daphne sensed she did not want to talk about it.

Putting her glass aside, Shanta stood and stepped forward to the unfinished painting on the easel, 'You are an artist.'

'I try, but—' Daphne felt embarrassed by the title.

'This is marvellous.' Shanta stood in front of the picture. 'A Yakshi. Yes, you have caught her, rising out of her tree.'

'You can see what it is? You exaggerate Shanta, it's not right, I can't do it. I'm about to give up.'

'But you can.' Shanta was excited, pointing at the image. 'Raj said you needed help. You see the nose is not quite right, and the lips — with a little bit of adjustment—'

'Show me.' Daphne joined her, picked up a brush and handed it to her.

'May I?'

'Make it work for me—'

Shanta touched the face with the brush, stroking on a thin layer of paint while Daphne watched, intrigued. With slight touches Shanta adjusted the nose and the lips, refining their outlines, then worked on the jaw line and the chin, so that a younger more sensuous woman took shape.

'She's Indian at last,' Daphne gasped. 'Not European. She's young now and vibrant — with real character — a person with a spirit. Where did you learn?'

'A little at school, and practice—'

'No formal art training at all, is that what you're telling me? Self taught. A woman of many talents, Shanta. '

'I paint when I can.'

'Just like that.' Daphne laughed, pushing back the feelings of envy that went through her. 'Natural talent. And here's me grafting on — life's not fair,' Daphne carried on laughing.

'But you did the main part, I just finished it.'

Daphne laughed again at Shanta's praise, watching her add another small dab of paint along the neck and ease it along. 'You have exhibitions?'

'Some — when I can —' Shanta concentrated on the earrings and bracelets smoothing the paint on with a light touch.

'Your father and your husband must have helped you in that too? And selling? Commissions?'

'With the help of your husband.'

'Ben helped you with that too?'

'He got my cousin Jagar to contact galleries and helped me set up a little studio at home.'

'Ben did so much for you,' Daphne contemplated for a moment, 'that he never told me about. Neither did Carl. It's as though they kept you in the dark somehow—'

'I didn't mean to take over your painting—'

'You've done it perfectly well.' Daphne turned from the painting and found herself observing the smoothness of Shanta's facial skin, her eyes made up with blacks and shades of ice blue, her pupils darting as she looked over the painting. 'I'm pleased Ben found you, you've been a real asset to *Paint Clever.*' Daphne drew breath. 'You needn't worry. What Ben's left you will cover all your costs. You can pay your daughter's hospital bills, pay the women at *Kali Ko-op.* You won't have to sell your house.'

'Thank you,' Shanta smiled.

'I would like to see the co-op. It would mean a lot to me.'

'Of course,' Shanta replied. 'But do you think it's the right time, it's a long journey. And your health—'

'I'd like to meet the Devadasi women—'

'They work very hard,' Shanta said. 'It's to get them out of a bad way of life and sets them up with skills so they don't need their old ways to survive. In *Kali Ko-op* they learn to read and write in their own language as well as English. They learn sewing and embroidery skills needed to make the purses, bags and cushions and throw-overs we send to you to sell. They embroider the chunni scarves and kameez you get from us. Some learn to carve wooden boxes. There's a small area for weaving and dyeing. Others can paint pictures on fabric in old style Indian design. We even train women on computers, working with numbers, so they can do office work.'

'Does it really work?'

'A few have gone on to get office jobs, one has left and married a man who knows about her and supports her. Most stay for a long time living off what the co-op provides — and feeding their children. But you have to understand they've been forced into a life they don't want — a life of sexual slavery from a young age. As young as twelve, from their first period — it's true. You cannot imagine.'

Daphne shook her head. 'This sort of things really goes on — it's appalling.'

'Girls are made ready to dedicate themselves to the goddess Yellamma,' Shanta continued. 'That means they are wedded only to the goddess Yellamma through a special ceremony when they achieve puberty. The girls don't know what's going on, they are promised everything will be all right and told they are privileged. And then any man in the village can have her as his right, any time he wants. A Devadasi girl must always wear a necklace of red and white beads so she can always be recognised for who she is. All can know — especially men. They can never marry, and even people in their family, even Brahmins, can have them when they want. It's a tradition that goes back thousands of years when Devadasis were attached to places of worship — temples that were greedy for the money they brought in. Village people still believe if Devadasi women don't serve Yellamma properly by granting sexual favours to all men, crops will fail, they will starve and the well being of the community will be at stake. Others say by doing the sex work and being a vehicle for men to reach moksha, or heaven, they too will achieve a better life in the next reincarnation. But they are slaves, Daphne, there is no way out for them and I can only do a little for a few. But I was expanding, until—' She stopped herself.

'We can keep it going—' Daphne said.

'If they can learn a skill,' Shanta carried on, 'they can survive. You don't know how hard it is for a women to survive without a husband, to break free and make her own life. Some of our Devadasi women have learned to make and sell things and so, not being dependent on money from male visitors, or from begging, they can make a life for themselves with some dignity.'

'And all this — because—' Daphne shook her head again, 'of poverty—'

'If a family in a village in Karnataka cannot afford the dowry for a daughter, she cannot marry — and as she grows up the family haven't got the money to feed another mouth. Then there's pressure from local landowners who want to buy her virginity — at the age of twelve or thirteen. You cannot understand the pressures. The girls don't know what's happening to them, they're just told it's a once in a life time ritual and they're privileged to be selected and that they won't have to worry for the rest of their lives. They're never told that old men and married men will force themselves on them and they will go on to have babies, not knowing who the fathers are. That they are likely to get AIDs and will never be able to afford medication and will die young—' Daphne could see Shanta's fist shaking. 'Ben helped me set up *Kali Ko-op* to teach them skills. To show them a way.' She turned aside, her bottom lip trembling. 'With money we can keep this going and open co-ops in other villages. We can't let it go—'

'Any luck with the suppliers in Pune?' Daphne said.

'They are not quite what we need, their prices — I can keep bargaining, but—'

'We will save it, Shanta—'

Shanta watched her. 'Many women in your country are sex slaves too, if you only look under the surface. Women are brought in to India for weekends from Russia and Europe as sex objects for rich men of all nationalities. You think those women are free? And in that way we are still a colony.'

Daphne shuffled beside the painting again, the gin was starting to have an effect and the brightness outside burst into the room. The Yakshi was more alive now, a sensuous half smile on her lips. There was more work to do on her body, the tree and the background. 'I want to meet them — Ben would have wanted me to. Before we go though, I must visit the caves again.'

'We can go tomorrow,' Shanta smiled at her.

'When I came years ago with Ben the Yakshi I saw in the first cave — her glare was a though her eyes were boring straight into parts of me I didn't know, making me feel I was a living lie—'

'Tree spirits can be disturbing. You are painting one, so you feel their presence. But they are only ghosts,' Shanta laughed, 'Yakshi — painted ghosts.'

6

After a late evening meal Carl pulled Raj out into the warm night and they sat in the darkness of the hotel gardens. The caves of Ajanta, a kilometre or so behind them were lost in blackness. 'Have a smoke.' Carl took out a packet and they lit up. A canopy of stars pitted the sky. 'You remember that temple you took me to. Down near where your mother was born in Karnataka. Must be a couple of years ago now. The one with the carved bodies on the walls.'

Raj was watching the heavens.

Carl drew on the cigarette. 'That was some place. Some carvings,' he laughed. 'You pointed one out — one guy with three women. Three women eh? The acrobatics of it — all carved out on the walls. Amazing.'

Raj blew out smoke. 'You miss your wife?'

Carl looked at him, the features of his face just discernible in the faint beams of light from the hotel. He shrugged. 'That's over mate. You know how women can be. I didn't do anything wrong, Raj. She said, "It's not you, it's me. You get angry, think I need protecting. The love's not there—"'

'You miss your daughter, I think,' Raj said.

'Melody does her own thing, lives most of the time with her mother.'

'I've never met her.' Raj continued star gazing then turned to him. 'You worry about her.'

'She can look after herself,' Carl laughed. 'It's just that some of the guys she goes for are tossers. Young kids who don't give a monkey's about her. Yeah, you worry as a father. And there's all sorts of older men you have to watch these days. You never know if there's someone in business who wants to get to you through family. There's some nasty pieces of work out there. There's this Jake bloke I don't like. Worked for us and we had to get rid of him. Got caught with his hand in the till.' Carl stared at the stars with him. 'It was different for you growing up—'

Raj said, 'Kids pointed and laughed, picked on me. I was different. Until one day. The monsoon was heavy that year and the rivers deep and fast. This boy fell in — the brother of a big boy who was always beating me. Life is strange, isn't it? And this little boy always copied him and shouted stupid things at me. If I didn't do something he would be drowned. We are left with choices.'

'So you left him?' Carl watched his face in shadows. 'And now, the guilt comes back to you?'

'He was screaming. I felt a deep urge for revenge come inside me with a cruel laugh. I was frozen — couldn't do anything. And I looked at the palm trees swaying in the monsoon wind, backwards and forwards. I could see a shape there figuring itself in the flowing branches, a beautiful woman's shape. She was shouting to me, as though pleading. The next minute I jumped, I was in the water grabbing him and pulling him — and he was resisting — my enemy was beating me again. I had to slap his face, and he awoke from his hatred. We grabbed a branch from an overhanging tree and I hauled him ashore. I wasn't different anymore, I knew who I was, I knew what life was about—'

'What is it about?'

'Saving each other.'

'Do you think so? How do we do that?'

'We find our own way. We listen to the spirit in the trees — the Yakshi — it's like an old and forgotten part of our minds, a connection with things around us, I don't know, don't understand it all really — intuition — something like that, something that binds us to nature—'

'You're a bloody romantic, Raj, you and your superstitions.'

'Tree spirits can change your life,' Raj laughed.

'Come on, have another smoke. You and your bloody phantoms. Let's have something stronger, tastier.' Carl took a packet from his pocket and began rolling. 'With this stuff you really will start seeing things,' he laughed as he lay a little stream of grass in the open cigarette.

'You don't want to get on their bad side, that's for sure.'

Carl laughed. 'Anyway, what's to do round here. There's only pictures painted on walls, a couple of hotels, a few tourist shops, a string of restaurants. No local night life anywhere to be seen.' Raj smiled at him. 'There must be some wayward young Yakshi women around here, somewhere, if you know where to look. Every little town has one, doesn't it?' Carl rolled the joint and sealed it with his tongue along the gummed strip of the cigarette paper.

'Not with our mothers around,' Raj laughed.

'*Kali Ko-op* is just the same, whatever you think.' Carl shrugged, smirking. 'These girls have always been on the game. I mean it's part of who they are, they may get new ways to earn a living, but they'll always be the same at heart. I mean, this is between us, you and I.' Carl playfully wagged his finger at him. 'They may have learned weaving and dying and all that, but we all know what they get up to when they're not in school. I've seen it. I've seen them off with blokes. They can't get away from their old ways, it's what they've learned, who they are. You can't blame them. Do you remember that new girl when I was here last — pretty little thing — around nineteen — what was her name? Devi was it?'

'My mother keeps them in check,' Raj said. 'Those kind of girls, you need to use protection—'

'When she's not around, you can't tell me you haven't explored the place?' Carl lit the joint and drew on it. 'What do you think my dad was doing out here in the first place? Do you really think he just ended up at your mum's village? Do you seriously think, he was this pure and upright man my mum makes him out to be? Ask your mum.' He blew out smoke. 'But we don't want any of this coming out now, do we — my mum's too frail, and we want all this money from my dad to keep happening — so your business end won't collapse, we keep getting your stuff to sell and everything's hunky dory.' Carl slapped his shoulder, then handed the joint to his friend but felt his resistance. 'That is what you want?' Raj nodded.

'We can do it,' Raj said, but Carl could feel his uncertainty.

'Good.' Carl took the joint back from him and smiled. 'We don't want my mum blocking things.'

'You've got nothing to lose,' Raj's voice was firm in the darkness. 'Whatever happens you can go back, build your on line business, sell off your shops, have an inheritance and live a rich life. And my sister rots in hospital and my mother's business falls apart. You always did have it better than me — the cards were always stacked your way. Whatever Ben did, you were his favourite, not me.'

Carl was unfazed. 'It was always equal — as equal as it can get for us — you got your schooling, you lived a privileged life here. And what my dad didn't give you I made up for.'

Raj stood, staring up at the myriad of stars, then over to Carl. 'But will that always be so?'

'Like you say, I've got nothing to lose either way —'

'You worry about your mother —'

'I can handle her whatever happens.' Carl shrugged. 'It's in your interests to play along with me so I keep my mouth shut too.'

'*Paint Clever* would survive without my mum's supplies?'

'She hasn't got any supplies at the moment.' Carl was aware of Raj's rising temper.

'She will get some —'

'You hope. So you keep everyone happy. It's down to you, Raj.'

'You need us.'

'So play along. That's all you've got to do—' Carl patted him but he pulled away angrily.

'Like always.'

'Like always—'

They sat quietly with their own thoughts for a long time before Carl got up. 'You remember that temple down your way you were telling me about, the one with the erotic carvings? And Devi, do you remember her — pretty young thing. She is about nineteen isn't she?'

*****

Daphne hid her feelings of apprehension from Shanta as they entered the first cave. Memories from her previous visit overwhelmed her, the images of the Yakshi suddenly fresh again and threatening and she felt unsteady on her feet. A guide at the entrance in plain white kurta reminded them that only small torches were allowed and no flash photography.

Being the only ones in, darkness enveloped them. Daphne relived the childhood fear of night and all the visions it could conjure until Shanta flicked on her torch. They marvelled at the painting of the young Buddha in his palace, no longer wanting to lead a life of luxury and the attempts of his wife to use music and dance to keep him.

Daphne lit her torch and led Shanta to the two princesses and quickly remarked that the dual portrait seemed more colourful than when she had come before. Flaked and worn in their lower bodies over the centuries, but still alive in patches and islands of tone and colour, they seemed to have real lives, that they would go off stage any moment and continue with their tasks. Daphne guided her torch so they could explore the detail and to consider how their eyes and expressions said a lot about their differing characters. Hypnotised, they meditated on the image in silence for many minutes.

'It's amazing,' Daphne whispered. 'These were painted around five hundred AD. In medieval England the pictures we've got of people are flat, two dimensional drawings — like children draw. These princesses were painted with so much more depth at least seven or eight hundred years before that. And a thousand years before the Mona Lisa — and Rembrandt.'

Shanta nodded. 'The work, the artistry—'

Daphne was anxious to confront her phantom from the past and searched the wall for the Yakshi. 'There she is—'

'You have her expression in your painting — she's of the earth but reaching for the branches and the sky. You painted it all from memory?'

'That and pictures from an old book an art teacher gave me.'

'She's so alive, her hair in one long braid over her right shoulder — the details of the fingers holding the branch, the left leg wrapped around the trunk of the young tree — I can see why she has so much for you—'

Dizziness was coming over Daphne. The figure was moving in slow embrace curling around the tree. She moved with the smoothness and alacrity of a dancer, with lightness of step and smoothness of hand gesture. Daphne was losing herself in the image, felt herself being drawn into her world. Swinging around the narrow trunk, she slowed, halting with her hand outreached to Daphne, her eyes looking straight into hers.

Unsteady on her feet, she clutched Shanta's arm.

'You're unwell.' Shanta held her. 'We must go.'

Shanta led her to the cave entrance and sat her in shade on a chair provided by the guide. The brightness was suddenly blinding and she felt herself fading. Two Indian women tourists stopped to help.

Memories of the previous sighting of the Yakshi came to her repeating the mantra: 'The monsoon does not come to all parts of India, some places have no rain for years. The trees die, the Yakshi tree spirits—'

'It's very hot today, you must rest,' Shanta told her as an elderly woman in a green and yellow sari and flip flops made her drink some water, and another in a red sari rubbed Daphne's forehead with a cold wet tissue.

She sat in the shade, not near enough to the cave entrance to be heated by the blade of sunshine that fanned through, but still disturbed by the way the Yakshi had stared with her large brown-black eyes, gabbling something, making her feel her life was a waste.

'Rest a moment,' Shanta insisted, 'and we will get someone to take you back.' The guide, a tall crouching man, had alerted the office and a couple of men were on their way to help her down the steps to the entrance where a wheelchair was waiting.

Still trapped by the spectral world she leaned back wearily. 'All the back breaking work in life,' she said, 'and for what?' She looked up at Shanta. 'I should have been an artist. She told me that with her eyes—'

She could see the specks of the men who were coming to help her at the bottom of the line of steps. 'A rickshaw is ready to take you to your hotel, madam,' the guide said. The elderly women nearby nodded.

'She whispered in my ear: "I come to those whose lives are not complete, who have not found themselves."' Daphne's voice was still shaky but stronger. '"We must grow like a tree with firm roots and floral branches, and we must bend with life's winds—"'

'You're a poet too,' Shanta smiled at her, 'not just a painter.'

'My mother never thought I was any good at art,' Daphne reflected, 'but I can see why Ben wanted to work with you — all those talents at your disposal. You're so perceptive, so — I was deeply in love with my married art teacher Tommy. My parents put a stop — Everyone said how much promise I had, how precocious I was — and now that's all lost.'

'It's still there in you.' Shanta held her arm gently. 'We can paint together and find that girl inside you again.'

The two big men clasped hands making a seat for her and lifted her, carrying her down the flight of steps, never stumbling, always steady, their hands gripping under her. She waved the women helpers goodbye, letting herself be transported to the waiting rickshaw.

When Daphne had rested in her hotel chalet-room Shanta came back. She chatted to Daphne about her trips to Kochi, and the Chinese fishing nets along the river. 'They stand on the river bank, made of wood. The men dip the nets attached to them in and scoop up fish.' Shanta got her an orange drink and some nuts, which she turned down. 'A wonderful scene to paint.'

Still tormented by her past, Daphne could not concentrate on Shanta's small talk and felt the urge to unload. 'I should have run away with Tommy. It would have been reckless and stupid. But we could have found the money for the south of France to start with — he could have taught me to paint properly —' Shanta sat with her, sipping her orange juice. 'Somehow we would have got to Ajanta — when you're young you can do anything —'

'Well, you think you can,' Shanta laughed. 'When you're young.'

'But you can, if you believe enough — that's what being young is —'

'You trusted Tommy that much? Men say these things — and mean them at the time, but sometimes their promises don't come to anything —'

'He said he would and I believed him — at the time.' Daphne reminisced gloomily.

'A married man.' Shanta looked at her. 'With children?'

Daphne sat up, memories reviving her. 'I bumped into him one day — oh, it must be over twenty years ago now. In the National Gallery. There's a favourite picture of mine there: *A Woman Bathing* by Rembrandt. It's such a tenderly painted picture. I can't tell you how much I love this painting.

Hendrickje Stoffels. Rembrandt's mistress. You can see how much he loves her by the way he has portrayed her. She is raising a smock above her knees so she can slowly wade in, and she's a bit unsteady, being barefoot, maybe there are stones and pebbles underwater that she can't see and might stumble on — how he's caught that look. The smile rivals that of the Mona Lisa, I swear: she has a radiance about her, the sort of aura reserved for holy people — like the Madonna for instance. She leaves a rich robe of Alizarin Crimson behind on a rock. Gentle light falls on her. How he masters light and shade. She comes out of a rich darkness of Umber and Sienna, so we see the right side of her face in light, but the other side in shadow. I can't tell you — I should find it on my phone, I—'

'Later.' Shanta said, 'Rest now.'

'She was only twenty eight in 1654 when Rembrandt painted her. He never married her even though his wife Saskia had died. And she helped him sell his work. But she died only nine years later, probably of the plague. Which makes this painting have even more resonance for me. She is coming out of the background of darkness, into light, but on into an unknown journey through the waters . . .'

'I'd love to see it.'

'You'll come to England one day and I'll take you to see it.'

Shanta looked at her.

'You will come, won't you?'

'And Tommy? He was there that time and you met him?'

'Yes, of course, I was saying. When I'm in London and have a free moment I pop in the National just to sit in front of the painting. And one day of course while I was sitting there he came and sat next to me. I was so engrossed in it I didn't take in who was next to me for a time, and he said nothing, until I turned and recognised him. We amazed each other and talked for over an hour. God, it must have been the early nineties. I was in my mid thirties and he was into his fifties. He looked much older — like an old man. His eyes were drawn in deep in the sockets, darkly, his forehead was furrowed and the lines around his mouth were deep and dark. He was a ghost of what he had been, and he looked beaten.'

'What did you feel?' Shanta said.

'Sorrow. Pity. And I didn't want to feel those things — I struggled against them. And there was still a small flame inside me for him, and he still had a sparkle in his eye. "He's got it right, hasn't he? Rembrandt?" he said and I nodded, but all I really wanted to know was whether he really did take the money and run from my mother. "Did you become an artist?" I asked him, but he replied with a question of his own: "Did you?" Then we both laughed because we knew neither of us had done it. We chatted about art, Rembrandt. I asked about his children and he told me how they had grown up and got their own lives, how he and his wife had split years ago. I persisted: "Why didn't you become someone with a name?" But he threw it back to me. "Why didn't you? You were always the most talented of the two of us." He floored me with that, but I couldn't let him get away with it. "My mum and dad forced me into the art business," I told him, snarling a bit as I did so, no doubt. "They broke us up. They said you'd demanded money, they'd paid you off to leave me alone, but I never believed it. I knew you would never do that."' She paused, hating the memory.

'Are you too hot, Daphne?' Shanta comforted her. 'Shall I up the air con?'

Daphne shook her head. 'You know he looked at me and then up at Hendrickje for a time and I knew. "You took the money, didn't you?" He stood up slowly, faced me and said. "If there's one thing I do deeply regret —" And I didn't let him finish and yelled at him. "You finished my art career." He looked away, then up at Hendrickje again, and back at me and said, "And I realised later by doing it, things would never be the same again, I would never be the successful artist I aspired to. There was nothing for me after you. Nothing." He looked down, then up at me with sorrowful eyes and I knew he still loved me. And the sorrow and pity I felt for him just grew and grew, as my respect and love for him just seemed to fall away. Then he stepped close to the Rembrandt and said, "Look at that, Daphne. Just look at the light and shade, the expression on her face." He was excited and I could see the old Tommy there. "Did you do it, Daph, did you get to Ajanta? The princesses?" I nodded and for a brief moment all the affection I had for him came back to me in a rush and I was nearly in tears. "You should have taken me, Tommy. It should have been you, we should have run together." I never saw him again. I heard later from an old friend who he had also taught that he had died. Hit the bottle, found himself homeless and –' She stopped her sniffles with a tissue.

Daphne leaned back on her pillows and Shanta reached for her hand and held on for a while.

'I should leave you to rest,' Shanta said but Daphne protested.

'Not yet.' Daphne feared if Shanta went she would end up depressed and in tears. She was quiet a moment searching Shanta's expression and trying to look into her experience as a bereaved woman. 'Tell me,' she said softly. 'Your husband – he really was your husband?' Shanta looked away. 'A married man, Shanta? And Raj? How can that be, in India?'

'If a man has money,' Shanta gave a smile of resignation, 'many things go on behind closed doors.'

'You must have loved him a lot.' Daphne was relieved to get away a moment from her own troubles, but anxious now to know everything about *Kali Ko-op*, there was so much she had missed, so much more to know, especially now that Ben had left so much money to Shanta. 'You could not have him all?'

Shanta drew back her hand. 'He told me many times he would leave his wife and be with me. They were just words in the end – and words don't lead to an inheritance.' She looked away.

'Inheritance?' Daphne was curious.

'When a married man dies, his mistress gets nothing.'

'And all this happened to you, too? Recently? Both of us have lost our loves. It must be very hard for you, I see it all now.' Daphne sat up and held Shanta's hand again. 'I'm here with you — all these things going on in your life, but now we're closer and know each other I'm happy Ben has thought about you in his Will.'

'You see,' Shanta said, 'the Yakshi brings new outlooks on life —'

'But the look in her eye, staring out at me, and whispering: "they wait in those parts for rain, trees and people. None comes. The ground is hard. Nothing grows. Trees die —"'

'Come with me to *Kali Ko-op*,' Shanta said. 'In a few days when you've recovered and rested and I have cooked you food and brought you things and we have got to know each other more. Raj can take us in his taxi and you can stay with me for as long as you want.'

Daphne smiled. 'That's just what I need. To see it for myself.'

'I must tell you though, there's a fascinating old story about trees in a forest in Jodhpur. It's supposed to be true.' Daphne motioned her to carry on. 'The ruler of Jodhpur wanted trees cut down for his palace and sent his men to a forest in Rajasthan, but a local woman heard about it. Her name was Amrita Devi — she knew the Yakshi tree spirit was inside every tree and so she clung to a tree trunk. Men took axes and cut Amrita Devi down with the tree she hung onto. But Amrita's daughter came and clung on to another tree, but they cut her down with it as well. More and more women came, at least three hundred they say, but all were cut down trying to save the trees and their spirits. They say no grass grows there now, there was too much blood. But when the prince heard he was very ashamed and said the forest must stay forever and no one must touch it. A law was made and now the Bishnoi tribe look after the forest, and they kill nothing there. They say it's true, all of it . . .'

7

There was little manufactured light near the small temple so the night sky shone with stars. The dark shape of trees hung around the central Gopuram, its pastel orange lost in shadows. When the moon slipped out of cloud it set a pool of luminescence around the front of the temple.

Raj had parked the old Ambassador at the end of the track that led through forest to the village.

'God, Raj.' Carl got out and surveyed what he could see of the building. 'That journey down here. I didn't think Karnataka was on the other side of the world from Ajanta. Man—'

'The state of the roads,' Raj laughed, getting out, passing Carl a cigarette and lighting them both, their faces flashing bright a moment.

'And the driving — and having to put up with your mum and my mum agreeing about everything.'

'India is known for its special highway code: horn and charge, and more horn.'

'And this outdated taxi of yours. God, man, when the money comes get yourself something more fashionable — and without springs that poke through the seating.'

Raj drew in smoke. 'They're both good friends, at least.'

'Such a relief to drop them off and have a bit of time to ourselves at last.'

'I come here sometimes, in the night like this,' Raj contemplated. 'Just to chill out and think things out alone. I look up and spot shooting stars, and satellites when they catch the sun. It makes you think about how small we really are with all our troubles.'

'Come on, show me again.' Carl nodded in the direction of the temple. 'Those wild carvings—'

Raj went to the car, coming back with a few candles which he lined up on the temple steps and lit one by one.

'You've heard from Melody today?' Raj said. 'I mean, you told me to remind you to keep in contact.'

'We were Skyping regularly in Ajanta — every other day. You're right, I haven't heard from her for some time. Must be busy with her party and all that. The last text was: *Have a good time in Karnataka.* She usually gives me more than that. I hope she's not unhappy about something.'

'How can a text sound sad?' Raj laughed, adjusting the candles so the light flickered, reflecting off the silver entrance door.

Raj handed him a small torch and clicked on his own..

'And of course I intend to have a good time here.' Carl switched his on. 'Show me again.' He waved the torch at the walls. 'I can't see anything. Where are they?'

'Some of Karnataka is wild, backward,' Raj said. 'Here's a carving of Shiva-ji and his consort Parvati. And here he is dancing in a circle of flames, and at the Churning of the Sea of Milk, the creation story—'

Carl played frustratedly with the beam for a time, flashing it up and down the tower and over images of Shiva and Parvati. 'Not that stuff. Where are they? You're playing with me.'

Raj laughed, settling his torch beam on a series of carvings at head height.

'Ah, you've found it,' Carl yelled. 'Or should I say – *them*.'

Several men were lying, sitting or standing in contorted positions along with numbers of females in various motions with them. In another frieze two women were helping lower a third into a position with a man lying on his back.

'Fascinating.' Carl explored the carvings with his hands, following shapes and bodies. 'Three women to one man.' Carl was quiet, fingering, Raj behind him smiling. 'And *Kali Ko-op* is just down the road from here,' Carl laughed at the irony. 'And Devi, the new girl—'

'We don't want to risk things—'

'We want this to go smoothly, don't we, Raj?' Carl threw the end of the cigarette away.

'Of course. We don't want anything to spoil it.'

'Spoil?' Carl ran his fingers over a group of naked women, the tips rippling on their over large breasts. 'How can moksha spoil anything. They get money. There's nothing like supporting the poor.'

'Not with our mothers around—'

Carl laughed. 'Don't play pure and innocent with me. The girls love you when you walk in the room, I've seen them. You can't tell me you haven't had the odd bite here and there with this right on your doorstep?'

'Let's go back,' Raj nodded to Carl to head back to the car. He pulled open the door and got back in.

'You scared, or what?'

'Come on.'

'We had a deal, Raj. You're not running out on me?'

'Another time—'

'You didn't find her then? — or you chickened out—'

As Raj turned on the headlights, the beams lit up a young woman in gold and red sari standing under trees.

'You did,' Carl laughed.

Long gold coloured earrings hung from her lobes and her wrists were covered in bangles. Round her neck she wore a necklace of red and white beads that seemed to look cheap compared to the other gold plated neck gear that adorned her.

'Like a princess. Just look at you. Come out now.' She looked down and he went to her, took her hand and brought her out into the main beam of the headlights, but she kept her gaze from him, her stare focussed on the ground in front of him and she stood silently. 'Twirl for me, Devi,' he said but she would not move. Taking her hand again he gently led her into a slow spin and she went with him, the traces of a smile on her lips.

'You've seen her, Carl. We should go now,' Raj called through the driver's window.

'Turn for me Devi.' She shuffled around gracefully, allowing her arms to wave as she went. 'That's it. Lovely. What does your name mean?' Still she would not look up at him. 'Devi?'

'Goddess,' Devi whispered.

'This is too risky, so close to my mother's place,' Raj called from the car.

'I can see that — a sparkling deity.' Carl watched her twirl again, her hair tied up in a bun with yellow flowers, and called genially to Raj. 'We're not backing out now. Get that bottle from the car, Raj, let's have a party and get to know each other.'

Raj started the car. Carl strode over, reached into the ignition and pulled the key out and stuffed it in his pocket, the headlights popping out. 'This is all right, it's just a little party, isn't it, Devi? Now get the bottle, Raj.' He turned back to Devi, took her hand and led her to the steps of the temple and they sat near the candles.

Raj was over in a moment handing him the bottle and three glasses. Carl picked up his anxiety and resentment. Devi turned aside when Carl offered her a drink. 'You live in the village?' She nodded. 'Come on, tell me more.' Carl coaxed her, but she tightened her shoulders.

'What do you care about her?' Raj snapped, pouring himself a generous portion of whisky and taking a gulp.

'School was very good.' Devi would not look at him.

'You couldn't carry on at school?' Carl poured himself a glass and sipped.

'I left when my father died. I had to help in the house.'

'That must have been a long time ago.' Carl watched her. 'What did you learn there?'

'We must learn English.' She gave a little smile, but still would not look up at him. 'Mathematics and history. I was always good at history. I liked stories about Gandhi and all that.' Forgetting herself, she smiled up a moment and her eyes sparkled. 'There's nothing to tell about my life.' Devi shrugged a little. 'I grew up in a village. When my father was gone I had to help my mother.'

'So you've seen her. Let's go.' Raj drained his glass.

'Don't mind my friend,' Carl smirked at Devi, 'he's not always such a bore.'

'This isn't Bollywood,' Raj grimaced, 'this is life. Is this what you really came to India for?'

'You left school, Devi.' Carl ignored his friend. 'And then what?'

'She was married to the goddess Yellamma. You know all that stuff—'

'Let her talk for herself. Be good to us now and offer her a drink again. Raj?' Carl smiled at his new protégé. 'You must drink with us.' He pulled the bottle from Raj, but before he could get a glass for her she had snatched the bottle from him. Tilting it carefully to her mouth without allowing her lips to touch the rim she took a swig. Carl laughed. 'We've got one here, then.'

Raj said, 'But she belongs to my mother.'

'Why did you become dedicated to Yellamma?' Carl asked.

'My mother chose me.'

'She'll give you a sob story.' Raj spat in a corner. 'About her family, about how hard it all is and all that. But you know the Devadasi tradition has gone on for thousands of years. They were courtesans in the palaces of princes and kings, singing, dancing, reciting poetry. They had wealth and power.'

'And now?' Carl interrupted and then offered her more whisky from his glass.

'She is a Dalit,' Raj said. 'She will not drink from your glass.'

Carl took the spare empty glass and poured Devi a splash of whisky and nodded for her to drink. She took a gulp without comment and would have finished the measure if Carl had not held her wrist gently to stop her. 'She can drink me under the table anytime,' Carl laughed. He liked her. Bending to her he took up her glass and put it to his own lips and sipped while she stared at him. Raj sniffed and looked away. Carl gave the glass back and motioned her to finish what was left there. She looked up at him again, then took it and sipped.

'You are mad,' Raj said. 'A Brahmin cannot dirty himself with the shadow of a Dalit girl in the day, but at night she can take him to moksha.'

'Why so tense, Raj. Chill, man. Have another joint. It's all right. Dance for me again Devi. I'm told Devadasi are trained in the arts — *all* of them.'

Raj was standing with arms folded. Taking her chunni scarf in hand, Devi danced several steps, twirled, motioned with her fingers as she turned and smiled at the men. Moving lightly she stepped around Raj, smiling and gesturing sensually at him. 'I can dance for you,' she laughed. 'I can sing you songs of lost lovers.' She rippled her hips in circular motions and lightly whisking her body round in skips and bounds, finished with her hands in prayer position.

'You've loosened up now.' Carl gave a short laugh. 'A different Devi, all extravert and — I like it—'

'Amazing what a few drinks will do for a whore,' Raj snapped.

'I said, "Chill, Raj."' He turned to Devi again. 'I don't know what's up with him.'

'We can't do this, Carl.'

Ignoring him, Carl said to her, 'You said your mother chose you. Why? Do you like the life?'

'I dance for men, I turn their heads.' She covered her laughter with her hand.

'Watching you dance, I know I'm in heaven,' Carl mused. 'So who is this goddess Yellamma?'

Devi remained with her hands in prayer position, bowed her head, then raising her face smiled towards Carl. 'Yellamma was the wife of the god Jamadagni.' She began to act out the story, emphasising parts with dramatic gesture. 'And every day she fetched water in clay pots from the river.' Devi lifted an imaginary pot, placed it on her head and pranced along, swinging her hips and laughing. 'But one day.' She wagged her finger at Carl and spun to Raj who was looking over his shoulder and did the same to him. 'While she was bending to the water,' she bent and imitated the action, 'she saw on the other bank a god making love to a goddess.' Devi sprang up aghast, her hand to her mouth. 'And she had a bad thought. She wanted that love.' Devi pretended to bite her lower lip. 'That bad thought brought bad luck, for all her pots turned to soap and the water inside ran away.' She threw her arms out melodramatically and gasped. 'When she got home Jamadagni saw what had happened and in his fury he got his son to cut off her head.' She quickly drew her fingers across her throat. 'But,' she paused again, pointing her finger first at Carl, then at Raj who was scowling at her, 'Jamadagni gave his son one wish. And he wished his mother to come back. And she did. But only to take girls from their families to obey her—'

'You see,' Raj laughed, 'a story of how a woman can tempt man with bad thoughts. You said it yourself, once a whore always one—'

'So it seems,' Carl nodded, smiling.

'Once she is married to Yellamma she cannot marry a man, but must be there for all men.' Raj pulled a packet from his shirt pocket and lit a cigarette.

'Or what?'

Devi put her hands on her hips. 'All the village is cursed. Women can't have babies, all the rice dies in the fields. Bad things happen. We have to serve her.'

'Sounds like a load of superstitious baloney.'

'My friend ran away with a man to Mumbai and her sister died the next week.'

'You believe that?' Carl sniffed.

'Can I dance for you again, sir?' Devi smiled.

The night was dark and warm. He looked up. A shooting star flipped through the eastern sky and died. 'Yes,' he said as a message beeped on his phone. Reading it, he called to Raj. 'She wants to ring me; she wants to talk.'

'You have a woman in your life, sir? She is very lucky.'

'My daughter, Melody,' Carl told her. 'I've been thinking about her.'

'How old is she?'

'Fifteen.' Carl tapped his phone. 'This Jake bloke's been hanging round her, my mate back home texted me on the way down here. Jake's my age for god's sake. Not satisfied nicking money from us — She's under age for god's sake—'

'Under age?' Devi watched him.

'A man cannot have a woman under sixteen. It's the law.'

'All girls I know would love to live in England.'

'It's eighteen here,' Raj drew on his cigarette.

'Police don't do anything here,' Devi said. 'Police come to Devadasi and don't care how old—'

Raj scowled at her. 'You want to live in England, but you never will.' He wagged his finger at her. 'You remember your place here. Jeldi. Quickly.'

'Everyone has to know their place according to you, Raj?' Carl challenged Raj.

'You wanted me to find her.' Raj scowled.

Ignoring him, Carl looked back at his phone. 'I must ring her — soon—' He gently took Devi's fingers and they smiled at each other. His palms were sweating as they walked hand in hand along the front of the temple. Stopping near the frieze of figures, he again explored their bodies with his hands. Drawing hers up with his, they traced the carved bodies before drifting into the darkness around the temple.

8

'I'm so impressed, Shanta. What a scheme.' Daphne sat herself near a smiling woman in her thirties who was sewing together purses. *Kali Ko-op* was contained in an old house with many rooms both upstairs and down. Crumbling at the outside edges, the dirty white building was situated in fields at the end of a track. The inside walls of the wide main room were decorated with paintings and hangings the women had made themselves. Around twenty women were busy working and chatting.

Shanta introduced her to Veena, a woman in her twenties in a yellow and purple sari who was weaving pieces of recycled fabric into rugs. Veena talked excitedly about her five year old daughter who was painting pictures next to her. 'We can get her into school soon,' Veena told her. 'She can grow up and get a good job and look after her mother.' They laughed, Veena showing Daphne how to weave in some of the fabric. 'You are good, you must come and work here.'

Several other children were skipping about or sitting helping their mothers. Teenagers Chandra and Meena, were knitting baby clothes when Daphne sat with them telling her what a wonderful place *Kali Ko-op* was, how much it had changed their lives. 'We can meet here,' Chandra told her.

'Not be on our own in our house,' Meena added.

'We can learn, we can be somebody.'

Three women who looked as though they were in their forties were painting icons of Shiva, Laxmi, Hanuman and Ganesh. One of them, Neela, talked about their friend Bhavna who had just got married. 'She was lucky,' Neela said, 'she found a good man. He knows she is Devadasi but he loves her.'

'A good man is hard to find,' Daphne laughed with them.

Neela leaned forward to her, placing her hand on her arm. 'Ben is good man. He look after us.'

'Respect us,' one of her friends added.

'We sorry,' the other said.

'Good man,' they all nodded.

'Thank you.' Daphne held back tears.

Other women were painting dancers, flowers and peacocks on little pots. Two girls who looked barely in their teens were painting little pictures of women carrying pots on their heads on the sorts of hand made paper Shanta supplied *Paint Clever* with and another two were carving tiny images of gods and goddesses out of wood.'

'What a wonderful place, Shanta, you must be so proud—'

'Ben's money and Ben's help—'

'He told me of course, but I had no idea what it was really like. It's doing so much for the women's confidence and esteem. And a place where they can meet and be themselves.'

'Their mothers and sisters come and help — even one or two brothers.'

'It's more than a co-op then, it's a community centre—' Daphne observed.

'I want it for all Devadasi in all villages.'

'You will, you will—' Daphne smiled, enjoying watching the women laughing and chatting while they worked. 'Some of the produce comes to us, but you have other markets locally?'

'We sell them in our shop in the village,' Shanta said, 'but we also take our wares to tourist places like Hampi and even up to Goa and supply shops and stalls. But it's not the money that matters, it's the women. They smile, they are happy, they have a life. Ben helped so much.' Shanta got one of the women to bring them pineapple juice and a bowl of nuts. 'We've been able to afford someone who comes in a few times a week and teaches them to read and write — in English and in Hindi. You can see their confidence rise every day. You can see them beginning to leave behind feelings of being dirty and worthless. He even helped pay for this old building to be renovated.' She stopped, hiding her emotions.

'Shanta?' Daphne led her out through doors onto the veranda out of earshot of the women.

'I cannot buy supplies for *Paint Clever*. Banks will not give loans.'

'Ben's money, Shanta —'

'Big debts. I have to pay the women. The little income the co-op brings. If I don't they have nothing to live on. They go back where they were. What good is that? It is worse — having known a different life —'

Daphne heard the voices, and two women singing as they worked. She looked in at the workbenches piled with materials and the walls hung with fabrics, several with lines of elephants head to tail across them. Large windows had red and gold curtains to curtail the heat and light, and although there was no air conditioning there were a couple of rickety fans on the ceiling, buzzing, and shaking in their holdings. And she imagined them all gone, the building dusty and empty except for the odd rat and the women on the street being propositioned by ugly old men.

'It's truly wonderful — they're so happy.'

'There are others who are learning culinary skills. In most restaurants you'll see men cooking and waiting, but we planned to open a small restaurant run by women.'

The brick and wood building from Victorian times had a long veranda that opened out to a road that led to the village, up a track between trees. It had been a local landowner's house, Shanta told her, and ironically a landowner who demanded it as his right to own several of the Devadasi women — although he was married with five children.

Two overweight men were relaxing in easy chairs smoking and chatting in the shade and being waited on by a young woman bringing cold drinks.

'We even have beds upstairs if one of the women needs to stay overnight alone. Men are strictly not allowed up there.' They laughed. 'Many of the Devadasi girls and women have what they call a husband — a boyfriend — and they can come around pestering sometimes. We need security, Daphne. You see we can't live entirely without men.' She clapped her hands and laughed. 'The two men you see up there, they are very good supporters of *Kali Ko-op* and all its ethics. If their boyfriends come there can be violence and we have to call the police. But strangely, being men, the police usually side with the boyfriends, seeing them as victims and the girls as predators. Can you believe it? Such is how things are here. So, we need the help of our own security system on the veranda.' She laughed again. 'They're not always lying about being waited on, you mustn't think that. They help with all the heavy work and they clear the land for growing—'

'Men do have their uses, then?' Daphne laughed with her. 'I'm so impressed, Shanta. All this you've done — on your own—'

'Like me, Ben believed in the Devadasi women — in their worth — that they could make something of their lives. If we can educate the women they can then have work and they can leave us and make way for others. And once they have work they can be independent and support themselves and their children.' The women chatted and laughed as they worked. Shanta looked away from her.

'It's very good of you to come and see us Daphne, we thank you. All of us.' Shanta was looking around the workers, as if searching for someone.

'It's the least we can do.'

Breeze wafted through the open doorway and windows, playing with the curtains and bringing with it the smell of onions, garlic, ginger and spices cooking.

'That smells just heavenly, Shanta.'

'You will have something to eat with us?'

'You have to ask?' Daphne smiled.

A woman brought cups of tea on a tray and the workers took a break, some going outside, others in a huddle laughing.

Shanta looked around again. 'They are all here. Except one.' Shanta watched them with the eyes of a worrying mother. 'I worry about her.'

'This should be a model for lots of places around India.'

'Devi,' Shanta continued about her truant. 'She's a new girl. Her father treated her badly and abused her. Then he died and her mother dedicated her to Yellamma — there was no money, they couldn't survive without the income a Devadasi can bring in and her mother is sick now and I don't want her going back to the old ways. She's bright, we can find some good work for her, maybe even send her to college.'

'When she knows the co--op is going to thrive now, she'll come running back, you'll see. I'm so pleased. I'm a sentimental old woman I know, but Shanta, I feel I've found a new friend in you. We can work together, I know we can. I can come over here, and you can come to England. Let's agree on that.' She held her hand out for Shanta and she took it and shook.

A woman brought in some homemade sweets, Ladoo, Jalebi and Gulab Jamun, and passed them around on a plate to laughter and cries. Shanta said something to the woman about Devi then turned back to Daphne. 'So many of the younger women find it hard not to go back to the old ways. We discourage it, and if we know someone is regularly doing sex work we suspend her for a while and offer her counselling — usually me, although I'm not qualified. But sometimes one of the women teachers helps in that too. The idea is to get them out of that way of life and to see that they are worth more than just the playthings of men. But it is a losing battle sometimes. Devadasi women often don't get past their mid thirties. I don't know if Devi herself is sick—'

'Can you contact her and find her?'

'Many of the girls are HIV and never get treated. AIDs is a big killer. We lost two last year in their twenties and now their mothers are looking after their children. It's desperate Daphne, the poverty, the–' Shanta banged her fist on the table with frustration. 'And the women carry it all. And are there for the men when they want them–'

'I'm sorry,' Daphne said.

'What else is there for her,' Shanta finished. 'The men in lorries they go with who truck up and down the country spreading disease.'

'What you have achieved so far, we can develop and expand.' Daphne reached for Shanta's arm and held her gently, and then pulled her into a hug.

*****

Devi clung to Carl's arm as they came back into the moonlight in front of the temple, and he held on to her, clasping her hand as though she was an old lover he had revered for years.

'We go–' Raj headed for the taxi.

'Devi's my friend, aren't you?' He pecked her forehead. 'My little babe.'

Raj cast a glance over his shoulder. 'You did, didn't you?'

'Come on Raj. Chill out, will you? Have a drink with us. Celebrate me finding my new love.'

Devi held on his arm, smiling up at him.

'You have to use them with these girls.' Raj had his hands on his hips.

'What are you on about?' Carl grabbed the bottle and handed it to Devi who swigged and laughed. 'You're a miserable sod tonight. Go and sit in the car if you can't party.'

'HIV,' Raj called to him with a sneer. 'You know these things, you've been around enough.' Carl stared at him for several seconds. 'You've been here so many times you would think you still owned the country. These village girls actually think if you don't use them it gets them free of it,' he laughed. 'Can you believe it.'

'Sit in the taxi,' Carl yelled at him, waving his free arm. 'Leave us alone.' Carl ran his hand through strands of her hair. 'You're a good girl. I know you wouldn't, but — we have something, don't we Devi?' He looked her in the eyes. 'You're not like the women in Mumbai, all loud and —' He reached in his pocket for a packet of cigarettes, found one, lit it and shared it with Devi. Raj got in the taxi and slammed the door. 'I must phone my daughter.' She started to pull away to give him some privacy but he pulled her back. 'Stay,' Carl whispered nervously to her. 'Having a daughter makes you see things differently sometimes, you'll do anything to protect them—'

The night was quiet. Occasionally in the distance at the end of the track a car would pass. The temple was on the edge of the village away from houses.

'I have a daughter,' Devi said.

Carl laughed. 'You're not old enough.'

'Her name is Chaunta,' Devi went on. 'It means the one who is brighter than stars. She is two years old now.'

'You had her when you were seventeen? You're like me, I was too young when I had Melody — twenty five, but still too young.' He laughed. 'I wasn't ready for it at all.'

'Nobody is.'

'You're right.'

'We have things the same.'

'It's like we've always known each other — like old friends —'

'In past lives,' she laughed with him.

'I can't believe you have a daughter. You Devi? You're too young—'

'You must phone your daughter now.' Devi nudged him.

'You're very good to me, Devi,' he gave her a squeeze. Pulling out his phone, he called. As soon as he heard her voice he knew something was wrong, it was not the cheerful Melody he met at weekends. Devi was watching him walking in circles. 'What is it, Melody?' he breathed anxiously. 'What? Tell me. Is it him?' Carl was walking, stopping, listening. 'You tell him to keep away from you. It is that Jake, isn't it. You tell him. Does your mother know? Tell me?' He walked again. 'It is him. He's a nasty bastard, Melody, you've got to — what does your mother say?' He stopped walking and listened again, his eyes meeting Devi's a moment. 'Get your mother to help you for god's sake. Melody, what are you doing? No, you don't love him. This is Jake. He's getting back at me — we fell out at work. No, Melody, he doesn't love you. He doesn't—' Carl was shouting. 'You think it's love, but — he's—' Shocked, he stood still, staring into the night. Devi went to him and held his hand, but he pulled away. 'No,' he yelled down the phone. 'No, no, no — you don't go through with this. You don't. You stop it now — Melody — no more tears, you don't go through with it—' She had hung up. He clutched the phone, leaving it in his fist, as though by crushing it the pain would go. Devi held her hand out to him again and he took it and she led him to the candles on the steps of the temple.

'Fifteen, she is. Fifteen. That scumbag is my age.' Carl stood up again and tramped around. 'He's done it to get back at me. Fifteen. I'll have him when I get back. He's dead meat.' He turned to Devi. 'She's pregnant. Three months. And she won't terminate. What's her mother doing, for god's sake?'

Devi stood with him, held his arm and guided him back down to the steps and held on to him, her face in the flickering candle light. 'You will have a grandchild, maybe another girl.'

'How can she be so stupid. He made her. Groomed her.'

'If you tell a child not to do something, it means they will go and do it.'

He held on to her. 'It's not her fault though. He targeted me — she's fifteen for god's sake. Fifteen.'

'You will help her?' Devi pressed him.

'You don't want your children to make mistakes, your own daughter, the baby girl in your arms messed up by some pillock. Dead meat, Devi.'

'You must go back to her and be gentle with her.'

'I've got to phone her mum. She's a head case, but—' He stroked Devi's arm. 'Stay a bit longer.'

'You must go back home,' Devi insisted. 'You have a family. Your family is who you are.'

Carl looked at her again. 'Raj over there says some of you girls have lots of money.'

She turned her gaze from him, twiddling her red and white beads. 'My mum says she regretted dedicating me all her life. I am a little child, I don't know what's happening to me. One day there's big festival for me and I'm just a girl, just beginning to bleed, to be a woman. They take my clothes off and put me in leaves from the Neem tree — that's all my clothes. They all tell I'm special — every girl wants this, my life is full of riches and fun.' She paused for breath. 'I am scared — I walk in the village naked in Neem leaves, and all the women cheering and all the men staring at me. And I think why the local men who have land are shouting numbers? My uncle tells me — they want to be the first to get you. And the one with all the money can have you that day. I was eleven.' She paused, gathering herself. 'I don't know what is happening — all these men coming to me — I thought I will die.'

Carl held her hands. 'I'm sorry.'

'It all goes to my family. My mother has a bad back and bad leg and can't do things. My brother, he takes my money. I pay for his clothes, his college. He beat me for more money to get a phone. And in town with his friends he laughs with them, tells them I am dirty and they can go with me.' She held back her tears with a flush of anger and pushed back her shoulders. 'I want to be somebody — a teacher, a doctor. They stop me—'

'*Kali Ko*-op — they help you. You can learn there, go to college—' Carl said.

'The women say soon the co-op will stop. No more money.' She held the necklace towards him. 'I can never marry — Yellamma will curse me. And who would want me? Is there a man in the world who would marry me?'

Carl stopped her talking, and putting his hand in his pocket came out with a roll of rupee notes. 'Take it. It's not true. My dad's money will keep things going. You must go back there.'

'For Chaunta.' She took the money gently, kissed the back of his hand, then kissed the notes and hid them in a cloth bag. 'My auntie keeps her safe. There is no father for her. No father's name to write down — then my daughter cannot go to school.'

'She can grow up in the co-op?'

'If I cannot get money for her,' she shrugged, 'she must do like me.'

'This life — just goes on and on? Generation after generation?'

'For thousand years,' Devi said. 'In old days all temples have money from Devadasi.'

'There must be laws against it?'

'Do you think policemen and judge don't want a dancing girl?' She laughed. 'How many politician come?' She paused a moment and composed herself again. 'I want Chaunta to go to school — not this — to be somebody. You have a daughter, you know this.'

Carl picked up his phone again. 'I must talk to her mum.' Devi sat while he stood, wandering about with the phone to his ear. 'You've got to stop this. It's madness.' He listened again for a long time then let out, 'You tell her. You're too soft with her, you always have been. She's under age. Get an injunction. Keep him away. Let me talk to her again. You know Jake, he's — listen, he was sacked for — he was caught red handed — it was nothing to do with me. Of course Melody listens to Jake's side of it — the scumbag's a liar. Of course he is. Get Melody on the phone now. You've got to get her to terminate—'

He hit his thigh with the fist of his right hand. Devi walked to him and lightly rubbed his shoulders.

'She says Melody is scared of me — of what I'll do. She says I've lost Melody—'

'You must tell Melody how much you love her.'

He looked at her. 'You're special, Devi. If your life was different you would not be here doing this—'

'I will be in school now,' Devi laughed, covering her mouth with her hand.

Carl stared at her. 'You're too old for school. What are you talking about?' He paused, thinking. 'How old are you?' She held her head down. He pulled her chin up with his fingers. 'Devi. How old are you?' She snatched her face from his grip. 'Devi?'

The moon had slipped behind a line of cloud.

'Fifteen,' Raj yelled from the car. 'She's fifteen.'

'No Devi.' Carl pulled her back to him. 'No, no. You're not fifteen. You're nineteen, Devi, twenty. If you want more money I can give it to you. You're not fifteen. You've got a daughter of your own. No Devi, don't joke with me. This is serious. You must be at least nineteen — you've had a daughter. Are you trying to get more money from me? Are you trying to scare me? I'm not having this, Devi, it isn't funny. After all I've done—'

Devi stood in front of him, head down, hands clasped. 'I was thirteen when Chaunta born.'

'No, no,' Carl looked up at the stars and shook his head. 'No, no, Devi, you're not fifteen. It can't be.'

Devi reached out to him and as he did not flinch she held on to him. 'You have a daughter, Carl, you must go.'

He felt tears welling up and pushed them back. 'Is it true? You had Chaunta at thirteen?'

She nodded and looked away.

They stood in silence for a long time while Carl struggled with a tangle of thoughts and emotions. Then he drew her to him, kissed her forehead and said, 'What can I do? To stop all this.' He shrugged. 'I don't know. Can I buy you a house? What can I give you? Is this real? Can I make it right? What can I do?'

'Save your daughter.' Devi held his gaze with hers. He looked up at the moon. 'All daughters must be saved.' She went on. 'All. Or they become like ghosts.'

They looked out to the stars and the little line of lights along a road across the fields. Devi pulled him round and faced him. 'Build a school.'

He scowled at her, puzzled. 'A school? Here? Can I do that?'

'A school my daughter can go to. A school for all daughters in the village. They can grow up and not wear the red and white beads.'

Raj flicked a cigarette butt out of the car window.

Carl said to her, 'I can do that, Devi? Can I give you that? Yes, I can do that. I can build a school here.'

Raj got out of the taxi. 'Be careful what you promise a woman like that, Carl, in India. She will take everything from you.'

'A woman like that, Raj?'

Devi turned away from him. 'He think he's better — I am just low caste — and woman—'

'I thought we knew each other, Raj. I thought you growing up with a mum like Shanta—'

'And you — with her — you tell me, Carl — and all the time you are making me find Devi for you?'

'Men hold onto old ideas—' Devi laughed then said to Carl, 'You give what you can give. And you give to your daughter.'

'Does Yellamma really curse those who cross her?' Carl asked.

Raj came forward. 'We can do so much with your money here, Carl, don't throw it away. I can find you investments and properties—'

'Her village needs a school. We'll build one, get teachers and pay for them until it's up and running.'

'If politicians and land owners will let you,' Raj laughed.

'Then we'll buy them too. That's how it works, isn't it?'

Raj shrugged. 'If that's what you want.'

'I thought you said life is about saving others.'

'We have to be choosy about who we save. India is changing, my friend, opening up to the world. It is becoming faster and more commercialised. Isn't that what you're here for also — business opportunities.'

'Then it will sweep away old traditions and they will become ghosts.'

Raj came over to the couple to address Carl. 'Traditions you love to indulge in? I don't think so, Carl. Be realistic, as long as men like you have the need, the oldest profession will thrive. Already many women who call themselves Devadasi in cities have websites of their own. The agricultural life will die, like it did in the west. Land will be farmed digitally. People will flock to mega cities of hundreds of millions, and you think there will not be women ready to serve men? Men's heads will always be turned by a pretty girl and a pile of cash. That is how men are. We must preserve our traditions too. When all the western companies come with all the same brands and all the same shops, there will be no more little businesses, no more individuality and character. Then we have made it. You want old traditions to go, Carl, they will and new ones will come. Who will give much of a damn about a little school in an unknown village in a backwater then? We are a new generation. We will rise and defeat the old. But we will preserve our pretty ladies.'

Raj stepped forward to Devi, took her hand and drew her up.

'What are you doing?' Carl stared at him. Beyond Raj he could see car lights waving their way along the track.

'This is my country, my traditions.' Raj stroked Devi's cheek with the back of his hand and she turned away from him.

'Leave her, Raj.'

Raj smiled. 'She cannot turn any man down. It is her tradition and it is my tradition.' He pulled her away. Carl was up after them, pulling Raj back. 'Not now, Carl.'

'What is it with you?' Carl raged. 'The jealousy? Always wanting what I have?'

'Get out of my way.'

'She doesn't belong to anybody.'

'Not even you,' Raj pulled her again. Carl grabbed Raj's shirt collar, pulling him close and bunching his right hand ready to strike. Raj stared into Carl's eyes, said, 'You think you can buy anything and anybody,' and pushed him away.

Carl readied himself to punch Raj, but was distracted by the distant sound of tyres on gravel. 'She'll have a school. For her daughter.'

The headlights of the approaching car lit up the temple tower as it turned towards them.

'Everybody in the village knows,' Raj continued wagging his hand at Carl. 'She's got AIDs, Carl. I told you to be careful.'

Carl froze. There was so much to make sense of. And the thought of having to face illness as well shook him.

The lights of the car streamed up the track and stopped. Doors opened and slammed, but Carl could not see who the figures were behind the beams. 'I'll look after you, Devi. You can have whatever you want, a house, a school, a hospital.' He was aware that the occupants of the car were approaching but could not make out who they were.

'What sort of brother are you, really?' Raj, still beside himself, held on to Devi. 'You were his favourite, always—'

The two figures were still behind the headlights. Carl heard his mother's voice. 'Brother? What is this?' Daphne stepped into the light.

Shanta followed her and seeing Devi called to her and she ran over and clung to her. 'We are looking for you Devi,' Shanta said, 'And you come here?'

'What else is there?' Devi was in tears. 'What could I do?'

Shanta frowned at Carl. 'You've been coming for years Carl. You've given us so much.' Devi was still hanging on to Shanta. 'All this time, Carl,' Shanta said, 'and you, and the girls.'

Daphne shook her head. 'How could you? What would Melody think?'

'I'll build her a school, get teachers, books, the lot. We can really help her, and the others.'

'On my money,' Daphne said. 'Are you in on this too, Raj?'

Raj sneered at her. 'You and your money, you think you can buy us all.'

'Shut it, Raj,' said Carl. 'I said, didn't I?'

'And you all did all right out of it,' Daphne looked up. The moon was high, dragging itself away from streamers of cloud.

Raj waved at them. '*Kali Ko-op* was all built on my dad's money.'

'What are you talking about?' Daphne laughed.

'Raj—' Carl cautioned him again.

'My dad's money — all of this—' Raj kept on.

'Your dad?' Daphne laughed again, bewildered. 'Ben you mean. My husband.'

Carl said despondently, 'Don't Raj.'

'Ben was my dad,' Raj pointed at Shanta. 'Look at her, she'll tell you. Tell them, mummy-ji. Tell them.' Shanta pulled her chunni scarf over her head and drew Devi close, kissing her hair. 'My perfect faultless father. And her. A Devadasi woman — the lowest kind—'

'You're educated. Your father made sure of that — you have a degree,' Daphne challenged Shanta, her face still buried in Devi's hair, the chunni scarf covering her. 'You're from a good background — I don't believe any of it. This is—' She looked at Carl and he looked down. 'Shanta? This isn't true — the man you loved, the married man—' The words tailed away with realisation.

'My mother was my father's other woman. He fell for my mother's charms,' Raj gave a cynical laugh. 'All these years you didn't know that? Where were you?'

'Enough, Raj.' Carl pulled him but he shook himself away.

'She was a temple Devadasi — only one with ambition.'

Shanta raised her head and called to her son from the darkness. 'You had a life, Raj — you had everything — a privileged upbringing, everything we could give—'

'You think I didn't get beaten up and mocked, your name thrown about with laughter — the bastard of a Devadasi—'

'Because of Ben I got you in a good school, got you a life,' Shanta said.

Daphne's hands were trembling and she shook her head. 'I don't believe any of this. Tell me this is all — Carl?' She put her hand on her chest and pressed it there, wheezing, as if by doing so the truth could be held in.

'Tell you what?' Shanta threw back her chunni and stepped into the light. 'About your painted ghosts? Things from the past painted on the walls that we don't want to see? Parts of ourselves we didn't want but were forced on us. Is it that, Daphne? You know it better than me, the life you were denied when you were young — you cannot get it back, you cannot repaint your life. We do the best we can, we make up what we can, we build what we can.'

Daphne stood in a silvery pool of moonlight next to the temple steps near the candles, several of which had gone out, the tower looming above her. Anger rose in her as she accosted Shanta. 'If that wasn't enough, you come along and take my husband. All the time over here on business he was cosy with his other family. All your lies about a married lover that died — it was Ben all the time—' She coughed.

Shanta appealed to her. 'He was my only chance. What else was there? A life of men forcing themselves on me. He was my way out — he could open a new world for me and my daughter.'

Daphne waved at her. 'You can even paint pictures — better than me — and because you had the chance and I didn't. How could you Shanta?'

'He was mine too.'

Daphne yelled. 'You were his whore, his cheap mistress, his bit on the side.' She waved at Shanta. 'No Shanta, you are not my friend. I'll do everything in my power to block Ben's money to you — you cannot have it.'

She left them in silence and sat unsteadily on the temple steps. A candle died, leaving one with a low flame next to her. Carl looked over at Raj with a knowing glance and Raj looked away. Devi looked up at Shanta.

Daphne expected Shanta to go back to the car and sit inside, but she came over and sat with her. 'Your life was taken when you were sixteen. Mine was taken when I was twelve,' Shanta said. 'I had to earn my own living at twelve. My body was not my own, my mind was not my own, walking naked in Neem leaves past the village gaze.' She drew breath. 'Ben took me out of that. He loved me and he loved his son, Raj and a daughter that wasn't his. I deserve his inheritance. Does a woman want to depend all her life on a man? I was never free, I never knew who I was. But I loved him, knowing I could never find the financial freedom to be a free thinking woman, depending on no one. And now — I depend on you, Daphne—'

Carl nudged Raj. 'You see what I said. You see now? You get nothing.'

Raj scowled back, tightening his fists. Shanta looked at him and he turned away. Devi went over and sat with Shanta.

Daphne shook her head and stared at the ground. 'I can't. Not now. You're not who I thought you were, Shanta, these lies and betrayal.' She looked over at her son. 'Carl. You knew all this time. All those years of having a secret brother. How many years did you know? How long?' He shook his head. She threw up her hands in despair. 'Have you turned into what your father really was — a heavy drinking womaniser who keeps things from me? Who lives a lie? Is that it, Carl? What sort of a father are you to Melody?' She stood jerkily and wobbled. 'You're not having it, none of you. None. I'll put a stop to it somehow.'

They stood in silence for a long time. Daphne sat with arms crossed and head bowed. Shanta held Devi's hand and turned to Daphne, the candle flame flickering its last nearby. Shanta spoke quietly to Daphne. 'Did the yoga teacher tell you Daphne, about the uncoiling of the Kundalini at the base of the spine, the up rush of new consciousness, a wide awareness of the world — as though you are sitting on top of a train and can see all horizons around you at the same time. Life takes from us for a purpose.'

'You knew what you were doing—'

'The gurus say there has to be something more to life than simply what we see. Science tells you that anything you cannot experience with your eyes and ears doesn't exist. But what you saw in the cave temple Daphne, the Yakshi, was that not real to you? A painted ghost coming to you from deep in the past? You feel like there's another being inside yourself, one that has universal knowledge. One that shatters the idea that life is one brutal competitive mind and body race where greed and having selfish fun are the gods. Is this the world we want, Daphne? This big race to survive — and then we die and that's it?' She paused, holding her hand out to Daphne who still had her head in her hands. 'When I look at the paintings in the caves I get the sense that things are bigger than that, that death is simply a gateway to other spiritual dimensions — so we are ever linked to other people and inexplicably part of them. Being human is forever becoming aware, billions of us becoming more conscious in our own ways and finding our own truths. Through that, we change — which means we have to kill off our old selves and find a new self and purpose in society. And with that our spiritual knowledge of life grows.' Shanta edged closer to her. 'We were both denied that and forced to live lives that were not our own — just like poor Devi here. Ben gave me a way out, and a way out for my daughter and my son, my sisters and my mother — and many Devadasi girls that he helped me help. He saw how bad it really was, he knew how they suffered. He took on my suffering and healed it.' Tears were beginning in her eyes. 'He gave everything to help us to be free. Did he never make you feel free? Didn't he take you to your painted ghosts on the Ajanta walls? Didn't he show you the Yakshi tree spirit come to open your mind. We have to paint over those ghosts now, Daphne. We have to put them to rest. Then we can fit in better to life. All we have to do is give up attachment, to things and people and a past that denied us the right when we were young to be our true selves — that way we can find our true selves — now.'

Carl and Raj stood apart watching the women.

'I never did find it,' Daphne raised her head and gave a cynical laugh. 'My true self — at least when I did through Ben, when I did — it was smashed in front of me. By you.' She stood up.

'But you can help Devi.' Shanta looked up to her. 'You can change things for the women here.'

Daphne turned from her and headed for the car before Carl stopped her. 'We could build a school, mum. Really make big changes for people like Devi—'

'Raj, the taxi,' Shanta motioned for her son to open the car door for Daphne.

Having done so, he spoke to Daphne as she came over. 'You must help us, Daphne—'

She walked past him in silence. Devi jumped up and ran to her as she reached the car, bent before her, crouching, and touched her feet in a gesture of respect. 'Please madam.'

Daphne looked down at her eyes and gently eased her to her feet. 'You don't have to do that,' she said sweetly, 'you don't have to.' And turning to them all said, 'Take it. Have it all.'

Shanta stood. 'Daphne?'

'I'm not doing this for you,' Daphne said without looking at Shanta, 'I'm doing it for the Devadasi—' Daphne got in the car.

'I am the Devadasi,' Shanta said.

'Please auntie,' Devi said.

'Work with us, Daphne,' Shanta stood by the open window of the car.

Daphne turned to them, shaking with emotion. 'I said take it. All of it.'

The last candle died.

*****

Daphne dipped her brush in a mixture of white, dabs of reddish brown Burnt Sienna and Naples Yellow, the buttery yellow she loved, with a hint of Alizarin Crimson, that dark bloody colour. Work was still needed on how the light was falling on the Yakshi's skin, the right side of her face, the exposed arms, thighs and lower legs. Humming, she stroked paint sparsely over areas she wished to soften and lighten.

Next, she must darken the background with a mixture of Burnt Umber, Ultramarine with a dash of Purple Lake. Memories of Rembrandt's painting of the woman bathing guided her in her choice of background. She wanted to make it appear cave-like, as though the Yakshi is emerging from darkness, a figure of hope coming out of a void. The left side of her body is still in deep shadow, still attached to the darkness, as she comes forward into the light. Light sparkles too on the leaves of the branch she clings to with her right hand.

Daphne gasped, excitedly — the picture was taking shape, becoming real. It was not just an image of a Yakshi, it had the spirit and emotion of one. She seemed real, an individual, not just one of a crowd of similar faces. This Yakshi had a personality of her own.

She wheezed a little, putting down the brush. Feeling giddy she headed into the bedroom and slumped on the bed. She needed water.

What did the Yakshi say: 'Some years the monsoon does not come to parts of the land. They wait in those parts. Trees and people. And no rain. The ground is hard. Nothing grows. Trees die. We must know who we are, or we are dead trees, dead inside. When the rain comes it brings new life.'

Her painting was visible through the half open bedroom door, the Yakshi holding up new green growths above her head. The monsoon would be here in a few days.

*****

'Where is she?' Shanta said as they entered Daphne's hotel room down the road from *Kali Ko-op*.

'In her room, probably.' Carl nodded at the bedroom door.

He was about to head there when Shanta's attention was taken by the painting on the easel near the door to the veranda. 'She's done it. She's finished.'

When Devi came in the room with Raj behind her, she joined them around the picture. 'A Yakshi — Shalabhanjika. Who did this, it is so much like real — ?'

'Daphne,' Shanta said, smiling. 'She's a real artist now — who she should have been all her life. Now she's found it.'

'She's so real,' Devi pointed.

'Don't touch, it's still wet,' Shanta said and Devi drew her hand back.

'Mum,' Carl called through to the bedroom.

Devi was mesmerised. 'She look like she will jump out of the picture at me. Scary and strong. Look at her eyes.'

'I've only seen two other pairs of eyes painted quite like that,' Shanta said. 'The two princesses at Ajanta,' she nodded. 'Their eyes make their personalities come alive. And Daphne's done that. She's given her the power of the past. Like Amrita Devi gave the tree spirits when they chopped them down in the forest at Jodhpur.'

Devi was nodding.

'Mum,' Carl called again. 'Where are you? Come and show us your picture. You've got it at last. All those stupid things I said before — you can do it.'

Raj looked on, nodding at the painting. 'It is good. It has atmosphere.' He turned to his brother, whispering, 'I know a good doctor—' Carl took Raj's hand and shook it.

'Thanks bruv,' Carl said.

'She will do it won't she?'

'You needn't worry, the money will come to *Kali Ko-op*.' And looking Raj in the eye said, 'You will bring Devi along with us to the doctor—'

'Hanji — yes,' Raj nodded.

Devi turned from the picture. 'Auntie. Where is auntie?'

'Mum,' Carl called again. 'Where are you? We're all here, for god's sake. Probably gone out.'

Devi went to the bedroom door.

'It's so real,' Shanta could not keep her eyes off the image. 'She knows the spirit of the tree and she knows how to paint ghosts. This is so perfect. Where is she?'

Devi's screams echoed from the bedroom and they were silenced a moment. They found Daphne lying on the bed with Devi kneeling beside her, holding Daphne's hand. 'She's cold.' Devi was in tears. 'Auntie's hand is cold.'

'Get a doctor.' Raj went for his phone.

'Mum, no—' Carl stepped forward and knelt to her, holding her hand, then put his head on her chest. 'No, mum, no—'

While Raj spoke on the phone, Shanta eased Carl away so she could look for herself. 'She's cold, no breathing, no pulse. She's gone.'

'The doctor will be here soon.'

Carl choked back tears. 'Mum, no — The doctor can do something?'

'She's gone, Carl.' Raj eased him back.

Shanta stroked Daphne's face. 'She did find herself in the end, you can tell by the way she finished the picture — She left herself in the painting,' Shanta whispered. 'Her painted ghost.'

Raj helped his brother to his feet. 'She's free now, Carl—'

'So are we.' Devi smiled through her tears and putting her hands together in prayer shape she bowed to Daphne.

'We can be ourselves,' Shanta said.

The brothers hugged and Devi held on to Shanta.

Shanta held her close. 'A painted ghost in all of us — come to change us.'

THE GARDEN OF IZZAT BAIG

Neil Beardmore

1

2010

'You have to work at it,' Stella said. 'Over and over again.' She threw her brush down, the tip spreading an untidy slip of Alizarin Crimson over the palette. 'And smudge it out, and—'

The sun was pushing up towards its midday zenith and although the veranda and overhanging palm trees provided shade, the increasing heat was beginning to drain her. Ahead, the white sands of Bagolem beach fell away to distant hills at the north end, the hump of an island and the infinite turquoise of the sea.

Lena leaned forward towards her own picture, scowling critically. 'At least with acrylics you can rub it out and start all over again.' And leaning backwards she adjusted the red headband that enclosed her dreadlocks, now tinged with grey

'That's if you're quick enough in this heat — Acrylics dry too quickly. I have to get it right or it sets and then that's it, and I can't rub anything out or change things. It's so annoying.' She ran the fingers of her right hand through her own hair, the dark brown tint hiding shoots of grey.

'That's Goa for you, in April—'

The little brick chalet was one of a short terrace, each with its own veranda looking out to sea. Palms hung over the terra cotta tiles of the long roof. Seats on the verandas of all the chalets afforded views up and down the crescent shaped beach lined with restaurants and chalets, each framed with palms that waved in gentle breeze. Young men launched boats of tourists out to see dolphins and remote beaches, groups swam, laughed and threw balls or ducked each other. Women in saris tended to toddlers where the waves gave up to flat sands. A short way towards the island, fishermen sorted equipment in boats or sat mending nets, cigarettes hanging from their lips.

'If only we could do that with life,' Stella let out a short laugh. 'Rub it all out and start again.' She frowned again at her efforts to get some colour and shape into figures by the sea. Hers were stiff and stick-like, or gross, and the dog she had sketched was two dimensional, as though caught in pose in cardboard.

She had woken at five thirty with an edge of depression and anxiety, had wanted to sleep longer but her buzzing mind would not let her. Wandering out into the sun's early rays she had watched the fishermen haul up heavy boats, ten men heaving each creature up over wooden runners lubricated with black tarry oil onto the brow of sand away from the tide's reach. Hulls made of dark hardwood slats bound together with rope thickened by tar, they lay like huge insects, dark, asleep.

Men stirred piles of nets, pouring out silver trails of fish while an entourage of women in saris rallied with plastic bowls.

Stella wished she could paint that, and more, that she could portray the movement and atmosphere, could capture the smiles and cries. To paint the talk and laughter, to get to the soul of that moment, to catch even the man texting on his phone and the eight year old girl in a pink frock dancing it seemed with her matching pink bowl, trying to gain access through the forest of legs to the smaller fish. To get all that down would require more genius than Stella could summon. And would the girl with the bowl sell them, Stella contemplated, was she an important breadwinner for the family?

The moment evolved, the players changed position as though choreographed haphazardly, until the participants drifted away and the image dissolved.

You had to get into a scene in order to paint it, to go right into the spirit of what you perceived, for it was transient, it changed, disappeared, so that all the artist was left with was astute memories.

She remembered reading that Chagall in his twenties worked memories of childhood and perhaps he was never released from portraying his visions through childhood imagery.

You had to have a photographic memory, Stella told herself, to be able to cite the important gestures life presented to you, as well as the ability to interpret and present those visions as your own. And yet this had eluded her all her life: she was just not good enough.

'You try too hard,' Lena let out a short laugh as she worked her brush.

Stella took a rag and began to smear out her figures. 'You can never do that. I mean I keep trying, but I cannot get this bit right,' she tutted. 'The specks of people on the shoreline. Mine are stiff or flat meaningless blobs – completely lifeless.' She drew breath. 'Why does he do this to us?'

She stared ahead at a group of men swimming and calling to each other. It was Friday and in the late afternoon Bagolem beach would be populated with holiday makers from Mumbai, Delhi, Bangaluru and other flourishing cities. Goa was high on the list of families seeking to enjoy themselves. Children flipped in, shepherded by mothers in saris, soaked, but with joyful laughs. Men in shorts joined them, shouting and laughing. A small group of women in hijabs allowed the warm waves to sweep over their feet. There was no one in the world it seemed to Stella that did not enjoy a beach and the freedom of spirit it allowed.

She smiled for a moment, then turning back to her work, scowled at her inability to put any of that in paint. 'Why does Arun do this to us?'

'He doesn't do it to us,' Lena laughed back at her. 'We do it to ourselves.'

Stella watched her half sister a moment: a tall woman with little flab for someone in her mid fifties, but with sturdy arms, long fingers, and a face still young looking, but with a touch of melancholy in the eyes. Lena's father had been Jamaican, Stella's dad and their shared mother, white. Compared to Stella's ever expanding waist line, fat arms and double chin, all acquired over the twenty years leading to her late fifties, Lena appeared agile and lively, yet her expression now as she glanced at Stella betrayed a message of having lived highly but with the struggle of experience.

'Do you reckon?'

'It's a painting holiday, what do you expect? He's pushing us out of our comfort zone.'

Stella stared at her canvas again. 'Is that so?' Frustrated with her work she stood up for a moment and went to the edge of the veranda. 'Don't remind me.' More swimmers were diving through waves with yelps and she watched a couple of young men approaching people to go on boat trips. Beachside restaurants were still serving late breakfasts. Waves beat a rhythm as they fell on flat sand.

Bagolem was a place Stella kept coming back to, calling it her bolt hole. Last year she had discovered Arun painting in a studio cum shop at the back of the main road. Befriending him, she got him to promise when she came back again to give her proper painting tuition. She liked him so much she said she would help him find galleries and set up a bigger studio then. It was easy to get him to agree to teach Lena as well and this their first private session led by him had gone well for Lena, at least. Stella had not reckoned it to be so hard though.

'You're not giving up?' Lena loaded her brush with Cerulean Blue mixed with white, letting out a short laugh. 'That's not like you.'

Stella stared out to the horizon. 'There's things you can do, and things you can't.'

Lena glanced up from her painting. 'He's a fit bloke, I'll give him that.'

'You keep your eyes off him and on your canvas.'

They finished at one and headed for the Pink City restaurant for lunch.

They swam in the afternoon and took Martinis in the shade.

In the evening they ate at the Rocking Globe under lines of lights coiled around the trunks of palm trees and up through their branches. The banyan tree with massive fronds that reached back down to the sandy earth was also draped with purple and red lights. For Stella it was a wonderland.

On stage beyond rows of filled dining tables a singer crooned a slow jazz number about a fickle man. Tall, in her thirties, wearing a red dress, she wove magic notes to her audience with unpretentious flare. A bass guitarist, drummer and guitarist accompanied her, their soft backing tones never overwhelming her voice.

Stella was reminded of Lena in her heyday up there belting out her own songs. She never had red dresses, it was sometimes ripped jeans, or leather, colourful head bands, scarves, sexy boots, or even tops she had made herself in vibrant colours. She sold her songs onstage, prancing for her audience, exciting them, drawing them on until they were lost in her music. One night when they were both still in their teens Lena's singing was so intense Stella believed music actually had healing powers. She had watched people come alive, yelling, dancing, laughing — leaving all their problems in the dark while they awoke. She was older and more sceptical now.

She glanced over at Lena.

'The moon is up.' Lena nodded at the half shape hanging like an upturned sickle in the sky. 'Magic in the evening. Purple dusk gives way to night's deep canopy . . .'

'You see,' Stella smiled at her. 'You're a poet — no, a song writer —'

Lena's sudden laughter faded quickly. 'Nah.' She sipped her gin and tonic and turned away from her.

'You are — or at least you were — a song writer — and such a good one.'

'No I wasn't.'

'It might have gone now, but—'

'No,' Lena snapped.

'I was only saying—'

'That world has gone—'

The singer was bringing her song to a close, allowing the mellow tones of her voice to fade with the bass line so that it sounded like she was slowly walking away into the forest or along the beach.

They sat in silence, sipping, Stella watching her half sister grapple with memories that now seemed to have lost their glow. Lena looked troubled and tired, remembering perhaps as Stella did now those times when she stood up on stage and felt the awe of being alive, of sharing what you have to give. Lena told her when they were teenagers that once you have tasted the life of being on stage, you always crave for it. Once a performer, always a performer. Once you have warmed to the stage it will always warm to you.

Stella sensed the agony and conflict Lena was feeling, the yearning to be up there and the struggle with the dark side of that addiction. Lena had told her the stage can bring you down too.

The spangles of silver moonlight sparkled on the waves beyond the brightness of the banyan tree.

2

Stella was up early the following day, dabbling with her painting. On the beach five men were launching a boat for a trip, the tourists standing in a disorderly queue as the sea tried to reach their feet.

Lena came out of the chalet with two cups of coffee, setting them down on the table near her sister. A couple of lone joggers ran along the wet sand and a woman in her early twenties worked through yoga poses.

'Right, of course — We should paint—' Lena said.

Their easels stood behind them on the veranda, their paintings still up overnight.

'Coffee first.' Lena was reluctant to get into it. 'Anyway, Arun will be here soon—'

'To clear up the mess we've created on canvas.' Stella mocked herself as she sat with a shudder in front of her work. 'It makes you wonder what it's all about—'

'And then you find yourself having another gin—' Lena laughed.

'You know your trouble, Lena,' Stella joked.

Lena shook her head and gave her sister a wry scowl. 'You know me so well.'

'You've never really grown up,' Stella finished.

'Why not?' Lena sipped her coffee and settled by her painting. 'Everyone should know the child inside themselves.'

Stella gave a short grunt, then angled her brush and thrust a cross through the lower section of the painting. 'We never did see eye to eye did we? I could never discover why. Even when mum lost it with you I kept trying –'

'Maybe you should stop trying now, and just start being yourself.' Lena shrugged. 'When things get bad I just sing the blues.'

'That's a good way out for you.' Stella tried to disguise the rising feelings of resentment she felt: it did not seem like Lena appreciated any of the lengths she had gone to in the past to help her. Until Stella too, like her mother, could do no more and left Lena to drift away into her own world.

'There's nothing easy about the blues. Bessie Smith singing on street corners when she was a girl to make ends meet, being ripped off by managers and flooring them with her fists. Ma Rainey hiding being a lesbian by marrying a bloke. The blues is the blues, it's life. You're not the only one who's been there. Even Lena Horne –'

'Your namesake.' Stella turned back and started to rub out the angry cross with a rag.

It was too hot to paint in the afternoon, so they snoozed over gin and read used books from a shelf in a restaurant facing the sea.

By half four the sun was low enough for Stella to be drawn back to her painting, encouraging her sister, who moaned at first, to join her. They settled at their easels and began silently. After half an hour of intense brushwork, Stella leaned back, shaking her head. 'Damn, damn, damn.' She felt Lena watching her.

'Let go of the inner critic and just do it,' Lena said.

'What do you mean?' Stella replied sharply.

'You know, the one that's always telling you you're no good – like mum.'

Stella stared at her. Lena could always dress well. Her golden yellow top and long loose skirt accentuated her shape.

Nothing fitted Stella properly. Diets were a failure. And somehow the bright reds and maroons she was attracted to tended to exaggerate her size rather than shape it. 'She loved you.'

'Pity she didn't have the hands and heart to show it then, because all I got was ice.'

Stella raised her tone in defence. 'She was gentle and generous — in all things.'

'Are we talking about the same woman?'

'She was always good to me.'

'To you — maybe,' Lena said.

Stella shuffled uncomfortably. This felt like old times with Lena, the tension in the verbal exchanges. 'And when do you open your inner eyes and let it flow,' Stella said pointedly. 'Where's your blues gone?' Stella pushed her brush through the beach area on her canvas. 'If it was only that easy. If my hand would just do that, it would be all right.'

'That's what art is — taking risks.'

Stella frowned at her. Lena could sound superior and condescending sometimes. 'It must be like life, then.'

'Even doing nothing's a risk.' Lena shrugged and went back to her images. 'You're the one, you're the success.'

Stella wanted her to be quiet. 'I've got the money, you've got the talent. You call that success?' Stella scoffed at her picture. 'Things just come naturally to you. They always have — although you block them. Ever since—'

'What?' Lena scowled.

Stella found she could not go forward and putting her brush down, she fanned herself with a piece of card. 'The mountains keep coming back to me. I was with my first husband up near Badrinath as the flowers were coming out in spring. The snows had thawed and we were so high up and in love. I want to go there again. I can't tell you how much you would enjoy it, the snow hanging over the summits like lace—'

Lena leaned forward and slipped her hand into her bag on the floor, pulled out a silver flask and took a swig.

'Not again.' Stella caught her. 'You had so much this afternoon, Lena. I thought you'd given all that up—'

'It keeps the throat lubricated.'

'Honey and camomile is what you need.' Stella watched her sister looking up the far end of the beach to where a little river fanned out to the sea. Beyond it an island seemed to float around the edge of the mainland. 'Let me look at yours then.' Stella came over to Lena's canvas and gawped a second. 'There you see, it works. You're so damned natural at everything. It's all so easy for you.' Stella stood in the way of Lena looking at hers. 'Don't look at mine. No, no, you mustn't.' But Lena eased herself past.

'You can work on it,' Lena said.

'Never picked up a paint brush before and look at you,' Stella nodded at Lena's landscape. 'The sheen of light around the island, even the specks of people have shape and movement. Not like mine — and I seem to need to get every bit of detail—'

3

'It was good of you,' Lena began telling Stella over dinner. It was Red Snapper again for Stella and a Vegetable Balti for Lena. The Rocking Globe had a sand floor. Imitation lanterns hung around the wooden walls. There were no singers tonight, only melancholic background music too low to cover their chat or the sound of the waves. They sat with a view of the sea, darkened by night, but with lines of surf. 'I mean, coming here—' The words trailed off as though she seemed embarrassed for a second — something unusual for her, Stella mused.

'I had to do something to get us back together,' Stella said. 'And what with mum gone now — I want us to be sisters again, Life's too short—'

'Of course, I suppose—'

'What?'

Lena stirred her vegetables then said, 'You haven't told me. Perhaps that's what this is all about, bringing me here — to tell me—'

'Tell you what?'

'She left it all to you.'

'Not exactly.' Stella felt awkward. Although she had known this question would be posed to her at some point, she still felt unprepared to answer it. Their mother had long since banned Lena from the house. For years she had tolerated drug inspired abuse until a day had come when the door was locked.

'She left me nothing then. Not even a two pence piece. Did she?'

Stella gestured for Lena to calm down. But when Lena got hold of something she would not let go. Stella searched for words that would make it sound palatable. 'Your lifestyle, the—'

Lena scowled, pursing her lips. 'How do you get on stage before a rowdy crowd without a shot of something. It goes with the territory, Stella. I mean, you can't be singer without it.' She drew breath.

'Not so loud.' Stella looked around her at eaters snatching looks at them.

Lena took no notice. 'So I'm a risk. Big deal.'

'It takes a certain sort of personality — risks, I mean.' Stella tried to keep calm. She did not want a scene ending with Lena storming off.

'She thought I'd blow it all on stuff. I've been clean, Stella, how many years?' Customers close by were taking an interest now. 'Did you tell her?'

Stella looked down, placing her knife and fork aside. 'I tried with her, but she would not budge — and you would not come and see her — Lena—'

'I might as well have carried on.'

'And you would be pushing up daisies by now. How many times have I rushed you to A & E? And mum gave up bailing you out years ago.'

'And I wake up sweating in the night asking myself: why did you save me? You know what cold turkey is on your own — just a few mates hanging in for you? And now I can't write another song. It was like the pain and all the junk kept driving me on. I was nothing without it. I became nothing. I am nothing—'

Stella was about to tell her it wasn't true, but she got up and was off, abandoning her half finished meal.

The following morning Stella stepped from the veranda into the small garden and then down the steps to the beach. Three men were pushing a boat of chatting tourists through incoming waves.

Lena would be here with her for the next six weeks or so. Stella had set it up and paid for it all; they would have to learn to live with each other. She walked towards the estuary. The journey Lena had been on had caused suffering to her and those around her, but because she had given up that way of life she needed support. From childhood Stella had had to be patient with her, to learn to take it calmly when things got tight between them.

Slipping off her shoes she let the sea sweep over her feet again and sighed, reflecting on her past. Now that the split with Alan was complete, her sons were married off and living abroad, and now that mother had passed away, Lena was all that was left of family. She Skyped Ollie and Eric every week and chatted to the grandchildren, but it was usually painful, not being there with the little ones.

And Lena was alone — as usual — a sad loner with melancholic eyes. She sang the blues because she knew the blues. It throbbed through her: the lack of knowledge about her father, of her heritage, of where her voice had come from. It seemed right after years of estrangement to draw her close again.

They must enjoy themselves. Life was short and had to be fruitful. She had reached the river estuary, where the stream broadened into a delta of wet sand and narrow rivulets. Now the tide was out it was easy to ford even the deep parts. A favourite spot for Stella, she sat on a rock in shadows watching the activity of bathers in the main bay and fishermen mending nets under little open ended shacks along the river bank.

It was not just because of Arun that she had come back to Bagolem. Although in his early fifties he still had the freshness and vitality of youth about him, which made him naturally alluring. Yet there was a look of sadness in his eyes, and she recognised that he was suffering. He hid the loss of his wife

Lakshmi well. When he arrived each morning at the unfinished paintings he guided, advised and instructed the women sensitively. Stella liked his easiness and his smile, and how he encouraged her. Through his praise and help she felt her self esteem rise.

Yet when he was gone she again fell back to self doubt and discouragement. Through this picture she wanted to achieve something out of her own efforts that could outlast her. And she felt alone and vulnerable.

The holiday was not just about getting Lena back on her feet, it was about addressing Stella's own doubts, fears and insecurities.

'It's all different now,' Lena said when they were together again at their canvases. 'I mean, not out there. I mean, for us. We're different. Life changes us. We're renewed — and if not renewed — we're damned —'

'You're cheerful this morning,' Stella forced a laugh.

'No, I mean — life changes us. Makes us see —'

'That's one way of looking at it, I suppose.' Stella deliberately left the figures and concentrated on the hulls of several boats, some orange, green and white, others ice blue under the sun's relentless hammering. Mixing in white with Cadmium Orange, she softened the glow of the brighter pigment. 'I know it hasn't always been easy for you, Lena.' She looked up at the sister she still felt she knew little of. 'I mean, drastically changing your lifestyle and all that.'

The fact that she had never fathomed Lena bothered her, made her feel distant and estranged, and she struggled to find a way to undo that ignorance — if she could, if it was only Stella's doing and not Lena blocking her. Lena was that type: she put up a shell to protect herself which became a wall to keep her vulnerabilities intact. You could see it in her eyes — not their mother's but her father's eyes.

'There's been that great gap between us,' Stella tried to sound casual as she shaped the hull. 'And I wanted to do something to bring us together. That's all. It's nothing to do with Arun. I want us to be sisters again. I don't know, time seems very short sometimes, we're not here for long—'

'Now who's being serious and morbid,' Lena said with an ironic laugh. 'Of course—'

'You don't have to say it like that.' Stella was close to anger with her again. It was not always what Lena said, it was the sarcastic way that she said it that cut Stella.

'Like what?' Lena gave a slight shrug.

'I never know with you.' Stella outlined shacks behind boats and contemplated putting the figures of fishermen there tending piles of nets. 'Whether it's the truth or another poke.'

Lena did not reply quickly, the pause being filled by the sound of a long wave pounding down. Stella knew she would respond, it was an accusation that was intended to get one.

'Stella,' Lena sighed, putting her brush aside. 'How could I ever have got here without you paying for it all. I am grateful. ' She looked back at her picture. Stella was flattered for a moment, but sceptical about Lena's true intentions. History told her it was hard to believe Lena. Truth for Lena was a complex thing, so it was hard to know when you were listening to it. 'It's wonderful, Stella. Who knows, I might get something of myself back, find some rhythm, get something down, even—'

Stella paused again, studying her picture and trying to let the truth sound unforced and casual: 'All your jokes and tricks. You never were one to conform when we were kids, always challenging mum. Rebelling. Real cheeky you were sometimes and never short of getting a slap from her.'

'Tell me about it.'

'You think she did not like you?'

'Me? Born of a passing fling. With a black man. In those days? '

4

'The crescent moon hanging in the sky.' Lena leaned back in the wicker chair on the veranda and sipped gin and tonic. They had eaten at the Pink City restaurant and had surrounded themselves with candles, incense sticks and mosquito coils. 'The sea rolling in with its incessant rhythmical pounding.' Lena looked out at the dark sea with its lines of bright surf.

'You've had a little bit to drink, I think.' Stella let out a short laugh.

'But you see it don't you?' Lena pointed with her glass. 'The purple haze round the island, the lines of lights along the restaurants. You have to look, to take it in. It's magic.'

'It sounds like one of your songs.' Stella suggested.

'No,' Lena said. 'Not that. This is different. You don't understand. Watch—'

Stella was used to her sister inferring that she was a misunderstood creative who had a unique vision of the world. It made it hard for Stella to take her seriously sometimes.

She sat back allowing shadows to envelop her, responsive to Lena's sensitivity. That Lena blocked talk about music was a shame, it was what she had been really good at once; it was a flame that burned in her. Now that Lena spurned that past and scoffed at her abilities in song writing saddened and appalled Stella. It was who Lena was and without it she was not a full person. For her, giving up the addictions, meant giving up the lifestyle, the lot.

'The sky is so clear at night.' Stella took them away from the subject, knowing it could not be denied forever. 'And so deep and dauntless.' She sipped a moment.

'Like me then—' Lena mocked.

'Mum tried with you. Bought you a piano, paid for lessons.'

'I would have been better off without that. I could feel the resentment in her voice — the regret—'

'That's the drink talking.'

'What do you know?'

'I know you don't mean it.'

'I mean every word. I would have had a different life — no pianos, no songs, no sex and drugs and rock and roll—'

'A quiet life like me then, Lena. Two kids and two husbands, both unfaithful. A house on a new estate, a daily life of work and bringing up the kids. A boring life with the chattering classes. You think you had it hard. What I would have done to get up on stage, to be shagged in a back room after, to have sniffed a bit of coke — have been able to paint. You had it all, Lena—'

'And squandered it — that's what you think—'

Stella felt for her again. 'Because it's gone, doesn't mean it's lost.'

Lena scowled, pointing at her. 'Don't you ever say that.' For a moment Stella was afraid Lena might lash out. 'You told me to.'

'Many times. But you did it. You made it in the end. You can rebuild it all a different way.'

'You want me back there? OD? On the slab?' Lena thumped her fist on the side of her chair.

Stella looked past her, down the beach where all the restaurant lights sparkled. 'I can't help you Lena, I don't know what you want.'

Lena leaned back and laughed. 'You're right. For once, you're right. I used to hate you for all the spoiled things that happened to you as a child. The way your dad doted on you. But now, I can paint. And you can't.'

Stella was hurt.

*****

'I'm not happy, Arun,' Stella told him the following morning. 'My painting — too amateurish, too — I don't know—'

Arun had a short greying beard and thick straight hair. He did not smile often but when he did his eyes lit up.

Perusing her images, he said, 'A lot of energy and colourful points of interest, all vying with each other.' He stood back contemplating. 'We can work on it. It will come. Creativity in all its forms is good for the soul. '

He was wearing faded blue jeans and a loosely fitting shirt with paisley patterns. Having taken Stella's brush and demonstrated tones and strokes, he moved towards Lena.

'You can develop that bit of faint landscape, that distant horizon with generous amounts of white added to your Purple Lake. A sky made up of plain blue — Cerulean, Cobalt, or whatever — is too cold and has no dimension. So we add a touch of purple or pink to warm it here and there and to give it some depth — there you see.' Lena looked from her painting at him, then back at her work. 'Let me try,' he said and mixing pigments on her pallet with a pallet knife, he took her brush, took up the mixture and adjusted an area of the sky. Stella controlled her envy. He carried on: 'And you blend it in so it creates a sort of shimmer in the background.'

'That's cool,' Lena said.

'In that way it helps to bring other things forward — the subject in your picture — the orange and green boat which is central to your composition but which you've nicely toned down now—'

Stella watched her smile at him. She had that effect on men: had to flirt with them.

'You make it look so easy,' Lena continued holding his attention.

'I'm following your advice,' Stella interrupted. 'But the boat just doesn't work, Arun. I can't get the perspective right.'

Arun put down Lena's brush and came to Stella, standing behind her and looking again. 'Stand back with me a moment,' he told her. 'Can you see? The lines of the boat are not quite there, are they?'

'Aren't they?' Stella was resigned.

He took her brush and adjusted the edge of the hull. 'There you see, by adjusting the outlines, the edges of the boat and — this line goes this way — '

She smiled at him. 'I see. Yes. You are so clever, and so talented, Arun.' She liked him, and did not want Lena to spoil it.

'Where did you learn all this — in some prestigious art college in Delhi or Mumbai I should think,' Lena said.

'He's self taught,' Stella carried on painting without looking up as she spoke. 'Everything he knows he got through hard graft.'

'Just like me.'

Arun carried on adjusting Stella's boat. 'You start by looking at other people's paintings in galleries and books. You study how they do things and you just work and work. He looked at Stella for a moment, then went back to his task. 'After many years you realise something — it just comes to you — there is no such thing as a mistake in art — you just learn by things that somehow don't seem to come out right — '

Stella stopped him. 'You must have some talent to start with, surely. '

'Ah well you see,' Arun continued. 'The ones that don't work are the ones that in the end are the most important, because they lead into new ways of doing things. I looked at Indian art when I was young, then western art, including abstract painters. And I looked further east at the Chinese and Japanese artists. Like Hokusai, my favourite.' He paused a moment for thought and they watched him. 'The artist is like a guru, he never accepts that he knows everything, only that there are infinite numbers of things to know — that being an artist is being something fluid that forever changes and moves on. When Hokusai was on his death bed in his nineties he said something like: "please god let me live another ten years then I will have become a real artist."' Arun laughed. 'That should be the slogan of all artists. With the development of our art, so we change and develop. In India I suppose we would say it is a way of enhancing the soul on its journey through time to wherever it is going. But then in eternity there can never be a destination, don't you think, only the movement of the journey — if you believe in the endurance of the soul after death, of course. Scientists are very sceptical about such things.' He laughed again. 'But gurus and rishis — seers — are not —'

They were silent for a time, the moment being filled with the relentless sound of waves on the beach and the cries and laughter of those tossed in them. Hoping she could spur Lena to respond Stella said, 'Maybe if you had continued with the piano —'

'Why didn't you paint pictures before?' Lena replied.

Lena appeared ready to retaliate further, but was cut off by Arun. 'My wife played the piano,' he said. 'It was wonderful.' He spoke excitedly. 'Lakshmi learned some Chopin, Mozart and Bach, all those great composers. I came home one evening and she was playing jazz and blues. I had never heard her do that before, I just didn't know she could. She gave recitals of the classics all round the country, but I don't remember her playing blues and jazz again — not in public — not even for me.' Stella noticed that the memories seemed to trouble him.

'She sounds like an interesting woman,' Lena said.

Arun looked up the beach at the island. 'We took Lakshmi's body to Varanasi and sent her on her way to moksha — you know this — the release of the body from more incarnations, so the soul can be truly free — all the suffering is done and over.

My sons put her on the funeral pyre in one of the ghats and let her go on the next part of the journey—'

'It sounds cosmic,' Lena smiled.

'Have some respect,' Stella rebuked her, but Arun continued without noticing.

'We have to let loved ones go in the end.'

Lena laughed, ignoring Stella, 'Unless you're a guru or something.'

'Ah,' Arun sighed. 'Lots of them have taken the spiritual path because they were jilted. If it wasn't for unhappiness in love Bollywood movies would not exist.'

'Can you imagine that?' Lena laughed again.

Stella was stern in her sarcasm. 'Yes I can, actually.'

They all laughed.

Arun smiled. 'Love plays a big part in Indian and Pakistani stories and myths. The story of Izzat Baig for example.'

'Who's he?' Lena asked. 'What happens?'

Arun smiled. 'Some other time perhaps. We must get on. But never stop observing — it's what art's all about.'

'You can tell us later then,' Lena insisted.

'It's just a Romeo and Juliet story, it's nothing really.'

When Arun had gone Stella said to Lena, 'I don't want things to go bad with us again, Lena. I want it to work.'

Lena yawned. Families were coming out on the beach, chattering and laughing. A group of boys were playing cricket on an area of flat sand that the receding tide had provided.

'Just give me my half then.' Lena watched a girl paddling with her father.

'It's not as easy as that.'

'You don't trust me.'

'Not while you're drinking so much.' Stella watched her, readying herself for the tirade to come.

'All those binges are done, you know that. It finished me touring, that's for sure. You know why I drink now?' She eyed her sister. 'So I don't wake up every morning as a "could-have-been".'

'Why didn't you — there were opportunities, you had contacts.'

'You tell me then.'

'The men who hung on to you, took you along so your looks and your voice could bring them kudos and cash. The smack they plied you with, the lifestyle—'

'It was my fault then?'

'You got taken for a ride — abused.'

'So what is this? A trip to make me say sorry. So I know what goes around comes around. I messed up — so nothing from mum, then. Nothing. What did she do for me anyway? Always a trouble maker — that's me.'

'She brought you up.'

'So I could remind her of her mistake.' Lena waved her arms. 'Maybe just — maybe your dad would have come back, if it hadn't been for her — mistake.'

Stella slammed her glass down. 'Go and get your story — about this — Izzat — whoever he is.'

5

Arun looked over Stella's shoulder at her painting the following morning: 'The sea rolling in with its incessant pounding, the children's cries, the mothers in shalwar kameez up to their waists in the sea. You have got that there, Stella.'

'You're just flattering me—'

Lena put her brush down. 'I want to paint something more challenging. This Izzat Baig fella—'

'You can't paint the myths, 'Stella said with a laugh.

'Who says? '

'You're mad.'

'I'll have a go at anything. I bet Arun has.'

A warm breeze was coming in from the sea, ruffling the palm branches. It was still early enough for a few joggers to be out along the shore. Further up the beach in a line of shade a yoga group was working out.

Arun stopped his instruction, seeming to slip out of role for a moment. 'It's about Sohni, the daughter of a potter. And Izzat Baig, the rich travelling merchant.'

'Don't stop there,' Lena harangued him jokingly.

'He's teaching us,' Stella cut in.

'Tell us the rest. I mean — have you painted the story?' Arun turned away. 'Show us them, Arun.'

Stella was surprised a moment about how taken aback Arun looked for a moment. She tensed her shoulders. 'Another time, Arun, come on—'

Lena persisted. 'I bet they're brilliant. We haven't seen much of your work. Only that one of the ruins in the tropical forest. It was very good, but you must have a much wider range. You have, haven't you? You've done at least one of this couple—'

He shook his head. 'They are just works in progress — sketches and ideas—'

'Come on Arun.' Lena would not let go. 'You say "they" — there's more than one. Are they at your house? Can we come for tea?' She added with a cheeky grin.

'And you can try my wife's piano,' he replied.

Lena frowned and turned away. 'Maybe bring them here then?'

Stella had given up on her picture for a moment. 'How many people round here have a piano, Lena?'

Lena's lips were quivering.

Situated over the back of the small town and facing a rice field, Arun's house looked new and pristine, its wooden gabled roof supported on walls of warm crimson. Two large sofas dominated Arun's wide front room, each with heaps of cushions with reds, yellows and golds. Stella was fascinated by a statue of a sitting Buddha. Piles of incense ash and the stubs of sticks were strewn around its base. Walls were hung with brightly coloured drapes, some with lines of elephants bordering them. He showed them a small shrine to the goddess Lakshmi, the four armed icon with open palms surrounded by gold ornaments and half burned incense sticks. 'Lakshmi was my wife, and so Lakshmi is my goddess.' He smiled, lighting incense sticks and waving them around the image before sticking them in a holder in the shape of a lotus flower.

He had given them tea and they had chatted about how Bagolem was likely to be developed in the future. A hotel was planned down the south end, which would create more traffic, since there was only one road in and out and that would pass the new hotel.

Stella picked up Lena's impatience: she wanted to see the paintings and it would not be long before she became assertive about it. She amused herself by measuring the time it would take for Lena to blurt it out.

'So where are they?' Lena said after ten minutes of chat.

He took them to a table and pulled over a large sketch book which Lena opened. The first page showed a young woman carrying a pot.

'This is Sohni,' Arun said.

'She's beautiful,' Lena observed. 'Outstanding, Arun. The chunni scarf over her head, the pink and white shalwar kameez. The delicate earrings — And this is charcoal? And chalks?' Arun nodded. 'The way you have blended the colours — and her expression — serious — but there's a twinkle in her eye. There's another side to her, I reckon—'

Stella joined in. 'There's a bit of the naivety and innocence of youth too. She's still very young here — maybe only fourteen. There's a sense of uncertainty about her. That touch of Juliet as it were. There's a feel of impending threat — am I reading in too much?'

'But she's strong as well,' Lena carried on excitedly. 'I mean, carrying that pot on her head. That's what I like about it — the complexity of her personality — vulnerable yes, but in some ways proud and strong. You've caught the different sides to her.'

'They say Rembrandt could do it,' Stella rubbed her chin, looking closely at Sohni walking alone through fields, the pot on her head. 'Yes, and many others.'

Arun laughed. 'I'm not in that league.'

'You don't know how good you are,' Stella scoffed. 'I should take you to England and show you off there.'

Lena agreed: 'Why not?'

Arun said, 'We like to laugh at a story, but we like one that can make us sigh too.'

'So tell us about it then Arun.'

'Sohni is only young here — long before Izzat Baig arrives in her village. In this one—' He opened up at another page. 'She's squatting at her father's potter's wheel, and he's instructing her. She was her father's favourite from an early age. They say she put her hands on clay and made a shape at only two years old. Now, at thirteen she has listened to him and learned all the skills.'

'You can see that in this one. It's watercolour this time, Arun?' He nodded to Lena. 'He realises one day she will overtake him in what she can do—'

'Perhaps develop a cottage industry into a little factory,' Stella added.

'She's a clever and resourceful young woman with a business mind,' Lena read into the work. 'She will do well.' She paused, then said, 'What she doesn't need is some bloke coming along and sodding it up.'

Stella laughed.

'It's just a story,' Arun said. 'The old earthenware pots are disappearing in India. You know those big terra cotta brown ones with fat round shapes that women carried on their heads.' Arun mused. 'It looked so elegant, so iconic. Now it's plastic. Much lighter I suppose, but not so appealing. But in Sohni's day everyone needed earthenware pots, it was good business.'

Lena put the pictures side by side. 'You had a model?' Stella watched his response: he looked away and seemed to tense himself. 'You must have,' Lena went on. 'Someone local?'

'I tried different moods and poses in this sketch.' He pulled another one out of a small pile and placed it on top of the other two.

Stella leaned forward. 'Here she is again, a little older perhaps, making finer pots. She and her father have new clothes: they are making good money.'

'The village respects them.' Arun seemed easier now.

But Lena followed her interest: 'Was it your own daughter who posed for you? Or no, it was some local beauty you coaxed into your studio and paid for? The balance of her features, her flowing hair, she moves like a dancer — we imagine her moving —'

'You're too kind,' said Arun.

'But tell us the story,' Stella insisted.

'So you want to know now too,' Lena laughed.

'As the daughter of a lowly potter, Sohni was destined by her father and mother to marry a local boy of the same class. And her life would be a fruitful one,' Arun continued. 'As a potter, like her family going back for generations —'

'You know what, Arun.' Lena looked at him. 'I will be secretly on the look out everywhere for your model. In the shops, on the beaches. She must be somewhere.'

Arun shuffled through the pile and pulled out another sketch.

'She's older here.' Stella studied the image. 'More savvy.'

'Seventeen or eighteen I would guess.' Lena joined her. 'But still with some of the innocence of youth in her face.'

Arun pointed at the picture. 'The pots she makes are finer, stronger —'

'You can see that about her,' Stella went on. 'She's that more worldly and business minded —'

'But the tenderness is still there,' said Lena. 'The soft cheeks — and a body to die for — perfectly shaped. I am going to be on the look out for your model.'

'Oh, she went away a long time ago,' he dismissed her with a wave of his hand.

'Here's another sketch,' Stella pulled one over. 'Still using pencil, charcoal and chalks, I think. She's stacking pots in this one, with her mother. That's who she gets her stunning looks from. The mother's face is lined, but those beautiful eyes, those fine lips — you can see she was special in her day. This is wonderful, Arun.'

Lena sifted through the small pile, pulling another one out. 'What's this one? People on the move — Is this— ?'

'Yes,' Arun nodded. 'He's arriving in the village. Izzat Baig. A travelling merchant passing through with camels and goods.'

'Just a figure approaching at the moment,' Lena bent closer to look at him. 'We can't make out any details of his features yet. I can't wait to see him close up.' She sifted through more of the remaining sketches. 'Here he is.' She pulled another one out. 'Tall, rugged, with a bit of dust of the road on him. Oh yes, he's somebody all right. Look at his stance, upright, commanding, but with sensitive looking eyes. He's fit all right.'

'Fit?' Stella scowled smilingly at her sister. 'Let me see.'

'And here they are together, in this one. Her head's covered and she's bowed shyly away from him.'

'But he gets her to stand.' Stella was engrossed. 'The father isn't there and he wants to buy some pots — he's got to deal with her.'

'And here, in this little one.' Lena rushed through. 'You can see in the eye contact between them — the attraction. This is wild, Arun. She's going to fall in love with him, isn't she?'

Stella smiled: 'The electricity between them is wild.'

Arun said, 'It was love at first sight for him.'

'His gaze follows her around the room.' Lena was intrigued. 'At the wheel, sorting stock. He can't keep his eyes off her. These are all sketches. Will you work them up on canvas?'

'The best ones. I want to make a series that I can exhibit. There is a gallery I know in Kerala, and one in Mumbai.'

'You will easily sell them.' Stella sipped tea from her cup. Wincing she put it down: too sweet. At least Lena had not been at her flask so far today; she was so much better, clearer and fun to be with when she was sober.

'To some rich collector,' Lena added.

'I can hope.'

'You will,' Stella assured him.

Lena was back at the pictures. 'She's very shy in front of him — Sohni.'

Arun carried on with the story: 'She doesn't declare her love for him as quickly as he does. She respectfully holds back her feelings.'

Stella smiled. 'You have caught that so beautifully.'

'Is it true?' Lena watched him, looking for answers from him all the time, Stella perceived.

'They say so. Hundreds of years ago, so it got handed down to us this way. It happened in a village in an area that became part of Pakistan when India was divided during Partition in 1947.'

'Here's some more sketches of Izzat Baig as a young man — Stella, look — Get him, eh? Smooth features, thick black hair, an endearing smile — he's fit all right. So handsome it scares poor Sohni. She hides away behind a pile of pots.'

They laughed. Stella had given in to curiosity, not only of the story, but Arun's part in it all. 'And who modelled for him?'

'One of the boys from the fishing boats. You can see him working down there every day.'

'Yes, I know him,' said Lena. 'At least I think I've seen him. But what happened to your model for Sohni?'

Stella watched them both: Lena getting more involved in the story and the sketches, and Arun trying to remain in control. He turned aside and fiddled with some pencils. 'Probably married with children.'

'You don't know?'

'She went to another city I think. Pune, or somewhere.'

'You didn't keep track of your muse?'

For a moment Stella noticed Arun seemed nervous and to be holding back. He was usually so open and chatty.

She quickly found herself frustrated with the side track and wanted to get to the end of the story. 'So what happens next?'

Arun went to a chair, picked up a small bundle of pictures and brought them over. Stella pored over the top ones. 'He can't keep his eyes off her. And here's her father again. And who's this other young man? Her brother?'

'There's a problem.' Arun smiled and gave a little shrug. 'Sohni is already promised by her father and mother to a man of her class in the next village.'

Stella observed the travelling merchant in one of the drawings. 'Izzat Baig is dressed in fine clothes — his neat shalwar kameez — his beard is neatly trimmed.'

'This other guy looks like he's just fallen off a horse.' Lena mocked the smaller figure.

'Sohni must marry this man,' Arun looked with her at the bridegroom, smiling with her, then nodded at another sketch. 'Izzat Baig is asking Sohni's father for her hand.'

'And he waves Izzat away,' Lena pointed. 'Poor sod. He can't have his princess.'

Stella was ahead of herself again. 'So many sketches you've done, all the story. And this one — they meet — look at this one — in secret.'

'By the river,' Arun indicated.

'She's in love with him now, isn't she?' Lena turned to Arun again.

'Can they run away together?' asked Stella.

'The wedding to the local boy is small,' Arun carried on. 'They are a poor family. But there is music and dancing.'

Stella studied the wedding scene. 'You are so good at capturing characters in your sketches, they're recognisable and real. Look at these dancers. And who are these?'

'Hijra,' Arun said. 'Men who have become women. There is a long tradition in India, going back beyond the eunuchs in the Mughals' courts. They bring good fortune to newly married couples and bless them with fertility.'

'Dancing and singing,' Stella observed.

'But this isn't going to be good fortune and fertility is it?' Lena gazed at the wedding party.

'So what does Izzat Baig do?'

'Here he is now —' Arun handed Stella another small sketch.

'This is him? Herding cattle? A bit low down for a merchant, isn't it?'

'He gives up being a merchant,' Arun carried on. 'Tells the camel train to go on without him.'

'Gives up all his wealth,' Lena laughed. 'What a man.'

'He called himself Mahiwal — which means buffalo herder — and made his home in a poor man's hut on the other side of the river from where Sohni lived with her new husband.'

'Where have these kind of men gone?' Lena laughed again. 'Find me one.'

'In this picture she is standing on the river bank looking over at him,' Stella said.

'What happens next?'

Arun stepped back. 'Sohni can't swim, so she's using one of her big hard baked pots to hang onto and float over.'

'And they hug on the other bank,' Stella said.

'And they get up to things in that naughty little hut.' Lena held her mouth. 'What an amazing story. She left her husband and went off into the horizon with the cow herd, who was a wealthy merchant. It can't be bad.' Stella watched her looking at Arun who was ready to carry on. Lena finished. 'It can't be like that, can it?' Her affection for Arun was clear.

Stella laughed. 'The husband kills her and Izzat throws himself in the river?'

Arun was shaking his head. 'It is the spying sister-in-law —'

'This is her then, in this one.' Stella fingered the next. 'Watching from behind bushes as Sohni gets the big pot she's hidden in the rushes and pushes herself across the river to Izzat's hut. And the sister-in-law sees the shape of her lover on the other bank. They are hugging.'

'The sister- in-law tightens her fists,' Arun led them on. 'This can never happen. This will bring great shame on the family.'

'What does the sister-in-law do?' asked Lena.

'She finds Sohni's hidden pot in the reeds and swaps it with another pot. When Sohni comes back that night she takes the new pot and starts to swim out,' said Arun.

'But what's this.' Lena looked perturbed. 'She's sinking. And she's crying out to Izzat. Arun?'

'The sister-in-law swapped Sohni's hard baked earthenware pot with a soft unbaked one that breaks up in the water.'

'The witch —' Stella hissed.

'Izzat Baig hears her cries from the other bank and tries to swim out to her. The pot crumbles. They fall into each other's arms and are swept away.'

Stella and Lena looked on silently.

6

'A real tear jerker then.' Lena sat on the long sofa. 'A sad story of love and loss. It crosses lines — of marriage, of class and caste—'

'That's what gives it such beauty I think.' Stella stayed glancing at all the drawings.

'And why it's lasted,' Arun said. 'I must get you more drinks — and some snacks.' He left them, returning a moment later with juices and Bombay Mix and nuts and small pakoras on a plate. 'It would make a good song.' He smiled, placing the goodies on a small table in front of them.

Stella put a couple of pakoras on a small plate. 'You've still got your wife's piano?'

'In the back room, just as she left it. No one has touched it since she passed. I think only a special person could be allowed to open it and press their fingers on the keys—' He smiled, gesturing them to carrying on eating. Stella noticed Lena grimacing.

'Here's the last portrait.' Arun held up a canvas showing the figure of a young man.

'Oh but you've put a lot of effort into that,' said Stella, chewing. 'The youth, full of energy and love. He's waiting for her.'

Lena got up and walked over, taking the canvas in her hands and scrutinising it. 'It is you, Arun. You used yourself as a model in this one.'

He looked embarrassed. 'The story is not done, really.'

'But it is so much you, Arun,' Lena carried on. 'You've lost your Sohni, it's there in your face. The face of a man cut deeply by love, yet with the vitality of a young man.'

'You read in so much, Lena,' Stella said.

'A man still in grief for his wife —'

'Lena, have a thought for Arun's feelings —'

Arun gave a short sigh. 'It's all a myth really.' He gave a brief breathy laugh. 'Just like life — a conundrum — a bewildering maze we crawl through —'

Lena laughed. 'Getting most of it wrong as we go.'

Arun took the portrait from Lena. 'Life brings us one precious thing at least — experience — with which we can enlighten ourselves, or torture ourselves.'

Stella took a spoonful of Bombay Mix, spread it in a small dish and took finger-fulls. 'Very profound, I must say.' She meant to tease him, but realised it sounded ironic and mocking.

'You're so sceptical,' Lena lightly chided her. 'The man can see things, his art says so.' Lena squinted at Arun, saying to him, 'You have been there. Hell and back.'

Stella tensed her shoulders, pushing back her emotions. 'You think because I'm not an artist or singer my every day hells don't count.'

Lena turned away from her. 'Did they find their bodies?'

'Washed up on a sandy strip at the river bank.' Arun poured glasses of pineapple juice for them. 'Every year a group of people meet to remember the story.'

'It's become a cult?' Stella sipped her pineapple juice. Probably Lena was yearning for a dash of gin in hers.

'Just a rich man with a big house and wide gardens on an island in a river in the south. They get together in his gardens and watch a dancer perform the story of the lovers, accompanied by sitar and tabla.'

'Sounds marvellous,' said Lena and laughing added, 'When can we go?'

Stella cut in attempting to soften Lena's demands. 'By special invitation only, I should think.'

'It's not the real river, of course, that's way up in Pakistan now.' Arun appeared to ignore the pleas and the sibling rivalry. 'But they celebrate the story — like you might celebrate Shakespeare's Romeo and Juliet — they play it out through music and dance. And they call it: The Garden of Izzat Baig.' He sipped his juice again. 'It's all very secret and select. Only once a year. Yes, by special invitation only. For many hours through the night they perform without tiring as a tribute to the lost lovers. They say the music hypnotises the performers as well as the listeners. All are taken on a journey through the heights and depths of existence, experiencing moments of gravity and supreme bliss.'

Stella smiled at him, assuming he was going over the top.

'Where does it happen? When?' Lena said.

'Music has power.' He looked at her. 'You know this, Lena. Music is made for taking people on journeys inside themselves. The hairs on the back of your neck tingling, your stomach turning over, the feeling you might faint, or fly up to the stars. You have felt that, Lena, I know.'

Lena was quiet and unsteady a moment, Stella could feel. 'I'm not sure I have,' Stella said.

'It's a moment that is just as exciting in its transcendence as the feelings of first love.'

'I must have missed out on both,' Stella said with irony, smiling.

'Where have you been?' Lena joked.

'I heard you play the piano once and it was beautiful. Maybe if you had carried on with it you might have taken me to those heights.' Stella pushed her sister in reply.

Arun nodded towards the adjoining room. 'You could start by opening my wife's piano. It is in need of—'

Lena shook her head, he took note and carried on. 'Performers and audience are spellbound as the dancer acts out the story, her leaps and swirls express the highs and lows and her finger movements and gestures add to an enriching hypnotic experience. At the end no one talks or applauds, they sit mesmerised, and then they drift off in a trance. People say it has changed their lives, given them insights — that somehow their consciousness has taken a jolt and everything seems clear — problems just drift away. They say it takes you into deep parts of the cosmos and you become aware of some sort of essence — a sort of bliss, or godliness — an individual spiritual journey—'

'You do big up a story, Arun.' Stella joked with him at the end.

Lena sat forward. 'Have you ever painted that — the Garden of Izzat Baig? With performers and audience and everything?'

'I have thought about it, but never dared.'

'What are you afraid of?'

'What every artist fears. Failing to pull it off. Or thinking you have pulled it off, but in reality you have made a ridiculous mess.'

'You're better than that,' said Lena.

'And so are you. But you will not touch a piano — probably for the same reason—'

'It's not that at all,' Lena said sharply.

'God knows why she's like this.' Stella thought for a moment about his descriptions. 'It all sounds like a big hippy trip to me,' Stella chuckled playfully. 'A bit like getting off on weed.'

'More than any drug inspired trips,' Arun reassured her. 'Words can't explain. But you come out renewed, with a sense of purpose, as though your past has been shed like a snakeskin. You must have been there, Lena.'

'Once, 'Lena smiled at the memory. 'The guitarist's strings broke, and he was so stoned he just stopped playing in the middle of the song. And so did the back line. I carried on singing without them. Like the song existed on its own and I was just the instrument it came out of. It went on and on. The crowd were suddenly hushed. I was somewhere else — up high somewhere — a sort of place of yes — bliss — a place where nothing can touch you, you can come to no harm—'

'What were you taking that night?' Stella finished Lena's dream with a laugh.

'Nothing.'

But Stella couldn't fully believe her. Stella's sympathy for what Lena had gone through checked her frustration at her sister's reluctance to sing again and put her hands on the keys. Reliving again the moment she had seen Lena, the teenage girl, singing her own song accompanied by the piano, she could see music had always been an answer to Lena. And although music had never given Stella the same kind of highs since and she was sceptical of the kind of bliss it seemed to generate in others, she could see that Lena was not a full person without it in her life. 'You can get it again, Lena,' Stella said quietly. 'Without the other stuff—'

Lena was agitated now. And she hadn't had a slug of gin yet. 'Too much water under the bridge. Too many chemicals in the brain. I can't find my way back to that place.' The old tortured expression was on her face, Stella registered.

'I can take you to the Garden,' Arun told Lena softly.

'And me?' Stella said.

'You wouldn't get it,' Lena sounded bitter.

'You can both come as my guests.'

'If she gets bored, she'll fidget all night. And she does get bored quickly, Stella does.'

'She will enjoy it too.'

Stella felt the old resentments towards her sister rising. Just because she wasn't a musician herself did not mean Stella could not appreciate the cultural side of the event. 'Promise? It's just music and dancing. None of this highfalutin spiritual nonsense. The world's the world and that's it. Get on with it.'

Arun kept with Lena. 'You are very attracted by Sohni's story, I think.'

'There's some words to a song running through my brain. I keep fighting it, but they won't go: *"She runs through the moonlight, Sohni, Sohni, to hold her Izzat tight . . ."* '

'You are a poet.'

'I need my guitarist man, Sam, to work out backing chords and —'

'Would you work with me?'

'That would be amazing. Do you play guitar?'

'Give me the words and I'll put music to them. My wife taught me some chords —'

Stella watched her closely: she would shy away now, that was certain. And she was right:

'The song is not very good,' Lena ended.

Stella couldn't hold back her frustration around Lena. 'What is the matter with you? This is your chance to get back on the rails.' Lena looked scared. 'Get hold of yourself, for god's sake.'

'We can't force things,' Arun tried to calm them.

'Sometimes we do. Get to that piano, Lena and do your stuff. Do it.'

'Slowly,' Arun said. 'When she's ready.'

'She'll never be ready, she's been like this for years. A jobbing singer who could have climbed to heights — recording contracts, big tours. She could have become a household name. But for this piano business. I heard her writing songs on the piano when she was thirteen. How she worked at it, the sounds were amazing. She was god's gift. And she blows it.' Lena got up and strode to the table top of sketches as Stella went on, 'She throws it all back at us. Mum was distraught — bought you a piano, got you lessons. She would have scrubbed floors to get you a grand piano if you had asked, anything. And you drop it. Just a bloody phase you're going through.'

'No, Stella.' Lena was shaking.

'You're bloody impossible. You say I was spoiled. You got everything you wanted — all the attention. Did anybody buy me anything like a piano? One that had to be sent away? What's the matter with you?'

Lena seemed lost in herself for a long time. Arun got up and came over to them.

'I—' Lena began.

'What?' Stella urged her.

'It was a long time ago.'

'Thank god for that. Wise up, Lena. This man wants to help you.'

'I don't need help.'

'What then?'

'I cracked it.'

'The drugs, yes. Life — no.' Stella gave an ironic laugh.

Lena looked drained, but Stella would not let her go. Lena wrung her hands. 'My piano teacher.'

Stella recalled the man: tall, handsome. 'What was his name? What was it now? Such a nice fella. Barnett. John Barnett. He was so accomplished, such a charming man. He came highly recommended to mum—'

Lena seemed to freeze. She looked like she needed a drink and Stella was close to giving in to her if for that moment it eased the pain she was clearly going through. Lena scowled, bunched up her fists, looking as though she was about to break down. 'You're not serious,' Stella read pain in Lena's face a moment. 'He was a very good friend of mum's. He wouldn't—'

'Our little secret,' Lena said quietly.

Stella held her ground. 'No, Lena. Not that. He was a good man. Nobody knew when you were telling the truth, or telling us something to get our attention. And you did nothing? You said nothing? Why? No Lena, nothing happened.'

'He said he would kill me if I said.'

'And you didn't say anything.'

'And one day he said he would kill you. You'd have this strange accident — fall down stairs or something—'

'You would have said something.'

'I told auntie Jean. She said Barnett was mum's and her's best friend, he would never do such a thing. I was making it up because I didn't want to play the piano anymore and it was a way of getting out of it.'

'She was right. You had to be the centre of things all the time. And why now?'

'I don't know,' Lena was sobbing. 'This talk of Izzat Baig and Sohni in the garden, it brings it all back. I wanted the piano, Stella. I could see it would be the key to me writing the songs I wanted. I knew it even then. But every week I would have to do Barnett favours if I carried on. I can't touch pianos. I can't—'

Arun edged towards Lena. 'I'm sorry.'

'She always did like a drama,' Stella said.

'We have to believe—' Arun added.

'The drugs, the self harming, the lies, Arun.' Stella had to fill him in.

Lena turned away from them, asking Arun for pencil and paper. They let her go, sipped their juices and watched while she scribbled the lyrics she had told them.

'You can do it for me,' Lena called to Arun. 'Take the lyrics and make something. But take me to Izzat Baig's Garden—'

'You didn't say.' Stella appealed to her sister, bewildered. 'I didn't know.'

'You seem to know everything else about me.' Lena rocked a little on her feet, the pictures of Izzat and Sohni near her on the table. 'And when I was on stage the very last time I wasn't in some place of bliss. Nah. It was hell. I looked around me and saw a grim naked race for survival. All the nasty little things people have to do to get food in their mouths and shelter in their lives. Just like all the other animals. Survive or die — by whatever means. And you know I thought to myself in the middle of that song: what if we didn't have to fight to survive, we could rise to levels of creativity we can't dream of.' She waved over at Stella. 'Long ago I lost the anger of: "Why haven't you got anywhere? You give all in your singing and it falls on deaf ears." That rage gnaws at you — destroying the belief you have in yourself.'

'I'm sure you are gifted—' Arun said.

She gestured at Stella again. 'When you are young, men grind you down with their power.'

'You think I never had that?'

'We don't know what each other's pain is — none of us.' Lena seemed almost to be thinking out loud, tottering, as if close to being in trance. 'That's why we need art and music — to do it for us—'

'You always did over dramatise.' Stella tried to take it all in. 'Work on your new song then.'

'I will. I'll go so deep in it'll kill the memory of what I was pushed into being.'

'You always were more hard done by as a child.'

Lena was firm. 'Your dad and our mum had parted for a while. My dad comes along, passing through. You think — that if my dad hadn't come along, your dad would have come back. But not with somebody with a black baby. God no. If my dad hadn't come by, I would never have been born. You would have had them all to yourself—'

Arun cut in quickly. 'We should take a break. I'll get some food prepared. I can get someone in to cook—'

Stella chided her. 'You make yourself a victim and dramatise for effect. They're all dead now so what difference does it make?'

'It happened, Stella,' Lena said quietly.

'You get help and move on.'

'That's it then, box ticked, done that, faced it, put it away. Ignore what an imprint it has on you, how the scar becomes you.'

'Do as mum did.'

'What did she ever do for me?'

'She put her weaknesses and imperfections and hurts in a little box and pushed them to the back of her mind. That's how she survived.'

'I did that — feeding it on junk.'

Arun said, 'What happens to us we become and we pass that on to others. Gurus say if we could work through our past hurts we can be renewed.'

'We'll never be that good,' Stella replied.

'They say,' Arun continued. 'What is it about our nature that makes it hard for us to find empathy.'

'People will never change,' Stella kept on. 'Because we are who we are.'

'I need to go there, Arun.' Lena appealed to him.

*****

'It's no use, really,' Stella told him the following morning. 'I just haven't got the talent. You can do so much, then you find you can't push your abilities any further—'

Lena's stool was empty. The sea was pouring in along the shore, a group of young men were splashing each other and small groups of lively tourists were out strolling.

'But the orange boat is beginning to live. And the fisherman you've put there, he has movement — authenticity.'

'Do you think so? Or am I just paying you to say these things to me?' She laughed.

'Confidence comes with practice.'

'I wish I believed that.' She felt good with him alone — like it was last year. She had him all to herself. 'You never showed me those pictures when I was here before. Your secret, eh? You're not all you seem on the outside.'

'Lena is late?'

'She couldn't be bothered, today. It's just me, your favourite student. Now show me how to put in another figure along the beach.' She gently grabbed his arm and pulled him closer. 'I had such a wonderful time with you last year — those romantic boat trips along the river, under the old wooden bridge, the Brahminy Kites circling high up.'

'Will she come later? She hasn't given up altogether?'

'Who knows with her.'

'So much has happened to her.' Arun spoke softly.

Stella was still shocked and was grappling with her feelings about the revelation. It was always hard to believe what Lena said, there was such a history of lies and deceit, of craft and connivance. It was why mum lost it with her. Even as children she was known to bend the truth to get her way or to get out of things. That was all magnified with the addictions when she got older. Stella dare not contemplate whether what Lena had said could be true. She could not think about it anymore, it was too difficult and painful. She wanted them to be close as sisters but doubted it was possible. She had to put it out of her mind, it was too big. This thing could never have happened.

'Now, this figure. Help me, will you?'

He silently took her brush and prepared to smooth out some lines for her. 'She is so sensitive —'

Stella nodded for him to get on and alter her painting. 'You don't need to worry about her. Maybe it was a mistake —' He smoothed the lines of the chalets in the background, softened the green in the foliage on the island behind. 'I brought her over, when I could have had a trouble free time with you. Doing her a favour. I got hold of her when mum died. She said she'd dried out — I believed her.'

'I don't think it was a mistake, Stella.'

'Maybe not to you.' Stella felt challenged.

'The visit to the Garden will calm things.'

'I was thinking of putting her on a plane and sending her back home.' She pushed for a response from him.

He stopped painting. 'She's hurting.' And standing back he said, 'I think we need to adjust the perspective a little — that person way down the beach is too large compared to the fisherman — let me — Tomorrow night we go to the Garden. The next day we will talk about the images we gained from that, do some sketches and try out ideas we can work up into paintings—'

'Exciting.' Stella sucked the end of a brush. 'You won't fall for her charms, will you? I don't like to say it but you can see she has always been a bit jealous of me.'

'Her piano lessons?' Arun stared at her.

'The stage was the right place for her to develop her narcissistic streak—'

He put the brush down and considered the painting. 'She seems — broken — in many ways.'

Still holding her wet brush, Stella folded her arms. 'She's got you where she wants you when you believe that.'

'I do want to help her write songs again.'

'She won't stick at it,' Stella was adamant.

'You would let me help her?'

'Who am I to stand in the way?'

'I'm sure if I can get her back to the piano her whole life will change.'

Unfolding her arms she dipped her brush in a pot of water and then wiped it on a cloth. 'You can try.' She rubbed the brush heavily into the cloth again, avoiding eye contact. 'I came back here so we could spend more time together — you and me — I thought—'

'Yes,' he cut her off. 'Yes, when we have finished the course.'

Stella nervously drilled the brush further into the cloth. 'I thought — a meal together. You and me.'

Arun screwed lids back on tubes of paint and stacked them in a box. 'Let us go to the Garden, and finish our ideas after—'

'Tonight, I thought perhaps — The Rocking Globe restaurant.'

'We cannot leave Lena alone when she is like this.'

'She knows other people down town she can get drunk with.' Stella took the pot of water and slopped it over the rail onto the green spiky plants in the sandy garden beyond the veranda. Then she turned to him: 'I have hopes for us, Arun.'

He gave her a quick frown, 'If I try and help Lena with her songs, you might not finish the course?'

Putting everything down she sidled up to him, smiling. 'We were very close last year, Arun. I want that to continue and develop.' She took his hand and rubbed it. 'We agreed we'd make a partnership of it. And now, with my inheritance, you can build a new studio with a gallery and open up all your contacts. The world's open to you Arun, you just have to paint the right brushstrokes—'

7

When they came out of the small concert hall, they sat on a couple of wooden benches draped with green, red and gold fabrics, the dark star-spotted sky above them. Candles lit routes through the garden. Flickering light danced over the tropical greenery. A thicket of bamboo formed a crescent behind them, and on either side were tropical plants with great green leaves. Bromeliads proliferated, along with bougainvillea, pitcher plants, heliconia. Orchids hung precariously in semi-darkness. Palm trees towered over them, their branches unruffled in the stillness of night. Stella recognised agave plants and tall cacti — not native, but thriving in this atmosphere.

Hidden fans allowed drafts of air to waft around their feet, keeping mosquitos at bay. A giant banyan tree stood over the back near the river's edge, its branches and fronds draped with golden fabrics and tiny flickering lights.

The size of several football pitches, the garden was like a small jungle lit entirely by candles of all shapes, colours, perfumes and sizes. Paths led to quiet groves surrounded by palm trees and hung with brilliantly designed drapes. Some were occupied by groups or couples sitting in meditation on carpets with the whiff of incense around them.

From Stella's bench the sound of trickling water from a fountain nearly drowned out the distant hum of sitar and tabla. She was fascinated by the feature, the water shooting from the mouth of a pot — Sohni's pot. A pond spread out ahead of the fountain where carp lurked with streams leading to groves and grottos.

When they had first arrived Arun had walked them round, leading them down overgrown tracks and paths to sacred little sights. One grotto consisted of a mound standing in front of a rock on which a three foot high Shiva pranced, a circle of bronze flames framing him. Surrounded by incense the lively dancer sparkled in candlelight, making him seem alive and in motion, moving in a similar way to the dancer in the concert hall.

Another path led to a rocky arch that Stella and the others had to bend low to get through. The end opened out to a cavern containing a life size Buddha sitting in meditation, eyes half closed, body and limbs in complete relaxation, his lithe young body of smoothly carved stone.

A model of the Taj Mahal half a metre high stood in another quiet area, complete with reflecting pools, its structure seemingly golden white to Stella. Miniature fountains supplied the pools, and the whole was surrounded by tiles and mosaics of Islamic design with stylised Arabic writing.

Arun told them that the shrines represented various religions: Hinduism, Buddhism and Islam and that other grottos were planned to cater for all religions, including Sikhism – to be represented by a model of the Golden Temple – and Christianity – perhaps to be symbolised by a simple wooden cross. Each shrine and each meditation area was supplied by streams of running water that circled the garden, starting at the pool with the main fountain, working their way around and back, the fountain pool being the heart of the place.

Occasionally a young waiter in a white Punjabi Suit and tightly wrapped turban of orange or white or green drifted through the greenery taking drinks, sweets and snacks to people hidden in groves and caves.

Stella had been excited by the performance. The moods the sitar and tabla painted, from the slow and romantic of the lovers meeting, to the quickness of the flooding river inspired images of Arun's paintings. Most of the hundred or so audience in the space seemed enwrapped, eyes closed in meditation, or open in trance watching the dancer. Clad in tightly fitting leggings and a bodice of reds, yellows, golds, silvers and greens — with gold earrings, bracelets and necklaces — and with trailing scarves, the twenty year old leapt lightly across her space, animating the story with finger and hand gestures. Arun had told her there were two groups of performers taking it in turns throughout the night to prevent over tiredness.

Stella was engrossed, but did not see herself as being as immersed as Lena and Arun, or most of the audience.

They sat on the bench silently for a time, enjoying the mixture of sounds: the trickle of the fountain and running of streams, and the phasing in and out of the sounds of the sitar and tabla.

Arun looked over at the women and nodded: 'You see?'

Lena whispered: 'Don't talk now.'

Stella left her in her trance, and whispering to Arun said, 'Oh yes, it was very good. I'm not sure it took me to the heights you go.'

'Shush,' her sister hissed. 'You have to enjoy the silence that fills the space between the notes and the dance steps afterwards.'

Stella could not help but feel that she was trying to impress Arun.

'The smoothness of the sounds,' Arun said. 'Every time I come, even though I've heard it many times — it just transports me.'

'You can imagine each part of the story.' Lena seemed to wake suddenly out of her trance.

Stella crossed her legs. 'Very good, but just music.' She enjoyed the variety of plants in the garden, felt enclosed in a friendly jungle, expecting to hear monkeys chattering and parakeets calling. But the music trailed on, the distant whine of the sitar and the incessant tap of the tabla. She imagined the dancer with her smiles, her lightly shaking head, her finger motions and the turns of her feet. And the pleasant sound of the trickle of splashing water at the little fountain added further magic to the music. It was all pleasant, all of it, the garden, the music and the dance, but not in the way they were experiencing.

'Didn't you feel the flow of the river,' Lena went on. 'And the intensity when they are in each other's arms—'

'The tabla talks back to the sitar,' Arun added.

'And her dance — the green and the gold — the expressions and movement. Her hand and finger gestures. I was in your drawings,' Lena told him. 'There's that moment when he's herding cattle and he sees her approaching with a pot on her head. The feeling of first love, the youthful bliss — it's all there.' She paused a moment. 'You didn't get that, Stella?'

Stella laughed. 'It was good.'

'The wedding,' Lena carried on. 'The distraught Izzat Baig in the background, the unsure and uncertain bride, the arrogant bridegroom. It's all there in the music.'

'I like it,' Stella said. 'It took me to memories.' She laughed nervously, 'Perhaps not as far as you two.'

'That is good,' Arun said.

Stella felt they were reading too much into the event when it should be taken on the artistic and cultural level it was intended. 'It may take you places. It was very enjoyable, but not therapeutic — at least, for me. And I don't want to be dragged into memories. The past is the past and it should stay there,' she contemplated.

'But it can't,' Lena challenged her. 'It's part of the present, and the present is who we are. That's why it seemed so real to me.'

'I'm very pleased it did that for you,' Stella tried to sound genuine.

Lena continued, 'There's a part where Sohni is making pots and the dancer is spinning round and round. The sitar player has a smile of deep contentment. The music has possessed them with the story of life: the tragedies, the comedy. That magic moment when performers and audience link in appreciation. Yes, a sort of bliss. A place where words don't exist. Nothing of us is left then, the mind drifts untroubled. There is no pain in that place.'

'I can't see that—' said Stella .

'Music can redeem us,' Arun said.

'Can it? I'm not sure.'

'It helps us along.'

'I'm glad.' Stella wanted to be truthful without sounding like a killjoy.

Lena glanced around at the greenery, at the big black shape of the banyan tree over the back, its long dark fronds reaching back into earth. 'I was taken to a world beyond the piano.' Lena turned to her sister. 'It may have seemed, Stella, I was trying to be better than you all the time—'

Stella looked down, replying quietly. 'It did seem like that sometimes.' She did not know if her reply had angered Lena, or whether she was experiencing a rush of memories.

'Why did mum never tell me about Africa?' Lena fired up. 'About my heritage? In school it was always about Romans and slavery. Where were the black people who stood up and had a history? My identity was one sided. Why did I want my skin to be like yours? To be accepted like you. I scrubbed and scrubbed in the bath.' She stopped a moment. A circle of huge candles lit up the base of the trunk, outlining shapes and forms, creating lines of light and bands of shadow. And turning to Stella she carried on calmly. 'You knew your father and had something of him as you grew up. I don't even know whether my father even knows if I exist. But that's all I ever envied of you. What you wanted was what I had. You've always wanted that. Should I be hiding my talents so others won't be offended — or jealous?'

'Is that what you're doing?' Arun said. 'Making the piano to blame?'

'I was taught to hate it. I was a piece of exotic meat to be played with. He didn't play the piano, he played me.' She burst out, thought more, then said: 'The music makes me see things. Sohni dancing in front of me. The sister-in-law changing the pots — Everything we become has to be fought for. And those who cannot fight for who they are — just die away—'

Stella sat back shocked. 'Play the piano then.'

'When she's ready—' Arun interrupted.

'By one touch of the keys you could release yourself.'

'I was there when they were drowning—' Lena said dreamily.

'It's her choice, I suppose,' Stella shrugged.

Arun leaned towards Lena. 'Isn't that what the Blues is — going to hell and back?'

She nodded: 'On the nail.'

'I'm just hearing different things. That's all—' Stella said. 'It's all very beautiful—'

'You can go in again,' Arun suggested. 'They go on until dawn.'

Stella looked at them.

'We'll join you in there again in a while,' Lena assured her.

Perhaps there was more for Stella to gain, perhaps she could attain the heights they seemed to be transported to, but she doubted it as she stood up to go.

'I won't hold my breath.' Stella gathered her bag and headed past the fountain towards the hall. The swish of the water was replaced by the sound of tabla and sitar deep in a Raga, the two instruments bouncing trills of notes backwards and forwards to each other.

When she had gone Arun sat next to Lena. 'I'm glad you got something.'

'There's that long section — the bodies are washed up on shore and the villagers are dragging them back to the garden.

It's not simply music of gloom and loss, it's higher than that — the healing power of music.'

'Everyone says it.'

Lena laughed. 'Except Stella.'

'I'm not sure she's as tough skinned as she makes out.'

'You've got so much to give through your art — the music releases everything —'

'All the dark sides of ourselves.'   Arun looked away from her. 'It's too much —'

'But you paint your pain out. It's in your work, what you give to others.'

'Can we be forgiven?' he said and she looked at him. 'I'm not sure. '

She had not seen him look troubled before, his relaxed easiness about life had gone and she sensed the music had opened up old wounds. 'The music shows us the need to atone, but it does not give us atonement. We have to find that ourselves.'

'You've taken a lot from this,' he said.

'You're still grieving.'

'Yes, but the world is what we make it. Our mistakes, the wrong choices —'

Lena took his hand, wanting to understand the side to him he would not reveal. 'But we are also made by others around us. You've given me so much. Look how you've opened my eyes. I've found a new voice. I want to know you, and you won't let me in.'

He was shaking his head, his eyes welling. 'I can't hear the music.'

'I will only go to the piano if you take me.' She kissed his cheek, hugged him and they held each other.

Stella pretended not to notice as they parted quickly when she returned. 'Yes it is glorious, absolutely. I love it, but—' She sat on the bench near them, silent among the dark greenery, the branches of the banyan tree hanging like a lighted cloud behind them. 'So intense, I —'

Arun stood as she arrived. 'You were not transported in any way?'

'Magical music and a dancer too beautiful for words.'

'You were moved,' Lena said.

'Of course, in a way —' Stella felt an outsider, that because she had not been transported in the way everyone else seemed to be, she was excluded from their cult. 'I'm feeling a bit dizzy —'

'Can I get you some water?' Arun said. 'Or some juice? Something to eat — there's a buffet in the other hall — plenty of food there — Or I can call a waiter to bring some tea and sweets.'

'Water? I — something stronger?'

'No alcohol, I'm afraid,' Arun said. 'It can be seen to interfere with meditation —'

'You purists. Lena, your flask —'

'I left it behind.'

Weary, Stella held her hand out to her. 'I'll take it from your bag.'

Lena dived in her bag, took it out and handed it to her. 'It's against the spirit of things here, but —'

'It is the spirit of things,' Stella laughed at the double meaning, but remained agitated and unsure of herself and what she was experiencing.

'You can lie down and relax,' Arun said. 'There is a space with cushions you can use — or you can go to a shrine of your choice — '

'It's nothing really — just a hot flush. And things — pictures you have in your mind — memories — I don't know —'

'What do you see?' Lena said.

Stella swigged, exhaled and sat back. Images were beginning to flow through her mind uncontrollably. 'I think, I don't know. There was — you — at the piano — I—'

'I was playing?'

'At thirteen, playing so well.' She drew breath shakily. These mental intrusions were hateful. 'Until he came—' They were right. It was like a trance, a place where pictures flicked through your mind film-like. Only you could see them and be hurt by them.

'John Barnett?' Lena gasped. 'Were you there?'

Stella was confused. 'So many memories. You file them and you cannot remember which are real and which are—' She was confused by what she saw. Images continued to roll through her vision, entangled with memories and the surrealistic state of dreams. Nothing was fixed or certain. Only painful.

'You knew?' Lena tensed. 'You saw him with me?'

'I don't know.' Stella trembled. She struggled to see what was real and what was distorted in the visions that she could not shake off.

'When I was thirteen, you saw me at the piano and you saw John Barnett — doing what he did? What do you mean?'

'I do need to lie down.' Stella made to get up, but Lena pulled her back down. 'I mean — I don't know.' She did not seem able to control her mind or her body, the flashing images and shaking fingers. She hoped she might faint, but everything was becoming clearer.

'You saw him do that — and you did nothing?'

'I don't know where that damned music leads you. I don't know.' The images in Stella's mind were as stark as if happening in front of her now.

'You knew that? All the time?'

'The music, Lena, the dance—'

'You never told anyone?' Lena raged. 'All that time nobody believed me — and you knew. And did nothing?'

'I don't know,' Stella held her head in her hands. 'The music. You end up not knowing what's real—'

'Make yourself know.' Lena grabbed her arm and shook her. 'Or I'll throw you back in there and you can know some more.'

'Is it a real memory? 'Stella fumbled through the daze.

'Do you know what it feels like? Being told that your memories and experiences are a lie — that you made them up to get attention and to hurt people you didn't like? Everything is taken from you. I wished I was dead. The times I cut myself. The OD's. Because I hated myself. I was the bad one who did bad things.' Lena calmed, then said: 'Why did you not tell?'

Stella shook her head. 'I don't know.' She was lost in a slice of time she had lost long ago. Images mixed with feelings from teenage years that rolled into feelings of the present. The remembered feelings were clear but the present ones were of fear and confusion.

'Don't keep saying that,' Lena kept on. 'You didn't tell because you were afraid, or because you were jealous of me and wanted me hurt? Which is it?'

'I was a kid too — I — can't remember—'

'How many times? How many, Stella?'

'Once.' Stella pushed back tears, admitting pictures lucidly to form themselves. 'By accident. The door was ajar. I saw him kissing you — I didn't understand — I couldn't believe — and then the week after, you stopped the piano. The rows — I—'

'You were sixteen. But you knew—' Lena pushed her aside and stood watching the fountain.

The faint sounds of the sitar and tabla echoed down to them, filtered by the cascade. Lights through the jets of water created miniature rainbows.

'Perhaps,' Arun looked at Stella. 'You were afraid the same thing would happen to you?' Stella took a tissue and dabbed her eyes, choking back sobs. 'Or it was too much for you and you blotted it out all these years, and the music brought it back for you. The mind can hide traumatic memories from childhood.' He watched the flickering candles sending flame-light dancing over the greenery. 'I sometimes wonder about Sohni's sister-in-law. She thought she was doing the right thing. Perhaps she wasn't overcome by malice and jealousy as we would like to believe. Perhaps she — within the values of the time — thought — she was doing everything right. That the affair would end, that Sohni would go back to her brother. And then—' Arun drew breath. 'And then at the height of the second movement of the music I find myself asking what sort of life did she live after. Did she tell anyone that she had swapped the pots, or did she keep it to herself? Did it eat her up inside and make her sick and kill her? Or did she somehow rationalise that she had done nothing wrong? Or did she live with a kind of denial about it for the rest of her life? It fascinates me. How did she live? And how long did she live? And did her brother — Sohni's husband — know she did it? And was he an accomplice? Or did he not know at all? And did he blame his sister for the rest of his days?' He let out a short sigh. 'Ah, we shall never know.'

Stella whispered to her sister, 'I did not know — until — the music — it was all lost, gone— '

'Convenient.' Lena refused to turn away from the fountain and face her. 'I can't believe that.'

'You were children,' Arun tried to pacify them.

'So?' Lena turned to Stella. 'We should know — what did you feel in there?'

'It was too much for me—'

'You never believed me.'

'I brought us here — for us to find out this — I didn't realise — and then I saw—' Stella fumbled through tears, trying to find words to express the genuineness of her feelings.

'It was the least you could do.'

'The music brings all sorts of changes—' Arun contemplated.

'I brought you here, Lena.' Stella tried to find some inner strength, 'To give you something—'

'Out of guilt?'

'In those buried memories—'

'I should catch the next flight home and never talk to you again.'

Stella was thoughtful for a time reflecting on her affection for her sister and her understanding of the shock of what Lena had gone through and how it had moulded her life with all its addictions. 'I hope you won't do that,' she said. 'I can understand, and I can't stop you. But Lena, you have the piano. Nobody can take that away from you — Barnett, me — nobody—'

'You can't buy me back again.'

'I always wanted it to be right — whatever you thought — or think now. I didn't want this — I wanted to make you happy, to—'

'Atone?'

'The memories were gone, Lena, I swear — buried — blocked — I couldn't understand the trauma — all hidden away inside waiting for the music to set it free—'

'I'm the one who's supposed to be the drama queen.' Lena gave a cynical laugh.

Stella stood, went to her, placing her fingers on Lena's shoulder but she pulled away. 'I brought you here so we could share something, and so that I could hand over something of the inheritance—'

'You want me to believe that? I don't want it. It's not mine.' Lena kept her back to her while Arun watched them.

The music had stopped for a moment. It was quiet except for the fountain. Pieces of Stella's life seemed to slip into place, the past had a meaning. Circles could be completed if she gave into the love she felt for Lena, if she understood her pain.

Arun said: 'I'd underestimated the power of music and what

it can do to us—'

His words sparked something in Stella and she felt suddenly buoyant and jokey. 'Get off your cloud, Arun, and get back down to earth with the rest of us.' She laughed. 'You can't hide it — neither of you. I might have known, Lena, you'd nick my man. And Arun, we were going to build galleries. I guess I deserve it.'

He sat quietly, letting them talk.

'Stella? Will you help him?'

'I've lived it all wrong,' Stella experienced a sense of release and freedom. She had wanted Arun, but felt the need to put her sister first now — let her have the pleasure of the love she deserved and had been denied throughout her life. 'That life of quiet conformity, doing all the right things with family; nursed my dying mother, forgave my angry father.' She paused for reflection, 'Did everything right as far as society's concerned. Except one thing. I saw something that I did not understand, which terrified me and which I should have talked about and shared — I'm sorry—'

Lena let her shoulders relax and turning to her looked in her eyes. 'You were a kid. We both were. It was a long time ago.'

'I was your elder sister. I let you be broken.'

'You buried things you couldn't understand.'

'Your touch on the piano was light and sensitive, transporting me through my imagination. You thought you were struggling to get phrases right, all that devoted practising, but you had the gift all the time. Your music could take me to heights. As a teenager, I could not handle all that. It was too much. I ran away from the things I saw — and I lost the realisation of where music can take you, how it can heal and inspire you—'

'You don't have to be afraid—' Lena said, drawing her into a hug. 'We're together. Sisters.'

Stella felt the warmness of her sister's body against her, and held on to her as she sobbed.

'It's funny,' Stella smiled through tears after. 'I always wanted to paint. And I'm no good at it.'

Arun got up and joined them as Lena dried her eyes. 'You're developing, Stella — like all of us — at your own rate.'

'Always the optimist and charmer, Arun. You're too kind. I'm not a good artist.'

'When we're small we have that little voice of greatness inside us. Life, parents, teachers tell us we'll never be any good. So that little voice turns on us and tells us we're no good. And we grow up believing it.'

'Were you renewed in there, too?' Stella asked him.

'I must go back in.' Arun sounded distant and evasive.

'You miss your wife,' she said softly. 'I know how painful it must have been being with someone who is slipping away. You must have loved Lakshmi very deeply.'

Arun began, 'It was —' But he stumbled, confused, not being able to find the words and sat back on the bench.

Having tossed her tissue in a nearby stream and straightened herself with a smile, Lena said to him, 'We see that pain in your paintings. That self portrait of yourself as Izzat Baig.'

'It was not Sohni I painted —' he said.

'Was it our wife, Lakshmi?'

He shook his head and said, 'Janini — Not my wife —'

Lena touched his shoulder. 'Was Janini your model? She must have been very beautiful — young and —'

'You loved her,' Stella said. 'I saw it in the portrait. 'You painted Janini and you possessed her, shutting out Lakshmi.' Stella's mind was clear.

'I could not help myself,' he gabbled. 'I was lost, I was trapped — Lakshmi and I had not been close for years. Her moods, her depressions. She would not take her medication —'

Lena said, 'Your wife knew about Janini?'

Stella sat with him, holding his arm. 'How did Lakshmi die, Arun?'

He shook his head.

Lena sat on the other side of him and squeezed his fingers.

His face in his hands he broke into sobs. 'The music takes you places you do not want to go.' Body bent, he was shaking.

'It doesn't lie—' Stella held on to him.

'Lakshmi came home early and found me with Janini — I always loved my wife. The piano she played — how it took me places. But the years of days she spent in dark rooms — it was hard with her — the craziness of how she was — highs and lows and rages when she would not take her medication— I found Lakshmi hanging in the banyan tree—'

The sisters sat holding him while he sobbed.

'You fell for your young model. What happened to Janini?' Stella said.

'Janini ran. Hid herself in the billions of India,' he said as Stella gave him a tissue and he wiped his eyes. 'We can't escape our karma. Janini loved me. After my wife — she ran — and took the baby—'

Lena said: 'You have a child you don't know?'

'There's nothing left.' Arun continued dabbing his eyes.

Stella was aware of the sound of sitar and tabla. Hundreds sat in the hall, spellbound, each individual going through their own unique mystic process. 'You can have the studio and galleries I promised you.' Stella urged him, 'Lena and I will help you—'

'You can't do this — now. What you know — of me—' As he straightened and looked up Stella took a tissue and began wiping his tears.

'But you must find Janini and the child,' Stella told him. 'A single parent in India without an income can't survive.' She felt a new strength inside, a power that could carry her on. And she knew Arun better now that she saw his vulnerabilities.

'My sons will not talk to me,' he said.

'I'll help you find her.' Lena held his hand.

He turned to her. 'You would come with me — after this? Is it right to look for her?'

She nodded and he forced a smile through his tears. 'I know her family in Mumbai—'

'We'll go and find her—'

Taking another tissue from Stella he wiped his face. 'Only if — There is a piano in my house, Lena. You must come and play it and write songs—'

'Yes,' she said. 'We can write songs together, Arun. 'And you too, Stella —'

'You want me to?'

'Come on—' Lena yelled enthusiastically, pulling them both to their feet.

As the slow brightness of dawn was infiltrating the foliage they made their way passed the open door to the concert hall and were halted by the spectacle. The sitar and tabla reached a climax, the players' fingers working rapidly as the sound echoed through the place, thrilling the audience. Lost in the frantic melody, the dancer flashed across the stage, flipping her hands in gestures, moving her limbs quickly and supplely. For Stella the dancer was Sohni aching for her lover, Izzat Baig. Then she was Lena searching for lost chords, ending up as Janini, somewhere out there, waiting for the father of her child to come to her.

A line of candles lit the route out of the garden as the great hanging plants began to glow a brighter green.

'Music rescues us from who we are,' Stella thought to herself. She was no longer afraid.

A VIEW OF GLASS MOUNTAINS

Neil Beardmore

1

2010

The rucksack on Ria's back might as well have been full of rocks it was that heavy. It was two in the afternoon and the sun was hot for March, but it would soon be eclipsed by the white ridges above and the cold would kick in quickly. She stared at the high mountain lines moistened with salty expanses that fell into grey shadows and was mesmerised a time, reminding herself that these giants were the home of the Hindu gods. Even though the road to Dharamsala that she travelled was high up in the foothills the front line of peaks were like great waves about to break over her. On the other side the hills rolled into green valleys.

The sound of a single drum beat intruded on her concentration as she stared, its slow rhythm imitating to her the heartbeat of the mountains. She imagined a melody with lyrics singing to her: *'Come, come, come to the peaks, soar through us like an eagle. See the gods sitting here.'*

As she turned she found a figure behind her. Tall and with a rugged frame, she wore a sari of orange and gold neatly wrapped round her torso. With a wide grin she beat the little hand drum and chanted a few words Ria could not understand. She had sharp features, almost man-like and her arms were thick, her fingers broad and fat. Her eyelids and lashes were heavily encrusted with black make up, her sunken cheeks rouged and the eye sockets deep and hollow, out of which shone a gaze that disturbed Ria.

The drummer stopped in the road, chanting and singing and smiling, then pirouetting with a flip of the feet she danced a little for her. Embodying something of both male and female and with an apparent strength and intuition from both, she carried on her show for Ria.

The figure danced round her, and round again, drawing Ria in. Entranced by her melodies, she was compelled to watch her as she circled, the bangles on her arms rattling in rhythm with the tiny bells on her ankles. Mesmerised by the glare of her eyes directly into hers, Ria was trapped in the circle the dancing drummer circumscribed. As the sound of the drumming increased and the dancer sped round her, singing and laughing, Ria tried to shake off her fears. Not only that she would harm her, but the connection Ria felt with her.

She should run. She was at the edge of the village of Patrinath now with only a juice seller nearby. Even with a heavy bag she could make a dash.

The drumming stopped, but the dancer still blocked her path. The figure's sudden smile eased her a little and she held out her open palm to Ria, her thick fingers painted with henna. Everyone had told her not to give to beggars and Ria turned to go, but the dancer blocked her path, smiling up at her, her open hand under Ria's chin.

'A few rupees, you can give. A few, madam.'

Ria's fingers trembled.

'You give, and I will bring you good luck and many babies.'

'I'm not ready for that,' Ria laughed. Her stare held Ria and she read anger there and hurt.

'You will give, and I will bless you.' She smiled. 'You are from the west. You have riches and many things, you can give to the poor, to feed her. I will give you many many blessings.'

Ria hesitated.

The man at the juice cart called out to the dancer, and she turned a second, allowing Ria to step away, but she turned back with a gaze that seemed to go right into her, as if she was reading something of Ria's inner self. Ria suppressed her fear.

There was another yell from the vendor: a rattle of short angry syllables directed at the dancer as he came over. The dancer did not move, howling something back. The vendor waved to Ria to go, then raised his other hand as if to strike the dancer but she shouted back. The slap fell on to the dancer's neck, she whined, tried to strike back but was blocked by the vendor.

'No,' Ria shouted, but she could not stop the next whack from the vendor. The dancer stepped away, pulling her ragged sari back to shape and glowered at Ria. A myriad of emotions from hatred to compassion raced through Ria along with the anxiety that something about the drumming dancer was familiar. Gathering herself, the dancer checked her earrings and started walking in the direction of a row of shops.

'Dirty.' The juice vendor sneered a laugh. 'Dirty people. No give money.'

'You didn't have to hit—'

The man laughed. 'Man dress as woman. Mad man. I make juice for you. Come—'

Selecting a pineapple from the pile on his cart, he lopped the top off with a small machete, and slicing it again on a board, he loaded the pieces into a machine that he turned. Juice oozed out of the mincer into a cup below.

'Here—' He handed her the mixture and she drank. 'They come here.' He waved his hand again. 'You do what they say. Or. Curse.' He laughed again. 'Stupid people think like that.'

'Who are they?'

'Hijra — man who want to be woman.' He laughed again. 'I say to my son — you be real man.'

'Real man?' Ria said.

'Real man take what he want. Strong. No sissy. Not let men take from him.'

'There's too many men like that in the world already,' Ria said, but he just looked back at her with a puzzled grin on his face. 'There's no need to hit—'

'Hijra will rob, hurt, steal baby boy. Bad people, you stay away. I am helping you, saving you. You must give me some rupees now.'

She looked at him, thinking whether just to walk away, but he scowled and she was suddenly more afraid of him than she had been of the hijra. Diving her hand in her bag she came out with several notes, slapped them in his hand and walked away.

'I save you,' the man shouted after her.

She did not turn.

Instead Ria carried on towards the family's house. Tramping half a kilometre she found a track to the left which she descended. Mountains were to her back now, the steep rocky route led down the edge of a fierce stream, then veered towards a group of concrete houses. The water tumbled on to a larger valley below of green where trees trailed into the misty distance of lush foothills.

The concrete house was perched on the incline, a small place with an unpainted wooden door and concrete steps with a rusty iron rail up the side, apparently leading to a top room and flat roof. The smallness shocked her and she could hardly believe a family of four could live there.

The sound of a woman singing drifted down from the top of the building:

'Come little boy, little man,
Come into the world and do what you can,
Come little life, come sing with us,
Blessed and loved with soma and sweets,
Join in life with all its treats.'

Ria left her bag at the bottom of the stairs and as she climbed up she expected to see her half sister Sadie singing to her baby, little Krish, on the roof. A panorama of snowy tips to the back and a green valley sloping steeply ahead made her draw breath as she got to the top.

Sadie nursed her son without looking up then rose, leaving Krish in a chortling bundle and gave Ria a hug. Ria pulled her close but she seemed stiff and Ria doubted a moment whether Sadie wanted her there.

Sadie had pale-blue eyes, unlike Ria's dark brown eyes, and thick curly hair of faded chestnut, to Ria's flat black locks. Sadie often joked they did not look like half sisters. Ria joked that no one would guess; and people never did. They shared the same mother, but Ria's father was Indian.

'You made it then,' Sadie smiled.

'I didn't mean to disturb you, I — it's so lovely, you and the baby, the mountains—'

Sadie stooped back to her son, who giggled upwards to her, and waving a line of hair from her eyes she sang softly again.

Ria watched. There was one thing certain about the mountains: they were silent. Always. And always there, like giant buildings, a city towering over the speck of you. How would they be at night she wondered, with no light: silent buildings, cold and black, holding up the stars.

'It's so special.' Ria ignored the tension she felt from Sadie. 'The air is so fresh. The Himalayas. At last I get to see them. Home of the gods.' She wanted to hold the baby but was hesitant to ask. 'I came through Patrinath,' Ria said. 'Smallish village, isn't it? I can't wait to go to Dharamsala. All the Buddhist monks, the Dalai Lama.' Ria was anxious to make a good link with her sister early on. 'Didn't think I'd get here this late.' She looked down the green valley at a pile of smoke miles away slipping up in a windless line. 'The trains were packed and—' Ria continued, wanting to cuddle the baby but scared a moment of Sadie's reaction.

'Oh. Indian trains,' Sadie sighed, laughing. 'Tell me about them.'

Perhaps Sadie was trying too.

'But the Himalayas, Sadie, I never imagined. Just — fantastic. Like giants with lacy cloth around their peaks.'

'You haven't changed,' Sadie said lightly, looking up smiling at Ria while attending to her son.

'Their sharp lines scrape and scratch into the sky.' Ria turned to face them. 'When clouds are dashing it's like the peaks themselves are moving—'

'They're just mountains,' Sadie shrugged cheerfully.

Ria lost herself a moment, thinking out loud: 'Yet somehow, sometimes, they seem like, I don't know, protective and comforting or something.'

Sadie rocked Krish.

'The others?' Ria said. 'The family?'

'Inside. Some of them. It's okay, they all speak good English. Only use Hindi amongst themselves. Probably Madhu is downstairs studying. Her mum Padma cooking, or washing—' Sadie waved her arm towards the downstairs area. 'That woman never stops. What an auntie Padma's been to Ijay — and now to me. Without women India would grind to a halt.'

'And Daya?' Ria said. 'I've heard so much about her — from Ijay. I can't wait.'

'At the shop with her dad, Bijal.'

'It's good of them to let me stay, I mean—' Ria said.

'It's small. You should really stay in a hotel.' She paused for Krish awhile. 'Of course Padma is Ijay's auntie really, but me being married to him and all that — she's an auntie to me —'

'Does a half sister count?' Ria laughed.

Sadie rocked Krish again, then looked over to Ria. 'Daya and Madhu sleep downstairs, mum and dad in that room down there.' She waved downwards towards a door. 'And me and Krish in that tiny space next to it. You'll have to sleep with us. And no snoring or kicking in the night, right? — I know you.' She laughed.

Ria sat with them on a low bench. 'How is Krish?' she said, gaining confidence. 'Let me hold him.'

Sadie handed him over, Ria took him, cooing and then sang:

Be happy and wise, marry well,
Find money and good fortune,

For Laxmi looks over you,

Come to the temple and ring the bell . . .'

The sound of traffic along the road to Dharamsala carried on the wind and at the back whorls of misty cloud were covering the peaks.

'My brother, Hari,' Ria said. 'Our mum reckoned my dad brought him to the mountains.' She played with Krish. 'Lovely little boy, aren't you. Just a little darling — I mean Hari, he is my twin — How mum knew where they went I don't know.'

Sadie leaned back, smiling. 'You can't believe all she says.' She drew breath. 'I'm not going back to her.'

'Little Krish. Smile up to the mountains. That's it. Giggle and laugh. He's gorgeous, Sadie, you're so lucky.' Ria drew breath. 'She doesn't want me. New bloke. Jack.'

'It's like a dating agency, her flat.'

Ria was pleased they had found something to agree on.

'She gave me the usual—' Ria enjoyed the new ease.

'Huh.'

'The place isn't big enough for me and him.'

The apartment in Kilburn was the top floor of a Victorian house. Two bedrooms. It was spacious enough. Dealing with mum's drinking and binges of calming pills, Ria thought Sadie managed better than she did.

'What changes?'

The baby chuckled up to his auntie.

'I don't like him anyway.' Ria added. 'The way he looks you up and down—'

'You always had a knack of landing on your feet, Ria, that's what I always liked about you.'

Ria did not know whether to take that as a compliment or a dig.

'I used to wonder what it was like for you and mum, before my dad came along, and Hari and me were born—' Ria left the sentence hanging, trying to find a way into Sadie. 'You were always so close to our mum.'

Sadie shrugged. 'When my dad had gone, I had to be. Then your dad comes along full of India.'

'But one day dad and Hari were gone. I mean, I was just a kid. And my dad disappears with my twin brother—'

'They were all you had to hang onto then?'

Ria was unsure whether she was being sarcastic. 'You know—'

On the open sun roof of the house Ria could either face the mountains, or face the valley with her back to the snow tips and imagine they were not there. As she looked up at the peaks again the sight of cloud dissolving from the ridge inspired memories. Ria reckoned she must have been about six when dad got her and Hari together, excitedly showing them gifts. He had come back from a trip to India. Unwrapping gold and red paper with swirling patterns with elephants in lines, trunk to tail, he pulled out bits of twisted cardboard padding, then rustled tissue paper. Inside was a glowing model.

'Glass mountains,' dad said as he placed the model on the kitchen table.

Hari gasped. 'They're so real, dad, like real mountains. How?'

'A piece of quartz,' dad said. 'Look. The base is black rock - like earth. The lower line is purple — the mountains. And the top is pale and clear, like glass.'

'Or snow.' Ria remembered her joy.

'It could be snow,' he nodded. 'There's a place in the Himalayas they call The Glass Mountains because early in the morning when the sun shines at a certain angle on them the snowy peaks glow like glass—'

'Wow,' Hari was full of wonder.

'This is a model of it. My friend in Delhi made it for me.'

Her father placed one hand at one end and one at the other and gently easing, pulled a part away at each end, leaving a chunk in the middle. Each section was about two inches long, and the same in height. Ria recalled the beauty of its smallness and sparkling clarity.

Taking one piece of the carefully-fitting jigsaw joint from one end, he gave it to Hari and nodded for him to hold it, and the other end he held out to Ria who rolled it through exploring fingers and sniffed and tasted it.

'This is for me.' Her father took the centre section. 'Now we all have a bit.'

She remembered her dad's grin of joy and Hari's shining eyes. Two years later they had gone.

'Wherever we are we'll never forget each other,' dad had assured them.

As they sat playing, pulling them apart and putting them back together again, bending close to squint at the miniature range, she was aware of someone else at the door.

'I got you this, Sadie.' Ria's dad handed her a parcel which she pulled apart. Ria remembered Sadie as bright and chatty as a child, but she was always serious and quiet when Ria's dad was there.

A little bronze elephant sat on her palm. Sadie watched inquisitively, turning it around, but then glancing over at the mountain puzzle. Ria knew then Sadie wanted a piece. The little elephant sat on a window sill for years under thickening dust, falling only a few months back and bending its upturned trunk.

It had not been easy for Sadie, Ria pieced the memory together as she watched the giggling baby's hands grasp at the sky. Her father had gone off with another woman and never made contact, Ria's dad had come along overshadowing her and suddenly she had a new twin brother and a sister she never got on with.

Two months before coming to India Ria's bit of the glass mountains had disappeared. When Jack and her mum were out she had searched the flat for it but was disappointed, feeling a hollowness inside — as though she had lost her brother forever.

Was it life that was strange? Or people?

When Ria's dad had gone missing with Hari, their mother had hit the bottle. And it was then that Sadie got some sort of relationship back with her mum, for a time at least.

Clouds were now filtering away from peaks. 'Do you know, Sadie, my bit of the glass mountains went missing.' She looked over at her sister and spoke softly to cover traces of accusation. 'Do you know where it is?'

Sadie continued to coo to Krish.

Ria giggled with her at the baby, then continued to Sadie. 'That's what I went looking for at my mum's. Yeah. And to get some of my things. I knew she and Jack were out.' It was best to fill Sadie in on her situation back home. 'I go round the flat one day, then I remembered the attic. I found this old suitcase up there, Sadie.' Then she felt uncomfortably like she was trying to justify herself. 'Full of cash. I mean loads — thousands — got to be. Maybe more. I guess it was Jack's from scams or something. Or was it my dad's? I mean, big time. I mean, that much. I was thinking then, it wouldn't be right—' She paused, turning back towards the valley where the line of smoke had panned out flatly in the windless sky spreading a pall over a distant village, and tapped her foot. 'But I must tell you, you know that stupid boy I was with — Terry. He went off with some kid in a band a week before. Then the restaurant I'm working in burns down.' Ria bit her thumb nail a moment. Someone was singing in a nearby house. 'And the row with Jack and he tries to hit me and tells me to get out of my own home. What else was there? And then there it is. I'm face to face with all this dosh. And I mean Sadie, it was like fate was staring me in the face and saying: "Go and find your brother." All those sparkling notes. I stared at the cash for ages, fumbling it through my fingers. I reckoned I deserved it. I mean pushing me out of home. Compensation.'

'Some story. And all that cash. Wow.'

'The accident was such a shock,' Ria acknowledged. 'You and Ijay were so close — the perfect couple. So many of his friends at the funeral. And he never got to meet his little boy.' She nodded at Krish and sent him a little smile. 'You'll be all right, sweetie pie.'

'I've got Krish. He gets me through.' Sadie smiled away tears. 'You're just in time, anyway. We're taking Ijay's ashes up to his bit of land soon. Up the hill.'

Nothing had been straightforward in Ijay's life. The BMW had come off the road near Manchester. Driving alone, he could have fallen asleep, although rumours indicated he smoked lots of weed, was a connoisseur of drugs, that he had debts — through dealing. Another story had it that the accident was more sinister than that, that he had enemies. Girls at Ria's restaurant who knew him said it was scams, talked of a train of other women. Ria knew Ijay was good at keeping things from Sadie, so probably she had no knowledge of these theories.

'You're gutted, I know,' Ria tried to reassure her. 'It's been so tough for you. I wanted to be here for you.' Ria hugged her again, but she was still tense. 'I mean his aunt Padma must be in grief too.'

'They're all trying to help. They're being sweet to me, cooking for me, looking after Krish.' Sadie smiled. 'But I do need my land back.'

'You've got land here? How?'

'All Ijay's money — he put it into a piece of land just up the hill here—' Sadie nodded towards the mountains. 'It belongs to me and Krish now.'

'Ijay left you something then.'

'He was going to build a house on it for us. His dream. Live here and grow mangoes, the mountains above and behind us—'

Ria concluded Sadie really knew nothing of Ijay's double life, or she ignored it. 'Like gods protecting you.'

'Bijal set it up. People from England — even Indian people from there — can't buy here. Uncle Bijal had to do it in his name and set it up with Ijay.'

'And it's nearby? That's exciting, Sadie. A project for you—'

'It's rough ground really. Ijay's dream was to grow things, build a little house we could go to. Six months at home, six months here—'

'You still can — on the hills under the mountains — amazing. What an inheritance for Krish. I can't wait—'

'When we take up the ashes, you can come — But it's no use to me now. I need the money. I've got to get Bijal to sell it.'

'You won't keep coming back? To your own bit of land?' Ria looked at her.

'I've got contacts in London, shops and stall holders. They'll sell anything from India.'

'You've always been strong, Sadie,' Ria felt closer to her sister. 'I mean when my dad left you were there for me—'

'You would have been taken into care.'

'I'll always be grateful.' Ria reassured her. 'And there's just a chance I might find Hari. They say the Glass Mountains are somewhere around here.'

'It's a big place. None of the family know of him,' Sadie said. 'I remember sticking up for him at school once. Anyway, you're calling yourself Ria now. What's all that about?'

'One day I got up singing at an open mic in a pub in Camden. I used my real name, Parvati — which I never really thought suited me. An Indian bloke came up to me after and said he could get me some singing work but I had to change my name. He came up with Ria. In India Ria means "singer". He got me a few gigs, but it turned out he was ripping me off. And all the bad stuff going on, I came here. In English Ria means rebellious woman.'

'You got that bit right.' Sadie laughed but she looked tired.

2

Padma was small with intelligent darting eyes, and coming out quickly from the kitchen, flung down the basket of washing she was carrying and rushed to hug Ria when she got to the bottom of the stairs to the wide courtyard in front of the house. Her body was thin and fragile, as though shaped by years of surviving. Sadie joined them with Krish.

'When we saw you, you were a baby,' the little woman said, flapping warm arms round Ria and looking up at her. 'Now you're grown — all grown. My Parvati — Too long — why you don't come to us.'

'Ria,' Ria said, noting that Padma's English was quite good. 'They call me.' She laughed nervously as Sadie came down the outer stairs with Krish. 'It's my pet name now,' Ria laughed again.

'Parvati is a good name — wife of Shiva,' Padma said. 'Ria. You come to my house. You come and eat and sleep. And with your sister.' She shook her head. 'Your poor sister. Ijay was a lovely boy, always helping. And now, kismet — he is gone and we're all in tears. Ijay, he's my brother Lakshan's son. He cannot believe his son is gone —'

'We're all devastated,' Ria assured Padma. 'It was all so sudden. I met Lakshan and Ijay's mum at the funeral in Manchester. Such lovely people — and his mother so lost without her son. We all miss him.'

Ria was uncertain of herself. She had assumed having an Indian father everything would come naturally to her in India, but things seemed different and strange, so she kept something of herself back. If she wasn't going to upset people and make herself look silly, she was going to have to go slowly and pick things up as she went along. 'Here,' Ria pulled a gift wrapped in gold and green from her bag and held it up to Padma who took it tentatively and held it to her chest with a smile. Ria hoped she would enjoy the perfume she had bought for her in Delhi.

'You are your father's child, you and Hari—' Padma told Ria and turning to the kitchen door, she called for her youngest daughter, putting the present aside to open later.

Madhu was about nineteen and she looked fresh with clear eyes. Giving Ria a smile she hugged her briefly. Her hair was brushed back in a long pony tail with pink hair grips at the front, and she had silver earrings, not too long, and wore a shalwar kameez with yellow flower patterns. Madhu said, 'Ria, at last, we meet. I heard all about you.'

'She is studying,' Padma nodded at her daughter.

Sadie took over: 'Madhu goes to a local college to learn business and IT.'

'Then a degree,' Madhu smiled.

Padma smiled at her daughter. 'My clever Madhu. She is the one who will be big. She will have businesses — like her father.'

'Look how hard he has to work,' Madhu said. 'He's just a tailor. And now, they make clothes in factories. Who wants clothes made for them anymore?'

'He works very hard,' her mother added.

'He should have a factory and make clothes for big names in England.'

'Where will the money come for a factory?' Padma told them. 'Banks give nothing. Hotels in the towns here and Dharamsala — uniforms, they need from Daddy-ji.'

Ria watched Madhu as she challenged her mother again. 'How long will that last? Daya and I will get married — it's costly. Anyway Mummy-ji we need food and drinks for our guest.'

'All ready inside. I will get now,' Padma obeyed, going inside the house.

Madhu waved for Ria to sit, and the couple sat on a bench in front of the house, with Sadie in an upright chair with Krish asleep.

'It's good to meet you, Madhu,' Ria said. 'And to be in India. I should have come ages ago. It makes me feel in contact with a side of myself I didn't know much about. You like college?'

'If you have a degree you can go to Dubai, or Canada, Australia. They want Indian professionals — not like England — it's so hard to get in there now. All the immigration rules. Nobody even tries now. All the talent from this country goes to other places. We won't have to bother about a little tailor's business when India gets bigger.'

'Daya will go to college too?' Ria said.

'My sister and my dad will be back soon. She helps him in his shop in town.'

'Your shalwar kameez is so beautiful—' Ria went to her bag and rummaged.

Sadie said, 'Only the best will do for Madhu.'

'I brought you these,' Ria handed Madhu a packet. 'Pens. I couldn't carry much. Not on my own. You see—' She nodded at her backpack. 'But they are good ones — special.'

Madhu took them and put them aside with a brief glance.

'I thought, you know,' Ria tried to hide her embarrassment at the smallness of the gift. 'You're studying, you might need pens.' But she knew it would not cover Madhu's scorn.

'What we don't have here is modern technology, phones, i-pads, that sort of thing.'

'Yes, yes,' Ria gabbled nervously. At the edge of her vision she noticed a wry grin on Sadie's lips.

Madhu leaned back. 'You have everything in England.'

Padma came out of the house with plates of pakoras and cups of tea and nodded at Madhu and the basket of washing but Madhu acted as though she had not noticed.

'Everyone has cars,' Madhu took plates from her mother's tray and handed them out.

'I don't,' Sadie looked at Madhu. 'We're not all as rich as you think.'

'We don't need cars in London.' Ria tried to soften tensions. 'We can get around on buses and underground and taxis. It's very easy.'

'You must eat,' Padma instructed them to fill their plates. 'Nobody in England worries about anything.'

Madhu gave a saintly smile. 'You do have everything there.' And handed out cups of tea. 'One day I'll have a good job somewhere in the world, that's all that matters to the family. I will send money home, of course.'

Padma began hanging washing on the line that stretched from the house to a pole along the low wall at the edge of the courtyard. Beyond the wall which served sometimes as a bench, the green land fell steeply half a kilometre away to where the stream flowed.

'How much more studying do you have to do?' Ria tried to reconnect with Madhu, but she just shrugged. 'My restaurant where I worked burned down.' Ria tried to keep conversation going.

Madhu kept up her smile. 'Don't you have a degree?'

'She's lucky,' Sadie said to Ria, nodding at Madhu. 'Without Daya working in the shop — only one person can study —'

'Shush now,' Padma called over to her daughter as breeze from the mountains rippled the line of washing she had hung up. 'Ria is tired. You must rest now . . .'

*****

Sadie woke Ria at eight in the evening. The darkness overwhelmed her as she came out onto the veranda and the mountain air was cold. A single light bulb hung near the kitchen door, the blade of its filament skeletal against the night. Nearby a small fire burned in an iron bowl on the veranda. Ria shivered and Padma came to her with a shawl and draped it over her shoulders. 'Come and sit near the fire. Bijal is here, and Daya. We will eat.'

'You shouldn't have waited for me.' Ria looked over at the family sitting cross legged around the glowing embers. 'You should eat, you must be hungry.'

'Daddy-ji likes a fire,' Madhu told her, pointing at the man squatting half in shadow half in the reflected glow.

'He always makes a fire at night,' Sadie said.

Ria watched them a moment, their faces lit up. Behind them the mountains were black and mysterious in their gloom. Above the ridges the sky with its trail of stars was paler. It seemed that the tiny fire was there not only to warm everyone but to stand as something, a symbol of life and survival against the odds of the bleakness and power of nature.

Bijal stood, came to her and shook her hand with a smile. A small man with wrinkled face and a cheerful glance, his eyes searched Ria's in dim crimson light as he promised soon to take her to his shop. 'You are welcome,' he said. 'We loved Ijay — auntie's brother's son — he was full of fun. But we have Ijay's son, Krish. My daughters and my wife will look after you. We must eat,' he continued. 'It's a small place, but you are welcome. All my life my wife has been by my side, without her, none of this would be possible. Let me tell you, she is a clever woman — she knows how to guide her husband. That is the most important thing in a marriage — not making food — guiding him, giving him ideas.'

'Ria,' Daya came to her next, throwing her arms round her. 'The name suits you so well.' A little taller than Madhu, but less slim than her sister, Daya had a broad smile and hugging Ria closely but gently, Ria felt her shoulders were a little tense. She smiled sincerely, and Ria held on to her hand a moment too long, feeling she had found someone she could get to know well.

Daya urged Ria towards the fire and the bowls of food and plates set out on a sheet beside it.

They ate dal and rice and spicy vegetables cross legged round the fire.

Having finished, Ria was revived, and excusing herself to go to her bag she came back with gifts, giving one to Bijal and the other to Daya.

'They're very nicely wrapped,' Madhu pointed at the presents, unnerving Ria and reminding her she hadn't wrapped Madhu's pens.

'You know I love books,' Daya undid hers. 'Indian birds. It's wonderful.' She held the book up in the light so everyone could see while Bijal pulled his gift from its wrapping.

Padma threw a couple more small logs in the fire bowl along with some paper to get more light and heat as Bijal held up a shirt made up of reds, golds and greens. Ria was aware of Madhu watching her carefully. And Sadie was probably thinking badly of her giving a shirt to a tailor. But she had found it in Camden and thought it was just the thing for him, forgetting at the time his occupation. She was apprehensive of making any more mistakes.

'It's wonderful, Daddy-ji,' Daya took it from him, shook it, then held it up in front of him. 'The colours, just you.'

'Good, very nice,' Padma began stacking dirty plates. 'Now he can take me out. He always wears plain shirts. This is good for him.'

Bijal laughed. 'We can go and watch films, eat in the big new restaurant.'

'It really suits you Daddy-ji,' Daya kept holding up the shirt. 'How much in love they still are — he wants to take care of her still, it's so nice.' She handed the shirt to him. 'And Daddy-ji's shop is doing so well. We have a new contract coming to supply a hotel with uniforms, it's so exciting, things are going so well. And Madhu can continue her studies. What else can we ask for?'

The family talked over cups of tea until the fire dimmed and the cold and tiredness drew them to their beds.

Ria was snug under her duvet with Sadie and Krish, but going for a pee meant going down outside stairs and squatting in a freezing shack whose contents seeped down to the stream.

*****

A breeze fluttered through red and green curtains in the kitchen doorway as Ria pushed through the following morning. Sunlight seemed to search out all crevices leaving few slim shadows. As she was going in Daya was coming out with a couple of round stainless steel food tins. They surprised each other, Daya nearly dropping them, Ria helping her to save them, and the two laughing.

'Daddy-ji's lunch,' Daya said. 'Dal, vegetable and roti. He will be out soon and we'll go up to the shop. You can join us later. Mustn't drop.'

Ria felt an intuitive understanding between them. Daya's long black hair was bunched in a pony tail, the end hanging over her left shoulder. She had on a cerise and black Punjabi Suit with pink chunni head scarf around her neck but not pulled up over her head.

Sadie was already up and awake, jiggling a plastic toy with a bell for Krish. Madhu, sitting in a shaded area of the veranda, had on thick rimmed reading glasses as she studied a book.

'I can come with you,' Ria said.

'Rest first,' Daya insisted and followed up quickly with, 'You know I love books. Your lovely gift, Ria, I opened it last night. We sometimes see the mountain hawk-eagle circling with its cry. And the black-lored tit nests in the shrubs at the back of the house. The book is wonderful. And Daddy-ji will look so good in that shirt. In a few days Madhu can take you places.'

Bijal came out, some material draped over his arm. 'Into the mountains, Joshimath, Madhu can take you,' he told Ria.

'That's miles away,' Madhu looked up from her book.

'You can see Nanda Devi, the highest mountain in India,' Bijal continued.

'You can't get to Badrinath yet,' Madhu looked back down at her book, 'it's still snowed in.'

'When we got married,' Bijal said, 'I took Mummy-ji to the valley of flowers near Badrinath. It's so beautiful and so sacred. Mummy-ji was young and beautiful and danced and laughed in the flowers by a mountain stream.'

'Devout Hindus go there.' Daya stood near her father. 'There's lots of temples. The gods sit right up on the tips of the mountains.'

'You would think she went to college, too,' Madhu looked over, smiling.

'Madhu is the lucky one,' Bijal watched his younger daughter. 'We could see when she was little how clever she was.'

Ria noticed Daya look peeved by her father's comment.

Padma brought out another small tin and handed it to Daya. 'Daddy-ji had just started his shop when Daya was born, we could never afford enough for her, but she has been such a good daughter, haven't you?'

Bijal smiled. 'She could not pass her exams. Madhu could. Daya is so good in the shop.'

'You know so much,' Ria said to Daya, embarrassing her.

Madhu called up from her book again. 'She can tell you all about how the mountains were made.' And Ria could not tell if Madhu was scoffing at her sister or not.

'She doesn't want to hear all that,' Daya laughed nervously.

'But I do.'

'We've got to go,' Daya said.

Sadie jingled the bells and Krish giggled up at her.

'I'd like to hear all that,' Ria insisted.

Bijal took the tins from his daughter, said his goodbyes and headed up the track towards the shop. Padma went back inside.

'You can tell her,' Sadie said.

'India,' Daya drew breath, 'the whole continent—'

'See, she can't wait,' Madhu and Sadie laughed to each other.

'All the land with all the weight of billions of people,—' Daya went on, 'is drifting northwards into the rest of Asia, pressing into China and Mongolia, centimetre by centimetre—'

'She knows all about that stuff,' Madhu nodded to Sadie.

'And?' Ria got her going again.

'It's been doing it for millions of years. And the constant pressure is pushing the Himalayas up, bit by bit, making the mountains, little by little. The youngest but highest range in the world—'

'And we go up with it here,' Ria laughed looking at the ground near her feet.

'Yes.'

'You need a college degree, Daya,' Ria chuckled. 'That it then?' Ria urged her, realising Daya was sometimes shy, not pushy like her sister.

'All those mountains draw the weather to them. If it wasn't for them we wouldn't have the monsoon. No rain. It would all be desert. Nobody here.'

'She got that one from the Geography Channel,' Madhu cut her off.

Daya looked hurt a moment, but recovered. 'You love the game shows and the soaps.'

Madhu slammed her book down and began playing with Krish.

Daya smiled weakly, a look of hurt on her face a second, and lightly touching Ria's arm guided her a little way along the path and stopped. 'Look up there.' Ria followed the wave of her hand towards the snow capped ridges. She could feel Madhu's and Sadie's eyes still on them, but they were more distant, their voices not out of range, but less effective.

'In the early morning,' Daya was serious, 'the sun shines on that line of peaks. On a good morning with no cloud the sunlight just smacks on them like they are flat pyramids and the light reflected back is simply blinding. Just for twenty minutes at around the same time every morning. I just have to stare. It's why they call them that — the glass mountains.'

3

Ria's dream of a tiny temple among snow tipped mountains was broken the following morning by a shake. 'Ria. Ria.' Thinking there was an emergency she pushed herself out of bed and pulled a blanket round her pyjama tops, while Daya stood over her. Ria shivered. 'Come on. Quickly.' Sadie and Krish were already up playing on the roof.

A searchlight of sunlight had cast a path across the veranda as they crossed it.

'Look. Up there.' Daya motioned to the mountains. Brightened by early morning, they blazed back reflected sunlight. Slips of cloud added trimmings to their summits a moment with mild wisps of white, only to evaporate leaving a dazzling mirror. Mountainside surfaces seemed flat and glassy, like a huge prism that forged rainbow colours into a vast shaft of light that plunged down valleys, dispelling shadows, leaving a trail of stillness, tinging the landscape of foothills with a frosty brilliance. 'The glass mountains,' Daya said.

They stared.

'Lord Shiva-ji,' Daya began. 'They say he sits in the mountain tops. Sends out his enlightenments to humanity from his third eye.'

Ria relived the girlhood excitement of seeing the model of the glass mountains with her father and brother, and imagined the light she saw now would extend its magic to the future, and that her brother could be found, that he was safe.

'They say Lord Shiva-ji sits on Mount Kailash, deep in the Himalayas. A mountain shaped like a four sided pyramid and rivers flowing to all parts of the earth,' Daya said. 'I've never seen it, but they say no one has ever climbed it — or is even allowed to. Jains and Buddhists and Hindus gather to worship there. They say it's the centre of the world.'

'It sounds such a magic place. The mountains are so dominating, yet so silent.' Ria took in what she was saying, still staring into the distance as the reflected sunlight faded slightly.

'Your inner voices are thinking a lot for you,' Daya watched her.

'I'm not used to the quiet.'

'You like the clang of the city? You've seen Delhi with all its noise. They say Mumbai is worse.' Daya stood near her in the reflected light which, like the aurora of an eclipse, was fading. 'Mystics say it's good to be in the silence of nature, it's the first step in meditation. If you can allow that chattering part of yourself that bubbles away to still itself, it helps to open up the third eye.' Daya laid her index finger on Ria's forehead between her eyes. 'Symbolically it's the eye to insight and knowledge. In some forms of meditation the idea is to release the Kundalini, or snake energy and insight from the base of the spine, right up to the head and into the third eye.' She smiled. 'We have the knowledge of the gods then.'

They were silent together enjoying the loss of reflected light and staring out at the colours of the trees and buildings in the valley until Ria slowly became aware of the noise of the world waking. Vehicles were moving on the distant road up near the town along with pedestrians. Occasionally she could hear the laughter of children on the way to school. And Krish's chuckling filtered down to them along with Sadie's baby talk.

Padma was already in the kitchen and Bijal had headed for work. Madhu came out with a phone in one hand, a cup of tea in another and a book under her arm.

'There's a lovely story about Lord Shiva-ji,' Daya almost whispered. 'He was meditating and his consort, or lover if you like, Parvati — who you are named after. Parvati rushed up behind him as a joke and threw her hands around his head and in front of his eyes. You know the game children play of "who is it?" Shiva didn't play the game. Blinded by her hands — the whole world went into darkness — his third eye suddenly formed so he could see and control the world.'

'Do you think I will see things with mine?'

'Of course. I think you already have. Stay in India long enough and it will happen.'

'Is she filling your head with that mystic stuff?' Madhu looked over the steam from a cup of tea.

'Keep your eyes open and your intuition and you will see things,' Daya said to Ria.

Madhu put down her tea and fiddled with her phone. 'That's all a bit old fashioned really. Modern Indian girls don't want any of that stuff anymore, they want make-up and nice clothes. Do you really think girls on cat-walks in Mumbai are thinking about Shiva's third eye?' Madhu addressed her sister. 'You know what a cat-walk is, Daya?'

Daya looked down, then out to the valley where the greens were softening with the effect of the rising sun, and back to her sister. 'There has to be more in life than gold earrings and bright saris—'

'You need that if you're going to get married—' Madhu warmed her hands around her cup.

Daya answered her quietly. 'No rich boy is going to come knocking, Madhu. Not to us. You think Daddy-ji can afford the kind of dowry those families want these days? Some of that class expect a new car, or at least a new TV.'

'Nobody wants to be left on their own.' Madhu looked up to her sister. 'Do you want to get old and nobody wants you. Mummy and Daddy can't look after us.'

'I don't want you to expect too much, that's all.'

'If we just accept everything that's given us, then what? It just goes on and on. I marry some boy who works in a shop and live in his house and do all the jobs his mother tells me to.'

'The world isn't like the Bollywood movies, Madhu. That's how it is for us.'

Madhu looked back at her phone. 'I know boys in the village with cars.'

'Their daddies' cars.'

'We can have that,' Madhu stared at her, then flipped to Ria, 'can't we Ria?'

Ria looked over at Madhu but did not know what to say.

Daya scowled at Madhu and seemed suddenly tense. 'You're not seeing him? You're not?'

'I talk with anyone I like. I can't help it if boys like me, I can't keep them away.'

'Not Prem,' Daya's voice lowered. 'You mustn't see him.' Madhu stiffened and did a little shake of her head. 'Not him. He's not good for you.'

'You'll be left behind and I'll be in one of those houses up on the hill,' Madhu waved at some big buildings half hidden among trees up on the slopes on the other side of the main road near the village. 'I'll have a degree in business, a good job.'

'He doesn't love you,' Daya was urgent. 'I've heard about him. He plays with girls. He's Christian, he won't marry you.'

'What will you be doing then? An old woman running a tailor's shop?'

'You can't trust him.'

'Or you'll end up with the cousins in Delhi, you know what they're like,' Madhu said. 'So strict, never let you do anything. They would force you into a marriage you didn't want. So selfish and big headed they are.'

'I'm trying to help you,' Daya went on.

'You never want my happiness,' Madhu headed for the curtain to the kitchen, flipped it back with a wave and disappeared.

Sadie carried Krish down the outside stairs. 'Feeding time,' she whispered as she went in the house.

Daya looked at Ria resigned, 'I don't want her to get hurt. It's still hard for women here, even the educated ones. You can end up with the wrong sort—'

Ria laughed nervously, 'You keep clear of those kind of guys—'

'Not marry them and stay with them for the rest of your life,' Daya carried on her concern. Traffic noise sounded from the main road behind her and Ria could hear a woman singing in a house a hundred metres away. 'You can't have a boyfriend here, in the villages and small towns.' She drew breath. 'If a girl got pregnant and wasn't married she might as well be dead. You cannot imagine the shame it brings on the girl's family. And if she's poor—'

'Thank god it's not like that back home,' Ria said, her thoughts drifting. 'I keep asking myself questions. Why did my dad take Hari and not me? Why did they desert me? The glass mountains you showed me — my dad gave me a model of them. There must be something in it.'

'Sadie can help you?'

Ria shook her head. 'She's not the same without Ijay.'

'It was so sudden, poor thing,' Daya rubbed her fingers.

'Nobody knows for sure,' Ria whispered. 'I mean, how it happened. I mean, Sadie doesn't know. You mustn't tell. But you're just like a sister already. It's just that, well, some of my mates at the restaurant knew him. He got into a lot of scams.'

Ria read the shock in Daya's expression. 'You don't think it was an accident?' Daya said and then, 'We shouldn't talk badly of those who have passed away.'

'He was involved in stuff, growing big loads of weed and selling it. That's what they say. And dealing other stuff too. I shouldn't be telling you all this. I don't think Sadie knows any of it. It was just talk at the restaurant when he died. He was clever at making money and it was getting hot for him.'

'Poor girl. No wonder Sadie — I'll keep trying with her,' Daya said. 'And Ijay wanted the land there. Not for—'

'Growing weed? That's how he lived, Daya. We'll never really know —' Ria shivered under the blanket she had thrown over her shoulders when she came out. Although the sun was rising, the cold air of the mountains had not yet been burned away.

'Every family has secrets,' Daya said. 'And you never really know with people. When Ijay came here he was so respectful to Mummy and Daddy and so helpful to the family. We all loved him. I would like to remember that side of him. It makes it more important for Madhu and me to find the right man. We have to know as much about them as we can. But you're cold — you must get dressed.'

Ria guessed from Daya's expression that she wanted to say more and was curious. 'You have found somebody to marry?'

'There is someone in Patrinath. Mummy-ji is the only one who knows. I've met him a couple of times. Madesh.'

Ria was excited, 'And?' Daya looked away. 'What's he like? Do you think you could marry him?'

'There's something in what Madhu says. And Madesh's family have a business. What other choices will I get?' Daya kept her gaze on the valley. 'Maybe Madhu is right. The only other way out for a woman is education. Here I am working so she can go. I hope she does find her dream boy and live out Bollywood dreams.'

'I think she already has.'

'It can never be anything with Prem.' Daya turned back to her. 'I do know him, Ria. He plays with girls like they're his toys.'

Ria's concentration was interrupted by the distant sound of a drum beating for a moment, followed by silence.

4

'Have you ever worn a Punjabi Suit — shalwar kameez?' Daya came to Ria's room the next day. She had come back from the shop to pick up her father's lunch and took the opportunity to have a quick chat. 'I'm sure the right colour — it would look good on you —'

Ria again noticed the distant thud of a lone drum beat. 'Once, when I was little, thirteen or something,' Ria said, 'I was invited to an Indian wedding. Was I scared, and didn't really want to go. I mean if the girls at school saw me I would die.' Daya sat with her on the edge of the bed. A broad blade of sunlight spread in the room from the open door. The place was piled with baby clothes, Sadie's dirty washing and a small heap of baby toys. Sadie had taken Krish on the sun roof. 'But you know when my friend's mum put it on me I felt the Indianness suddenly flow through my body. I can't explain, I hadn't known it before you see, I was just English at school, and now like, it shook through me.'

'Through all the chakras,' Daya said.

'In front of the mirror I was Indian, and I had never seen that about myself since my dad gave me my part of the glass mountains. At school I had to survive, just like everyone else, so all that was hidden for ages.'

'We must go to town and get you a suit — or Daddy-ji will make you one.'

Ria heard the sound of another soft drum beat followed by silence and then the squawk of a distant bird of prey.

'I wore black trousers to school,' Ria went on. 'We could wear black skirts, but I never did. Always wanted to keep myself covered —'

Daya laughed, 'Like a good Indian girl.'

'Anyway I liked those black togs — was glad to get back in them after the Punjabi Suit,' Ria was serious, but Daya laughed. 'I dressed myself up every morning in front of the mirror, in secret. Knotted my tie. Then one day I remembered something: an old trilby some passing bloke of my mum's had left behind — a must. A bit of make up. Had to tie and pin my hair back first, then on with the hat, tilted this way and that. Posed for ages.' They laughed. 'Can you believe it? There I was hat and all. A bit of heavy makeup. I was quite flat chested in those days so I could pass as a boy. Posed for ages. Needed a walking cane to add a final touch.' She laughed. 'I could have been in the movies. I danced and pranced. But it was a laugh and I felt good. Then Sadie came in and laughed at me. Then I hated it. God I was late that day and got a mouthful. Always hated it then. I'd forgotten all that until now.'

'You never had the closeness to your dad — or even your brother — that I had,' Daya said.

'You've always been close to your dad?'

'I couldn't ask for anyone better. He is so good in so many ways — loving, caring, and full of jokes and fun. It's just — he's a bit stubborn in business and slow to move, but Madhu and me keep on to him about that. He is special, not like some of the fathers I know in the village.' Daya smiled. 'I was on the roof the other day when Mummy and Daddy were alone downstairs. I think they must have thought I was out, but I watched them and listened. He had brought her a necklace of yellow flowers and he put them around her neck. She was a bit reluctant at first. "No, silly, I'm too old," she said. "You're never too old for me," he laughed in reply. And she said, "You're a silly old man." "Silly, but not old." He laughed with her, but she was tense and went on about him getting the hotel order and how important it was. He fobbed it off with a wave of his hand. "They know me, I just have to show my face" And then,' Daya leaned close to her in a whisper. 'Do you know what he said? "Do you remember when we swam in that stream? We had only been married a while, we were young and — we found that little waterfall with a pool underneath it. Cold as ice, but we swam." Mummy-ji tried to stop him, saying someone might hear. And I could hear, hidden up on the roof. And then he says,' she cupped her lips in her hand a moment. '"Naked. Off with your sari. We should do it again." She tried to shake him off by taking off the necklace of flowers and hanging it by the door, but he only followed her and held her around the waist. I had never seen this before with my parents, Ria. She told him to stop it, but he went on about the waterfall and how naked they were and how free they felt then without a care in the world. She said: "We are not young anymore." And he said, yes, I remember now: "You are as young as you want to be in your heart. Love has no walls." Isn't that a wonderful thing to say, Ria? But you know my mother replied straight away. "Not for men."' Daya leaned back a moment in thought. 'How right she was. But Daddy-ji kept fooling around with her saying things like: "And a man asks himself why she can't be his little cherry again?" He's such a romantic. Who can ask for anything more. But she wasn't having any of it at that moment: "There's things to be done, food to be cooked,"' Daya smiled. 'And that was it.'

Ria helped Padma cut vegetables for dinner and took care of Krish while Sadie had a nap. It was late in the afternoon when Ria, Sadie and the baby went up to the shop and sat with Daya, watching her sell shirts and materials while her father sat at the back with a sewing machine, surrounded by fabrics.

In the evening Bijal lit a fire in the bowl, Daya and Madhu set out the blanket and brought in the food. They ate chickpeas and okra with rice and roti as it got dark.

Bijal said, 'Very nice. Daya is taking care of you, Ria? I couldn't live without her. She keeps the shop going, gets me customers, talks to them, smiling — and then she goes in for it — the kill — she makes them buy something.' They all laughed.

'Daddy. I'm not that bad,' Daya laughed with them.

'She is. Under the calm she is determined. She could sell you a view of the mountains — and she could seal it in a can and sell you that too.'

'Daddy.'

He turned to Sadie and Ria, 'Sadie, Ria,' Bijal talked excitedly, 'I must tell you how I became a tailor.'

'You can't tell them that, his wife was stern.

'That I was a thief?'

'A thief, Daddy?' Madhu scowled.

'Bijal – nay, –' Padma scowled at him.

'I was only a boy at the time and used to hang around the shop that sold men's shirts. The owner, old Rajesh, used to go out the back for a cigarette. I watched him and watched him, and one day when he went out there I took one of his new shirts from the front of the shop. But as I ran out he was coming back in the front, having met some friends round the back and walked with them round to the street. I crashed into him and there was no escape: he had me by the collar. I thought he would get a policeman and have me beaten, but he was a wise and good man, old Rajesh. He knew my father had died and I was the eldest son and had to get money for the family.'

Padma added: 'Bijal had to stop going to school and go to work when he was eleven.'

'Old Rajesh said,' Bijal went on, '"We are going to make a tailor out of you. I need help here. You run about for me and make tea, and when you are ready I will show you things, and I will pay you."'

'What a good man he was,' Padma said.

'And how we end up in life,' Bijal mused. 'We do not know our path. Good old Rajesh taught me all I needed to know, all the skills and all the contacts. And when he got too old, he handed the shop over to me because his sons had gone off to work in Delhi.'

When they had finished Sadie and Ria began to help clear the dirty dishes, Madhu excused herself to study, while Daya talked to her father, 'I promised I would take that man's jacket to his house tonight, now that it's finished.'

'You stay with Ria and Sadie and look after them. I will go. It is too dark for you,' Bijal said going inside for the jacket, returning with it over his arm and heading for the village.

'He loves you all,' Padma smiled as she piled up empty bowls and headed for the kitchen. 'But you know he forgets things.'

When the washing up was done and things put away Ria found herself alone with Daya around the dying embers of the fire. Daya got it going again with paper, twigs and a small branch.

'It was never easy for my mother,' Daya said. 'Her father was always drunk, there was no money. She had to help her mother cleaning schools. She would have done well herself at school, but had to leave it so she could clean it. Can you imagine that? She has the brains of Madhu, she could study in her day. And she holds it all together even when things aren't going well—'

'What do you mean?' Ria warmed her palms over the glow.

'Daddy-ji has not been his usual self. Oh, he makes everyone laugh, but—'

'What?'

'He was drunk in town last week, so drunk he was struggling to stand up. Mummy found him and got me to bring him home. I've never seen him like that before. And now he keeps forgetting things. He would have forgotten about the jacket if I hadn't said. And when I got him home mummy said something that really shocked me. "All men are weak at heart. They will tell the world how clever they are, but really they are weak. I thought when I married your father that he would be strong and go out and shake the world, but he could not. And I looked at men, and at women, and I saw that I had to be strong."'

'He makes everyone laugh,' Ria said.

'Yes, he does, he's good to us.'

'You help him keep his business going, he's lucky he's got

you.'

Having put Krish to sleep, Sadie joined them, standing over the fire and warming her hands. 'I'm going to take the ashes—'

5

'Tomorrow?' Daya glared at Sadie the next morning. 'It's too soon.'

They had cleared away breakfast things, Madhu was inside studying, Padma was looking after Krish and Bijal was at work.

'People keep telling me to put it off. I'm doing it tomorrow afternoon.'

'You must wait,' Daya urged her. 'Daddy-ji and Mummy-ji want to come, and Madhu. And there's relatives from Punjab and Delhi. They all need time. And Mummy-ji will want a priest. '

'Ijay didn't believe in all that stuff,' Sadie folded her arms.

Ria said, 'We have to have some sort of ritual, Sadie. He belonged to them too.'

'I'm going up to the rock on the field on my land and who wants can come.'

The low flat thud of a lone drum beat sounded for a time then stopped.

'All right,' Daya said, 'I'll tell them.'

'I'll have Krish,' Sadie directed. 'You can carry the box, Daya,' and correcting Ria's puzzled stare went on, 'The box. The ashes, Ria.'

'Let my Daddy say: "Shanti, Shanti, Shanti." It means: "Peace " —' Daya looked over at Sadie.

'Whatever.' Sadie went inside and came back out with Krish. The sound of a single drum beat was coming from up the track that led to the road and the women stopped talking and turned

201

to look. Ria had heard its singular rhythm before and it had left her cold.

They watched the figure approach down the path singing. 'Shanti, Shanti, Shanti.'

Madhu came out of the house, breakfast cereal in a bowl and phone in her other hand as the drummer stepped up to the veranda still banging and chanting.

For Ria at first she was a stranger, a tall woman dressed in a white and gold sari, not new, but not yet rugged. What passed for gold earrings hung from her lobes, and she had several gold-like necklaces, and myriads of bangles along her arms. Her eyes were heavily made up, the rims with strikingly bright black. Her cheeks were over heavily rouged and her lips sparkled vermilion.

It was by her muscles that Ria recognised her, the thick manly biceps — the figure who had accosted her along the village road.

'You have a good English boy.' The drummer stopped, bending to the baby. Unafraid, Krish chuckled up at the new face but Sadie turned and pulled him quickly away.

Padma ran from the house, face in hands and laughing with joy, and the drummer gave her a smile.

'Daya?' Ria quizzed.

'Hijra. Not man. Not woman.'

'Ah yes. He was on the road when I came—'

Undeterred, the drummer thudded the hand drum again and gave a twirl. Ria was filled with a mixture of confusion, dread and admiration.

'Good English boy.' She pointed with her drumstick, 'I like a good English boy. He will grow up like Shiva-ji, strong with light. The gods of the mountains will protect him.'

The family stood aghast. Ria expected Krish to be the most terrified of all, but he was giggling in Sadie's arms.

Ria looked to Daya for leadership, but she turned to Ria with an expression that seemed to say: 'This is not going to be easy.'

'Shanti.' The dancer spoke clearly with a throaty voice. 'I bring peace. I bring blessings on you all and I come to you with god's blessings and love.' Turning to Padma and bowing she said, 'Auntie. Blessings on your house. Blessings on all.' She turned to them and bowed to each, saying Shanti. You will have good luck and fertility in this house, there will be good fortune. Love will flow here with the power of the Ganges River.' Seeing Krish in Sadie's arms her face lit up. 'New boy. Baby. You will be clever like Lord Krishna and strong like Shiva. From England.' Sadie stepped back, Ria at her side. 'A good English boy. I like. I bring good blessings and love to you.' Sadie grimaced at the figure, pulling Krish aside. 'To you all. May all your days be fruitful. May your mothers have boys. The gods of the mountains will protect this little one —'

Padma clapped her hands with happiness but Madhu next to her was scowling. Daya looked over at Ria.

'I will bless the boy today.' The hijra dismissed resistance with a glance of her hand. 'I am Diksha. Dickie to the friends I have here. Hijra. I bring him good luck. He will be blessed all his life. Good health, good marriage, good wealth. He will have many children. With all the power and ancestry of hijra I will bless this boy from England.' Ria stared at her, the mountains looming behind her. 'Auntie,' the hijra turned to Padma again, who returned a smile. 'Let me bless this boy in your house and let me bring the good luck from the gods upon everyone. This is a day of celebration. A new life, god's creation.'

'You can go now.' Madhu dropped her spoon in the cereal, but her mother pushed forward.

'Nay, 'Padma scolded her daughter. 'Nay.'

Ria's whisper to Daya was full of tension, 'What will he do?'

Dickie turned to Ria, sending her a laugh of recognition and giving her a wink. 'Madam from the West. You bring us beauty. You love our mountains, white and glassy. We bless all baby boys, make them fertile and protect their line. We give them the spiritual wisdom of Shiva and his strength. This boy will rattle mountains. Beautiful boy from England. Who is his sweet mother?' She bowed again to Sadie. 'It must be you, madam.' Sadie pulled the baby away.

Dickie stood still, held her hand out to Sadie, but she stepped back. 'The boy from England must be blessed. What is his name? He must have a name.' The family exchanged glances. 'I will give him a name. After a god. Lord Krishna, perhaps.'

Padma gasped, then dashed inside the house. Ria could see Sadie was disturbed that Dickie had got the baby's name right.

'You can't have him,' Sadie said. The sun was behind Dickie, shaping her in silhouette.

'You must leave him,' Ria pointed at Krish as Padma came back out of the kitchen with a plate of Indian sweets and offered it Dickie.

'No mummy,' Madhu told her mother, pushing Padma's plate of goodies aside. 'We send him away.'

'You're frightening my baby,' Sadie shook her head at Dickie.

Padma was still holding up the plate, as if in supplication to a god. 'The baby laughs, he likes her.'

'I am Dickie,' she went on ignoring the hostile looks. 'I come in peace to bless the precious child. He will eat curd and play the flute like Lord Krishna.'

'You're not touching him,' Sadie edged further back.

Padma offered the plate up again and Madhu pushed it away again, but Padma would not be stilled. 'She will curse us.'

'All he wants is money.' Madhu waved at her. 'You think these blessings are for free?'

Padma was shaking. 'We pay. Then she will not curse us.'

Daya stepped forward to Dickie and whispered until Dickie replied. Daya shook her head and they talked again.

Daya turned to the group. 'Twenty thousand rupees.'

Padma clasped her hands anxiously. 'Must pay, we must.'

Madhu said, 'No.'

And Sadie followed with, 'You get nothing from me.'

'Two hundred quid?' Ria gasped.

Sadie cradled Krish. 'It'll scare him to death.'

'The baby likes him.' Padma insisted. 'Dickie is gentle with Krish.'

'Two hundred pounds,' Sadie yelled. 'For what?' Curling her arms round the child she retreated near to the kitchen doorway.

Dickie beat a slow rhythm for a moment.

Padma held on to the plate of sweets, her hand trembling. 'They will curse us, my daughters will not marry, their sons will die—'

'Rubbish they tell you, Mummy,' Madhu cut in.

'No one's going to pay that much,' Ria laughed, shrugging.

Daya leaned towards Ria, her tone measured. 'This is a hijra. We've got to find a way.'

'I will bring blessings and good luck to your son and all your family for generations,' Dickie addressed Padma. 'You will have love and money. You will have lots of sons.'

'Two hundred quid,' Ria sighed, shrugging, 'I don't think so.'

Madhu urged her mother. 'You can't let him do this.'

But Padma stood her ground shakily. 'She will curse us.' And looking in her youngest daughter's eyes, 'You want to live, or die. That family in the mountains spat at a hijra and did not pay. The husband died one week since.'

Madhu dismissed her mother with a wave as Dickie went to Padma and put her arm round her. 'Auntie knows the love of hijra. I will take you to the banks of the Ganges River and we will bath and purify our bodies, like I purify little Krish here.'

'We are not a rich family,' Daya said. 'This is money to live on for months.'

Dickie eyed Ria. 'England is rich. This is pocket money.' The authority with which she spoke shook Ria.

'This will kill Mummy-ji —' Daya appealed to Ria.

'I can't just—' Ria began, but Daya nudged her and Ria went to her bag and rummaged, pulling out some ten pound notes which she took to Dickie, thrusting them in her hand. Ria hoped as she turned her back on Dickie that she would go quickly.

Dickie rolled out three ten pound notes. 'I think you will pay more for a good blessing. This is an English boy. Very special. Special rates to pray to the gods and purify him.'

'We have no more,' Ria held out her empty palms.

'You shouldn't give him anything,' Madhu said, crashing her bowl on the side, the milky cereal slopping out. 'They steal boys. Do things to them. Take their manhood.'

'We only take those that are ours,' Dickie said quietly. 'You need not be afraid if you treat hijra with blessings.'

'Sing, then go,' Daya instructed.

Dickie drummed a little, danced a few steps then sang:

'Little boy in the glass mountains, lost and new.

Baby child with skin like Krishna's blue.

Come from the snowy peaks to bring us joy.

Love, O love, sweet glorious boy.'

Then she stopped and drew breath. 'You pay now.'

Padma threw her hand to her mouth. 'Krish — He will die in a week.'

Sadie said, 'Leave us alone.'

'Like his father, he will die young,' Padma said.

'His father died in a car?' Dickie nodded.

Padma put her hand on her heart. 'Dickie knows, she has the inner eye.'

'We have to give her something more,' Daya urged Sadie who was sitting with Krish on her lap. 'She will not do any harm.'

Ria was scared a moment by the revelation about Ijay's accident and glancing over noticed Sadie looked shaken. Someone could have told Dickie about Ijay, rumour probably got about through villages, but it seemed unlikely, although somehow Dickie knew an English boy was here.

'Pay him, for god's sake, Ria. You've got it. Pay him.' Sadie nodded to her.

'Like his father, he will die young,' Dickie carried on matter - of-factly.

'Go,' Madhu yelled.

Ria reached into her bag again and turning her back on the group dived her hand in. Pulling out several twenty pound notes, she offered them slowly to Dickie who snatched them and stuffed them quickly down the breast of her sari.

Dickie danced, flipping her arms out as she twirled in circles. Ria was quickly entranced, finding her movements somehow beautiful and ungainly at the same time. Performed by someone who clearly admired the art-form and was sincerely attempting something of it, Dickie was heavy footed. Ria both admired and resented her courage and the sheer determination of demanding money and attempting graceful steps. Something made her shrink back from this formidable figure though, who forced herself on those likely to surrender to her, and those superstitious enough to be fearful of a curse.

Ria watched her audience, taking in Madhu's sour expression and Sadie's tense body. It seemed Dickie was oblivious to any kind of hatred or ridicule and twirled on without a sign of shame or sensitivity. Wherever she had been, it had been tough, but she had found a way through. Ria recoiled with a shiver at her own insights and she worried how much more she would have to pay to keep Padma's family protected from a curse. It felt preposterous, but at the same time essential.

The waving trail of arms continued along with skipping footwork as Dickie span near to Sadie, and suddenly facing her, she lifted Krish carefully from his mother, rocking and swaying the giggling boy, and laughing back to him. Sadie seemed too surprised to stop it, but seeing Krish so cheerful, she gave in. The dancer span him carefully, rocking him near her breast with the lightness of touch of a parent, and singing and humming to him.

Ria clapped a beat in time until Madhu frowned at her. Behind Dickie clouds had moved across the ridge and the sun was shut out for a time.

Dickie kept spinning Krish to the scowls of Madhu and Sadie, although Padma, pacified now, looked on laughing and clapped her hands. Dickie flipped her feet, jangled ankle bells, but all the time her gaze was in the eyes of the hypnotised child.

'Krish is laughing,' Daya clapped. 'He loves it.'

There were more verses in Hindi, then more thuds from the drum, then Dickie spoke in English again:

'Come little boy, little man,

Come into the world and do what you can,

Come little life, come and sing with us,

Blessed and loved with soma and sweets,

Join in life with all its treats,

Be happy and wise, marry well,

Find money and good fortune,

For Laxmi looks over you,

Come to the temple and ring the bell.'

The distant clouds which had enveloped several peaks thinned so a blade of sunlight blasted through.

When she stopped Dickie called for water and dipping her hands in the glass flicked Krish's face while muttering blessings. At that moment Ria noticed Bijal coming down the path from town.

'We need fire.' Dickie sounded confident now and in control.

It was opportune that Bijal arrived, Ria reflected, he being the fire-maker at night. The metal bowl he used was under the bench, still full of half burned twigs and branches and ash.

Dickie went on. 'Fire is sacred to the gods.'

Bijal strode to the centre of the veranda and faced Dickie. 'Go.'

Dickie scowled, seeming hurt and shocked, and immediately handing baby Krish to his mother, gathered her drum without words, turned and prepared to leave without any of the petulant challenging she had shown the rest of the family earlier. Ria wondered whether it was men that disturbed Dickie.

'Do not upset hijra,' Padma admonished her husband. 'Do not upset Dickie, she will bring good.'

Bijal waved her aside. 'Go now, get out.'

'No curse. We don't want curse. Please, Bijal.'

Dickie started up the track.

Bijal spat on the ground where she had walked.

6

Ria was haunted by events, wondering to herself if her encounter with Dickie on the road a few days before had sparked the dancer's interest in coming to the family. The image of the hijra singing and dancing stayed with her, leaving an impression which fascinated and disturbed her. She would not meet her again, so it did not matter, except as Sadie pointed out to her later: 'We paid a lot of money to shut him up and keep Padma happy.' Ria did not want to get distracted from her plan to find her brother Hari.

When the family had dispersed Ria remained with Sadie who was humming to Krish and rocking him in their little bedroom. 'I didn't want him dancing round my baby. It was only for Padma. So superstitious these village people.'

'Bijal doesn't believe in curses then?' Ria said. 'Did you see his expression when he sent Dickie away?'

'And Dickie jumped,' said Sadie. 'No threats and curses. He wouldn't do that for Daya. Or Madhu. That girl is so lazy. Only thinks about herself.'

Ria took Krish a moment while Sadie brushed her hair and put on some makeup with a hand mirror. 'They're so poor, we could have given that money to them.'

Sadie slipped in silver dangling earrings, turning her head from side to side to see if they hung well. 'If it wasn't for Daya doing all the work at Bijal's shop they'd have nothing. Madhu thinks she's some sort of princess out of a movie and Daya — always telling you what to do.'

'We have to try and be nice—'

'I need that money,' Sadie brushed her hair again. 'Ijay's land. It's my money.'

'The earrings suit you—'

Sadie scowled at herself in the mirror. 'We'll see who comes this afternoon.' Pleased with her appearance, her tones became warmer, 'I've got nothing back home, I have to have the money. We'll say a few words for Ijay. It's a glorious spot, you won't believe it when you see it.' Her eyes sparkled and her shoulders dropped, 'There's a trickling stream, trees for shade.' She looked as though she was about to cry but held on, took a breath and put her things away.

'Then you'll have something, Sadie. He actually bought it — all paid up?'

'Yeah,' Sadie whispered. 'It's a secret. Only people born and living in India can buy land. He found a way round.'

'He always was a clever boy.'

'He got Bijal to buy it,' Sadie went on. 'Gave him all our savings. Bijal bought it in his name.' She was excited. 'It's all good. I can get back what's due to me and start something up of my own.'

'You don't want to carry on Ijay's dream and live here sometimes?'

'We hadn't saved enough to build a house on it anyway, but you know what I was thinking,' Sadie spoke enthusiastically, 'I've got other ideas. I'm going to set up some kind of business.'

'Yeah?'

'You know, buying fabrics and artefacts from here and selling them back home. It's easy: Bijal has contacts with suppliers — you know Indian covers and cushions, wooden boxes, incense, that sort of thing. I've got plenty of contacts back home — shops and stalls who're mad keen to sell Indian stuff. I can do some online sales and build it up. I've got the links. All I need is the cash to get me started. I mean Ria, what else is there for me back home? I can't live with a baby with mum and her new boyfriend — who booted you out. And there's always a market for Indian things in England. Six or seven grand would be enough to get me going –'

As Sadie checked her purse and her makeup bag the light from the window caught her grey-blue eyes. It had only been a few months since Ijay had died so he had never got to see his son. Being in grief it was no wonder she was touchy, although things had never been smooth between her and Ria.

'Tonight I will talk to Bijal,' Sadie said firmly. 'I mean this has got to be sorted.'

'Do you trust him?'

Sadie looked alarmed a moment then shook away the expression. 'He's got to.' Pulling her bag over her shoulder, she nodded to Ria to pick up Krish. 'Are you coming to the village?'

*****

The mountains were already in darkness when Bijal got matches, slips of paper, little twigs and branches and a few coals to make a fire in the metal bowl. Swaying a little from side to side on his haunches making Ria think he had been drinking, he poked a lighted match in a cavern of debris. It was a struggle for him to get the coals alight, and his fingers so apparently adept with needle and thread all day, trembled as he created a grotto of twigs and placed the stub end of a lighted candle inside, so eventually it caught and fired up the coals. Still squatting, he warmed his hands. Every so often he would get up and go inside, coming out again with a grin on his face.

Ria intended to tell her that it was the wrong time, but when Sadie came out from having put the baby down she sat opposite Bijal in the light of a rising flame. Madhu was inside and Padma was preparing the evening meal with Daya.

'I need the land sold now, Bijal.' Sadie spoke to him over the fire, but he did not move or motion a response. 'For me. And

Krish.' Ria noticed Bijal tense a little. 'Now. I need it now.' He did not nod. 'I've got to start up a business,' Sadie said.

Ria held her hands out to be warmed and although she had a fleece on her back was cold.

'We will go tomorrow.' Bijal rocked on his haunches, but did not take his gaze from the flames.

Ria did not know whether Sadie had realised that he had been drinking.

'I must have it,' Sadie stared at him, but he did not look at her.

'Soon,' he said.

'When is soon?' Sadie was sitting cross legged, one hand clutching her waist, the other on her hip. Bijal kept his gaze on the flames, occasionally poking the embers with a stick.

Daya brought tea and they all sat silently watching the fire as the night drew in, waiting for Padma to join them with the evening meal.

Ria looked up at the mountain range, now black and formless against a backdrop of stars.

Agitated, she regretted she had not brought things up with Sadie earlier. Sadie never had a problem confronting her, and the more Ria kept putting it off, the harder it was becoming. Watching her, Ria's intuition was sharpened, thinking, 'Did you take my model of the glass mountains, Sadie? Do you know where my brother is?'

'When is soon?' Sadie said again, but Bijal seemed mesmerised by the fire.

*****

The sun was high when the troupe headed up the track from the main road. Rickshaws, buses and brightly painted Public Carrier lorries rushed by, horns active. The track upwards was steep for legs used to city streets, and made rocky by recent streams of rainwater that had attempted to make a river of it. Sadie had Krish in a papoose. Madhu, carrying the mango sapling was puffing a little, and Daya used the spade sometimes like a walking stick to pull herself along. Padma and Bijal stepped along with Ria carrying the large decorated box.

They went under a bridge of trees, the arch opening out to reveal the expanse of mountains above them where thick clouds were forming. Turning onto open land with jagged rocks and boulders, they followed a path upstream. Looking back Ria saw the cascade of water jostling its way down towards a bridge under the main road they had climbed up from, now several hundred metres below them. The line of water could be seen haphazardly finding its way further down to join the stream near Padma's house.

The mountains overwhelmed all things below them, buildings and people. An earthquake could only ever shake a little salt-like snow from the towers, the odd rock or two, but never crash them. The gods would not let that happen, Ria was dreaming.

The rocky land was covered in undergrowth with few trees, consisting of steep roughly marked terraces. Ria couldn't see much arable land: for things to grow bushes and undergrowth would have to be cleared — a big job. Sadie had told her it was about an acre in size.

To the right, a hundred metres up an incline of tufty grass a ruined building stood on a flat ridge, the rocky hillside reaching up behind it to a small peak miniaturised by the white peaks up behind it. Sadie had not mentioned it so Ria was not sure whether it was part of Sadie's land. Although the roof tiles were missing from the structure, huge sheets of blue plastic had been fixed over, giving the impression that it was inhabited.

'Did you see?' Madhu had noticed the building as well and called to Sadie. 'Up on that ridge, there's a ruin with somebody living there. That is your land, isn't it?'

'Where?' Sadie glanced up and seeing the structure, turned to Bijal, agitated. 'Bijal?'

'There is somebody there, isn't there?' Madhu persisted.

Bijal shook his head, motioning them to go forward.

'There better not be.' Sadie led them on, surveyed her little empire a time, considering different areas, then took them to an open space several metres from the stream. 'We'll plant here. This is the bit Bijal cleared for us. Thank you, Bijal. You've always been helpful with this place.'

He took the spade and began to dig but Sadie pulled his arm immediately and guided him a couple of feet away to another spot. Ria smiled at her sister's precision as Bijal obeyed, shovelling out soil and stones to a depth of a couple of feet. Madhu tidied the sides, Daya held the sapling straight while Padma began to fill in the roots with soil.

'Water.' Daya stopped the industry. 'Anyone brought a container?' She broke their silence again. 'Come on,' she called, heading for the rumbling stream and bending, cupped her hands to scoop a palm full. Dashing to the plant, she let go what drops were left.

'That's no good,' Madhu had her hands on her hips, but Sadie followed Daya with Padma next, and Bijal and Ria, they traipsed backwards and forwards with dripping cupped hands and a lot of laughter.

'It will be healthy now,' Padma nodded at the young plant.

Daya kept going after the others wearied, even smearing the leaves with dampness from her fingers.

Sadie took the box from Ria and ran her fingers round the gold edges.

'You can do it now,' Madhu told her.

Sadie lifted the lid and put her hand inside, coming out with a bunch of her lover's ashes and sprinkled it around the wet base of the young mango tree. The sun came out of mists over the back of mountains, the razor lines of ridges against the sky.

Ria watched clouds racing over and as she stared it seemed the clouds were still and the mountain lines were moving and remembered how quickly storms came up in the region.

Sadie threw handfuls of Ijay's dust down a few times, then handed the box to Daya who grabbed a handful of the grey dust and dropping some around the base of the sapling and some in the stream, she tossed the remainder in the air, singing, 'Shanti, Shanti, Shanti'.

Padma took some and spread it around the plant, then put her hands together for prayer. Bijal did the same, and Madhu came forward solemnly, letting a handful fall to the ground near the new shrine.

The sight of the remains of someone she knew stewed up in the bottom of a box made Ria nauseous, but she dived her hand in, grabbed the contents and sprinkled the last of him over the sapling. Madhu tipped the leftovers in a pile by the little tree and a turn of breeze puffed it away to the trees down the hillside.

An awkward silence followed with nobody knowing what to do next. Ria felt something needed to be said to send him on his journey. The vacuum left without the Hindu ritual Sadie had blocked was painful.

Daya said, 'Shanti,' a few times, but it was not enough, and she said everyone must say something good they remembered about Ijay, and something good about what he did, or good quality he had, or a little story about what he said or did.

Padma and Bijal gave a few words about how he had helped them with money to extend their house, how respectful he had been, how people liked him in the village, how he would have built many things on his land and helped many people through it.

Daya said things about how she and he had walked together in the mountains and how he had made her laugh. She went on about how charismatic he was and his quick wit. Madhu said he was clever and could build anything or fix anything. Sadie told a story of sailing in a little boat in the backwaters of Kerala with him, of their plans to build on the land and have sons and daughters, but she ended choking in tears.

Ria had to come up with something convincing. She had never really liked Ijay, although she could not put her finger on why that was, it was just intuition, until she heard the stories about him after his death. If what they said about him was true — which she reckoned it was, because different circles of people had said the same things about him — he had lived a double life and deceived Sadie. Despite her tough exterior, Sadie was naive when it came to Ijay's lifestyle, apparently believing everything he told her about being away on business. She was probably able to overlook a lot when Ijay told her he had fulfilled their dream of owning a plot in India.

'He did a lot for the family here in India,' Ria said, excusing herself with: 'I didn't know him very well, we only met a few times. But he was always buying Sadie things. And look at this wonderful baby boy he's given us. We're sorry you're gone, Ijay. We'll miss you.'

Clouds were gathering overhead and a wind had come up.

'We have to go soon,' said Daya. 'A storm's coming.'

The sound of the lone drum beat was unmistakeable, as was Sadie's utterance under her breath, 'No.'

A steady beat followed each step she took until Dickie, in a red and yellow sari decorated with patterns of lotus flowers, arrived near the group. Her arms were covered in bangles, she wore several necklaces and her long gold earrings swayed as she walked. Stopping by the stream and standing on a rock she appeared ghostlike to Ria. She had not made up her face thickly, although she had dark lines along the edge of the eyelids.

'Shanti. Peace to all of you. Let the soul of our brother rise up into the mists of the glass mountains, into the hands of the gods, to mingle with the clouds and fall like rain down snowy peaks and rivers, join the Holy Mother Ganges, become new life—'

Bijal shuffled awkwardly. Padma held her head up.

'No more,' Madhu said.

Dickie held her ground. 'I bless the spirit of the departed and send him on his journey to the after-world. We do it with peace —'

Sadie stiffened, 'Not with my money.'

Dickie threw her head back to the sky and increased the sound of the drum as heavy cloud swept over the peaks.

'Do something, Daddy-ji,' Madhu gesticulated to her father but he did not move at first. 'Daddy? You stop this —'

Ria watched how Bijal reacted. He seemed reluctant as he stepped forward with his hand raised, weakly telling Dickie to stop. It was not the same commanding gesture he had used before, making Ria curious now about the relationship between them. She wondered whether they had met before, and whether Bijal's previous anger had been manufactured to cover up things he knew. She became more curious when Dickie seemed to ignore Bijal's request, carrying on as though nothing had been done.

Dickie motioned to Padma to give her the box, picked out specks of Ijay's remains and tossed them in the air, singing:

Go in search of other worlds.

Take a boat across the river, pay the ferryman for a safe ride.

Meet the ancestors on the other side.

They come to greet with gifts and sweets

And news of lost souls in the deep,

There you meet your inner self,

Find the karma of your ways,

Things you achieved throughout your days,

Make peace with your deeds

And things done to others through

Your paths and ways,

Make your soul complete

Find chances that you cannot miss
In fast new worlds blessed with god's final bliss,
Come back again in a new body clean
Put on the coat of life again
Or with god's will slip away to moksha
Never here again, lost forever, unseen —'

Everyone was dabbing their eyes. Bijal wiped a tear from his cheek.

'We didn't ask for this, Daddy-ji?' Expecting more from him, Madhu frowned at her father who looked scared to Ria.

Ria looked the dancer up and down, perceiving a vulnerability she had not noticed before, and let her intuition guide her. 'He doesn't want any more money.'

Dickie nodded. 'I will do it free.'

Ria was still unsure of her, yet there was something in the sparkle of her eyes that endeared Dickie to her, something hidden or lost, or the residue of hurt and fear, which frightened Ria more. As with the others Dickie was strange to her, loud and belligerent and bossy, and she was reluctant to get drawn too close to her for fear Dickie would take advantage not only of her money, but of her emotions. To Ria, Dickie was a mistress at leadership, could get people under her spell quickly and with the alacrity of a confidence trickster. They should get her to go.

Dickie smiled. 'I will send this brother on his way for no payment.'

Ria thought she saw movement outside the ruin on the ridge. Another person in a sari had come out and was looking down at them.

'I ask you one thing,' Dickie put her hands together in prayer.

'You people always want something,' Madhu quickly flashed.

'You accept me here,' Dickie smiled.

Wind was flapping the young sapling and clouds were rushing around the sides of the closest peaks.

'Here?' Sadie picked up on his word. 'What do you mean "Here"?'

'We make our home.' Dickie bowed her head a little, palms still together.

Padma looked up the hill, following Sadie and Madhu's gaze, to the solitary figure watching them. Bijal pulled his collar up.

'Not here,' Sadie said. 'Not in that ruin. You don't make your home here. This is my land. Mine. My husband bought this.'

Krish started crying as the wind brought sleet.

The figure by the ruin went into the building.

'We have nowhere.' Dickie told her. 'This is our home.'

'No. This is not happening,' Sadie yelled above Krish's cries.

Dickie turned to the baby and Krish smiled up to him.

'Don't touch him.' Sadie spun away, starting Krish going again.

Dickie bowed to Sadie, then to all the group, and taking her drum banged a rhythm up the track to the ruin, leaving the mourners in silence.

'Bijal uncle, get him off,' Sadie shouted.

Sleet and snow swept over the group with a crack of thunder.

7

'Who is he?' Ria muttered when Daya brought her fresh pineapple juice in bed the following day. She could hear Sadie cooing to Krish in the shade outside.

Daya sat on the edge of the bed, a bundle of fabric under her arm. 'I can't stop long,' Daya said. 'I have to get back to the shop, if I don't get finished this morning — well, Daddy-ji's got this contract with a new hotel, all the new uniforms. I mean, it's big and it means the family's all right for the next year or two. But Daddy-ji needs to go to the hotel soon and sign it.'

'He is all right?' Ria sipped her juice.

'He gets up later every day and he goes out at night to his friend. I think they drink until late. He doesn't talk much now. I know he was going to see Dickie last night to get her moved, but where is he now?'

'Can Madhu help?'

'She's seeing that boy again. I know she is. She keeps denying it, says she's working late in the library, but she's seeing him. If Mummy and Daddy knew. The best I can do is to get them to find somebody for her,' Daya fiddled with fabric on the duvet.

'So the last thing you want is some, well, dancer, who won't get off Sadie's land?'

'I don't know how they got there,' Daya sighed. 'I mean Ijay came over here several times and set it all up with Daddy-ji. I didn't know the hijra were there until you did the other day.'

'All through the night, I could hear the drum banging in my head,' Ria laughed.

Daya laughed with her. 'It's a hard life for them — below the

221

Dalits even — outcasts. We should pity them really. They go back a long way. Some people say there's a tradition from beyond the eunuchs of the Mughal Courts hundreds of years ago.'

'They know what they want all right, and go for it.'

'They believe in who they are, Ria. I think there must be a lot of hardship and pain. They save and save for it, go through all sorts.'

'The operation?' Ria screwed up her lips then laughed. 'God.'

'No anaesthetic,' Daya said and they cringed. 'They must have conviction to what they feel about themselves and life. I think they only want to be accepted.'

'They just survive on blessing babies?'

'Dickie is like that, but there are some — well, you wouldn't know they weren't women. So beautiful, their faces so young. So vulnerable in a way. You look in Dickie's eyes, there's so much sensitivity there. Sometimes I think if we could just see them as individuals,' Daya watched her, 'trying to make something of themselves,' Daya said.

'Dickie can be in your face. I met her on the road before I got here, demanding money,' Ria told her. 'I was scared.'

'I suppose we're all threatened by what we see as different,' Daya said. 'But I don't think they will do you any harm. They get invited to weddings. Some people see them as a good omen, bringing fertility to the couple. Others drive them away.'

'And they can survive on what they make?'

'I think most of it goes to the Nayak, the leader of the group. A dozen or so live together.'

'Do you think more will come on then?' Ria was anxious for Sadie.

'I don't know. We only know of Dickie and her friend. They've got to make their money somehow. Some are, well, they do their work at night.'

'On the street?'

Daya leaned forward and whispered, 'Some people say that even married men go to them.' They giggled. 'They're still hated. Some parts of town are dangerous for them. Sometimes they are beaten and driven away.'

'I worry about Sadie—'

'Daddy-ji will have it sorted out. You'll see. I'm sure they'll move on and everything will go back to normal. I must go, he'll be wondering where I've got to.'

Daya gave Ria a hug, took her bundle of fabric and left. Ria was warmed by Daya, seeing her as another sister.

*****

Ria had rice, dal and mixed vegetables with the family that evening, although she longed for fish and chips and a bottle of lager. The group sat on cotton rugs around the fire in the bowl that Bijal had made, faces lit up, jaws in motion, the bare electric light bulb above them.

Even in the dark Ria was aware of the mountains. They huddled like a great creature crouching over villages and roads. In daytime, walking along the street or by the shops, she felt as small as a world to a star to them.

Bijal chewed silently, no one else spoke and Ria was aware of the tension between Sadie and him. Madhu was picking at her food, Daya was not eating much, and Sadie was eating quickly. Padma sat quietly next to her husband taking small mouthfuls.

'So what's happening?' Sadie stared at Bijal. He carried on chewing.

'We have to settle this, Daddy-ji,' Daya pushed the remains of her vegetable curry aside. 'We must talk.'

He looked up tiredly. 'I will talk to the police,' then took another mouthful.

'You said you would sort it last night,' Sadie said.

'I talk to the police.'

'Sadie's right,' Madhu put in, 'we don't want these people in our village.'

'Daddy-ji will talk to the police,' Padma intervened.

'You went up to see them on the land last night. You still haven't told us what happened?'

'He told them to go,' Padma said.

'And did they?' Sadie was fuming. 'For all I know he agreed to let them go there.'

'Daddy-ji wouldn't do that.' Daya glanced at Sadie. 'You have to give things time in India.'

After a pause, Sadie said, 'I will talk to the police with your uncle.'

'Daddy-ji knows the police,' Daya replied.

Madhu drew breath, 'If the police won't do anything, you have to think of other ways—'

'What ways, Madhu?' Daya quickly snapped.

Madhu shrugged.

Pushing her plate further away Daya said, 'We're not getting men with clubs and bats.'

Madhu smiled and leaning to her sister said, 'I'm sure Sadie will give us something for looking after the land.'

Sadie frowned at her.

'Daddy-ji is thinking of many things at this time,' Padma spoke and the group were silenced. 'He has the big contract. Not just one hotel, but many hotels. Tomorrow he must go up and sign—'

'They know me at the hotel. I have done uniforms for them before,' Bijal assured his wife. 'They do not need me to sign papers.' Bijal put aside his empty plate and wiped his hands with a tissue. 'Tonight I will go up the hill to them again.'

'Even if the land was sold, Sadie,' Daya leaned towards her, 'it would take a long time to get the money through. This is India — bureaucracy. You have to think about going back home and coming back again.'

Bijal tossed a short branch on the fire and it popped and crackled for a time.

'You can't just take rupees out of the country, Sadie, there's all sorts of complications.'

The meal ended in silence. Bijal stood up and left the family.

*****

Ria slept late and being the last up she was surprised to see Daya had not yet gone to her father's shop. She appeared to be trying to console her mother about something on the veranda. Padma was waving her hands and muttering agitatedly.

Sadie seemed to be ignoring Krish's appeal for breakfast. 'Bijal's not come back.'

Madhu joined Daya with their mother.

'Perhaps Daddy-ji has gone back up the hill with the hijra,' Daya grasped her mother's hand.

'The contract, the contract,' Padma was shaking.

'They will give it to him anyway.' Madhu laughed. 'They know him up there. Daddy-ji said so. He's done it before with them.'

Padma still looked worried.

Daya looked anxiously at her mother. 'If Daddy-ji is still up there, I will find him Mummy-ji.'

Padma wiped her cheeks with her pink chunni, turned and went inside.

Ria sat, rubbing her eyes while Sadie started breast feeding Krish in a shady corner.

Daya took Madhu aside. 'I know you're still seeing him—'

'Some of us want fun,' Madhu laughed.

Although she wanted coffee, Ria sensed Daya needed her there to hear so she sat pretending to fiddle with a loose thread in the cardigan she had borrowed, tucking some of it back and snapping the remaining line while looking out at the valley.

'Think of the family. All the town will know. The shame. You won't get a nice boy.'

'A nice boy. Who wants that?'

'You'll get hurt. Prem is just playing—'

'What do you know? A man has never touched you. I have to study,' Madhu pulled away. 'Then help Mummy-ji with the food.'

'You've suddenly got busy with chores then,' Daya replied, Ria picking up the sarcasm in her tone: Madhu seemed to do little to help Padma around the house. 'Now that I need you to come and find Daddy,' Daya said loudly.

'I'll come,' Sadie called over to Daya after Madhu had gone.

'You must stay with Krish,' Daya replied. 'Ria and I can go. Can't we Ria?'

'Now?' Ria was uncertain.

'We'll do what we can,' Daya put on her sandals. Ria's stomach was rumbling for breakfast, her face still unwashed. Despite Daya's pressure for her to wear a Punjabi Suit, she was still in her travelling jeans and T Shirt, with a pink woollen cardigan to keep out the cold.

Ria did not know what good she could do, but got the idea as they were walking that Daya thought she was the only one she could rely on, although Ria was struggling with her apprehension of going into Dickie's territory, feeling reluctant to get involved.

Morning cloud had evaporated leaving sun-blanched slopes and the glass mountains shone over them when they tramped up the pathway out of the trees. As they trekked upwards she could see the village unfolding below them.

The ruin was on a flat piece of land that fell away quickly to the stream, and with a wide viewpoint of the main valley and rolling green hills beyond. When they reached the rough wooden door with years of peeling paint, the place looked deserted. Daya banged, shouting, 'Namaste.' Silence. They looked at each other, then Daya knocked again, shouting, and thinking it was empty they turned to go, but the door was pulled back with a creak.

A squat figure in a sari faced them without smile or scowl. Bewildered, Daya hesitated, and Ria was apprehensive. The hijra looked them up and down.

'My father,' Daya began, 'Bijal.'

'Not here,' the hijra was about to shut the door, but Daya wedged her foot in the way. 'Dickie? Dickie is here?'

'Dickie sick.'

Ria was hoping nobody was there and they could trot off home and chat about Madhu's boyfriend.

'We must see her,' Daya stepped forward, her hand on the door.

'Very sick.' Dressed in a blue sari, the hijra stood, her feet wide apart. In her forties, she was stocky with thick arms and a round face.

'How sick?' Ria said.

'Very, very sick. Up here.' She tapped under her chin with her fingers. 'Not get up.'

'Has she seen a doctor?' Ria said while Daya kept her hand on the door.

The hijra shook her head.

'They've got no money to pay for one,' Daya said to Ria.

'We can get food,' Ria smiled at the guard, small and rotund in stature with thick black eyebrows. 'We can get fruits and vegetables for her.'

'No eat. Go,' the hijra said.

'But she should eat,' Daya persisted.

Ria was annoyed with herself for being drawn into something which she thought was nothing to do with her, a distraction from what she had come to India for. None of this brought her closer to finding her brother.

'Should we?' Ria hissed to Daya. 'I mean, you know what Madhu says we should do.'

Daya did not reply, looking away from Ria, and Ria picked up the disappointment Daya felt for what she had suggested. Ria thought Daya cared too much for too many people and that you just could not live like that all the time.

The guard flinched as though about to shut the door in their faces, but Daya resisted, grasping the edge surely. Ria heard a groan from inside.

'Go,' the hijra pushed the door, but Daya held on encouraging Ria to grab it with her.

'You have to get off this land,' Ria said, hoping to sound firm and decisive and get it over quickly. 'You have to go. It's my sister's.'

As soon as she had said it Ria sensed Daya's disapproval: she did not want them to be so direct so soon.

'We just want to talk,' Ria said.

The hijra did not blink. Daya let her weight on the door relax, and Ria felt her giving in. 'Ria. I've got to go to the hotel. Even though Daddy-ji thinks it's all right — can we take the risk?'

Daya had not finished when someone appeared behind the hijra in shadows.

'Daddy-ji?' Daya called through the narrow gap in the doorway. 'Daddy-ji?'

Bijal looked blankly at his daughter, showing only a little surprise in his eyes.

'You have come to sort things out with Dickie?' Daya called to him. 'You'll get it sorted out, I know you will—'

'We came to help you,' Ria said. 'Is it working?' She tried not to sound impatient.

'Don't forget the Raj Hotel. They're waiting for you—' Daya appealed to her father.

Ria saw him shrug his shoulders.

Sensing the hijra guard letting go her hold, Ria pushed the door back open with her foot.

Saying nothing, Bijal took a bowl to a tub of water and scooped.

'Daddy-ji?'

Bijal was wearing the shirt Ria had given him, although some of the greens and blues had been scuffed.

As the guard at the door stepped back, Daya edged her way in, with Ria following.

Turning, the guard went through a ragged red curtain. Blue plastic sheeting overhead created a gloomy sapphire light that touched jars and plates and bottles on tables and shelves.

Daya grabbed Ria's hand and drew her through the red curtain.

Dickie's face was puffed with welts and bruises, the large swelling over her left cheekbone shone a strange mauve in the blue light, and the right ear was inflamed. She lay on a low wooden bed that looked centuries old with dirty blood stained sheets.

'Diksha, Diksha,' Bijal said gently, dipping a dirty cloth in water and dabbing her wounds. 'Sweet Diksha, little Dickie —' Bijal nursed her as though she were a child.

The other hijra stood behind as Daya pulled the cloth from her father's hand and addressed him. 'You go, —' she told her father. 'It's late now. The contract —'

Bijal shook, tears in his eyes, as he knelt by Dickie, stroking her hands and running his fingers through her hair and bending, kissed her forehead.

Daya regarded her father for a moment, letting the cloth fall to the dirt floor. Ria's realisation came at the same time. Bending to retrieve the cloth, Daya wrung it tightly, then flung it in the bowl splashing Dickie's wounded face. Daya took two steps back, turned and dived through the ripped curtain crying, 'Daddy-ji, Daddy-ji, you can't — Not with Dickie. Not you, you can't do this —'

8

Ria was about to turn and go after her but Dickie grasped at her wrist and held her back and looking up at her said, 'Are you scared like them?'

'Let me go,' Ria yelled.

'There's something different about you. If we could explain, ' Dickie still held on to her and despite Dickie's thin damaged frame her grip was powerful.

'Explain what?'

'You're not scared like them.'

'Let me go.'

'Are you too scared to hear then?' Dickie croaked. 'Run away from the truth? Like Daya? It always catches you up in the end.'

'This is my sister's.'

Bijal quietly stroked Dickie's hair and forehead with a damp cloth.

'We didn't know. Not at first. We found an empty place—'

'You want me to believe that. You and Bijal set it up.'

'Bijal is a good man,' Dickie relaxed her grip and Ria pulled away.

'It wasn't his to give. You two making out or something?'

'People hate us everywhere,' Dickie sounded resigned to Ria rather than angry. 'You can see.'

'Who beat you?' Ria looked in her eyes.

'Boys with clubs and bats. There are even people in your family who hate me. I have nowhere else.'

The other hijra sitting in shadows grunted. 'People say all hijra bad. Some people take us to wedding. They like. We bring good luck. Sing song. Some boys in village do not like.'

'Mickie is my friend,' Dickie glanced over to her. 'She looks after me. I owe everything to her.'

'Boys beat you?' Ria softened.

'Beat,' Mickie carried on. 'Throw stone. We are not bad people. We give to people in the village. We want to bring good things, good luck.'

Ria could not dismiss Madhu's comments from her mind and was angered by the injuries she saw now.

'And you? And Bijal?'

'Bijal helps me. '

'How long?'

'Two years now.'

'You planned it all with him,' Ria suppressed her anger, feeling she should run after Daya but Mickie slid a chair behind her, a crude wooden thing with split matting, and motioned for her to sit.

'Bijal knows who I am,' Dickie said as Ria sat. 'Two years ago I was with a Nayak who beat me.' When Dickie looked in her eyes Ria felt Dickie trusted her. Yet she was anxious about the entanglement she was getting into and confused about how she could help. 'A Nayak is who you live with, a leader of the commune. You give all money to her – she decides. When I was with her first she was good, but she was jealous always of me and always had bad words: "You do not bring me enough money."'

A shaft of sunlight came like a laser beam through a tiny hole in the plastic roof sheeting, playing over her gesticulating hands. The room was dirty and smelled of damp. When Mickie lit incense sticks the tone changed and she felt how affectionate and loyal the two hijra beside her were – like sisters whose lives depended on each other. Bijal too, who she had forgotten in shadows, sat with the sweet aroma encircling him, letting life be what it was. Although she had impulses to get up and go, Ria was compelled to stay and listen.

'No,' Dickie went on, 'my Nayak wasn't always like that.' She paused, her fingers playing childlike in the beam of light. 'When I was a boy I knew I was not the same — the loud play-fighting boys with long competitive arms and legs — I knew that was not me. I loved dresses and make-up and dolls and — I was different, my body was not right for my mind. I was scared: you do not feel like other girls and boys but you don't know why and you don't know what to do about it. I was blessed that my Nayak took me in. My father didn't care about me, he had taken me away from my mother a year before, and he went off doing jobs, leaving me in the day. He often beat me if I didn't come home with money. My Nayak gave me food and shelter and I grew up with other hijra. They cared for me — more than my own family —'

'You had no other family?' Ria said. Mickie pushed the curtain aside and went into the other room.

'A sister once. I don't know what happened to her. She was taken away.'

'And you were snatched by your Nayak?'

Dickie's shoulders seemed to relax, and although the wounds masked the beauty of her face she was no longer angry. 'People think hijra steal young boys. They don't. With new born babies we pass money over their head to keep evil spirits away. We check them. If the boy has a lingam he stays with his mother. But some, they belong to us and we wait for them to come — we just wait, we never steal. I knew when I was taken in I would be all right, I had found people who would be my real family. I lived with her for many years. When I got older men came. Married men sometimes. Like Bijal.' She drew breath, glanced over to Bijal's smile and carried on surely. 'It's hijra. Who we are. You can hate us. You can beat us. But we are hijra. We are proud. When you beat us you are beating something you don't like about yourself.'

Mickie returned with a steaming cup of tea and handed it to Ria and she smiled and nodded in response. 'Dickie get tired,' Mickie said, 'After tea, you go—'

Mickie's words prompted Ria and she turned to Bijal. 'Uncle you must go to the hotel. You must talk to your daughter—'

Bijal motioned to Dickie to stop but she insisted on carrying on. 'I must tell her,' Dickie said. 'She must know.' And turning back to Ria asked her name.

'Ria.'

'That's a good name for you. I like it. Sounds English and Indian. I took the name 'Diksha'. It means "initiation." That is good for me. I was initiated into the hijra.'

'Few minute,' Mickie cautioned. 'Dickie need rest. Get well with rest.'

Bijal nodded.

'Bijal found me two years ago sleeping alone outside. He knew I might get attacked like that and saw that I was unhappy. The Nayak I was staying with shouted at me: "You do not bring in enough money, you are lazy, how can I live on this?" She was rich and she had got jealous and scared of me. I have ideas. I want hijra to be great. She could not see it. She said my ideas were too big and she threw me out. Everywhere we are hated and seen as dirty. And we live to that, we become that, and we become separated and only known as dirty sex workers. I do not want that. I want to change it. I ran away from my Nayak to set something up — a community of hijra, making and buying and selling fabrics and goods. And other things too — artefacts, tourist things,' Dickie smiled with excitement, 'I want hijra in the market respected for the quality of their work. Not just dirty people, sluts, but business people who know how to manage things, keep accounts, buying and selling and giving something to the community. I came to this bit of land for that. We will make this place thrive.'

'How can you?' Ria was sceptical and blowing steam from

her tea looked towards Bijal who looked away.

'It might take years, but others will join,' Dickie went on. 'Two are coming next week—'

'Long time,' Mickie said, 'but we will do.'

'You can really do it?' Ria sipped the sweet tea.

'I want all to be equal in the hijra house, not one dictator. A democracy, Ria, a co-operative. Is that good? Our business here will be a co-operative where everyone gains money and status and all the skills are recognised, and hijra can hold up their heads. I had that vision for years, but my Nayak thought she would lose all her power. Bijal has a big heart, he brought me here. This is where I am, this is where we do it. Can you see hijra in town and people coming to us as trusted business people? Can you?'

'With everyone against you?' Ria tipped back her cup finishing her tea.

'We need people to help.'

'I can't do anything—'

'Mickie came with me. She has the dream. What is life without a dream? Nothing. Drudge, hatred, stones on your back. Dreams give you hope, dreams dig you out of despair, they make you become somebody, they build your belief in life. We found this old ruin. Like a gift from the gods. We said to ourselves it must be true, this dream. Nobody lived here, so we said we would start now, spread the word to other hijra to come and join us — people to share our vision. So hijra are not just seen as child kidnappers who are weird and want to mutilate themselves.'

Ria's curiosity was awoken, but she did not want to be in the middle of the feud. She was also intrigued by Dickie's eloquence: she must have been educated in a good school and have learned English to a high level. Dickie had been good at hiding that when they first met on the road. There were many questions Ria wanted to ask, but she was concerned about how Daya was reacting to finding her father with his new lover.

'I want to make hijra accepted as part of everyday life. We can grow mangoes on the land and other fruits, we can trade fabrics, saris, chunni scarves, make-up, simple jewellery, icons and statues. Bijal can help find companies to trade with us, and we sell on. We can take our goods to Goa, there are many places to sell to tourists. Perhaps linking with someone in England so we can buy and sell. Nobody has done anything in India about solar energy — look at all the free sun we get. There's so much we can set up and do. Respect, that's all we ask.' Her bruised face glowed. 'Can you imagine? No longer living like sex slaves with little money and dignity. Many people would want us to come to their weddings and bless their children because we would be prosperous and bring good luck. Ria. You understand. You're not like the others. You listen—'

'But this is my sister's land,' Ria stood up.

'More hijra will come,' she held her stare at her.

Ria turned away and scowled at Bijal. 'What have you done, Bijal?'

'You will think about me?' Dickie said.

Impressed by the credibility of Dickie's ideas, but confused and anxious about how the situation could be resolved Ria said, 'I've got to go.'

Dickie grabbed her dangling wrist loosely as she was going, pulled it to her and kissed it. Ria recognised a change in her own views but still doubted herself. In Dickie she saw a young excited mind with determination. Dickie sat up, opened her palm and blew a kiss to her. 'Respect is what we ask. I lost my family, this is all I have—'

9

Resigned that there was little she could do, Ria felt impatient not to get too involved and to get on and find her brother. She was impressed by Dickie's enthusiasm, though. Sadie was almost impossible to work with, and Ria's influence useless. As she pushed past Mickie who smiled a goodbye and Bijal whose eyes searched her face for clues to what she might do, Ria mused she would have more luck trying to convince a tiger to become a vegetarian than moving her sister Sadie from her viewpoint.

Ria left the ruin, coming out to sunshine and far off snow tipped mountains. They did not ask her to come back, in fact they did not ask her to do anything, but she knew she was not done with them. Maybe they would get fed up and move on anyway, she shrugged. She could hear Dickie singing as she walked out under the peaks:

'Shiva rules the skies of our intent,
In the morning he rises in the east
And brings us the confusion of daylight,
Trips our egos with his enlightenments,
Throws us confusion, hurt and hate,
Falls and dies in the west,
Destruction, death and resurrection,
Shiva brings his change,
The certainty of the change the Buddha sent.'

She could hear voices a few houses away as she descended the path from the village to Padma's home and as she stepped on to the veranda she found Daya and Padma loudly tearful, holding each other. Madhu slammed a book down on the low wall fronting the space and Sadie was pounding about in a small circle thumping her thigh with her fist, baby Krish crying in a bundle at her feet.

Daya broke away from her mother, who stood bent alone, weeping, came to Ria and held her arm, 'Ria. Daddy-ji. How could he do this? Why? Mummy-ji is sick with worry. He's finished her. How can she live? The shame. Who will look at him again?'

Padma pushed away tears. 'Without my husband, we have no money. Everything is his.'

'People will not come to his shop,' said Madhu. 'You don't understand, when people know they will stay away. If he leaves Mummy-ji we have nothing. No studies, no—' Madhu's anger brought her close to tears. 'Who will want to marry us?' Madhu banged her book down again.

'On my land—' Sadie said.

Ria scowled at her, 'It's more complicated than that.' Ria could see Daya was struggling to find something positive although she was still in shock, a look of disgust for her father on her face. 'We must talk to him.'

Sadie stopped pacing. 'Calls himself an uncle, and sweet as pie to everyone, with jokes, and all this behind our backs. Now we know what happened — Bijal told him to take the land.'

Ria reflected that the motives of Bijal's action could not be denied. Again she felt in the middle of a quarrel that wasn't hers, trying to understand all sides, feeling ineffectual and not wanting any of it.

'You listen to them and not your own sister,' Sadie told Ria, 'All you want to do is find your brother. Even when we were kids you and Hari froze me out. I was glad when he was gone. Ijay is the only one who really helped — keeping contact with your dad's family in Manchester and auntie Padma—'

Ria paused, letting the reality sink in. 'You took it. My model of the glass mountains, didn't you?' Ria had not wanted to believe Sadie could have taken the piece she valued so much, but Sadie's coldness and jealousy indicated she was the culprit. Ria's anger was up. 'Did you even really know Ijay?'

'He was everything,' Krish's crying finally got to Sadie and she picked him up. 'Ijay stayed here lots with his auntie Padma. Anyway, mum said your dad brought Hari to the glass mountains.'

Ria struggled to hold back her anger. 'You treat Ijay like he was some god.'

'That's why you really came here. Not for me — or Ijay's ashes.' Sadie clung on to Krish unworried about the audience. Daya was sitting with her mother on the bench and Madhu was crouched by the wall. 'He was everything. Have you never loved, Ria?'

Ria was suddenly aware that her fists were clenched by her side. 'You looked the other way then with his scams.'

'He always looked after us.'

Ria shook her head, smiling ironically. 'You don't even know whether it was really an accident—' This was the argument that they should have had years ago. It had to come out. They had to shout at each other and then move on, with or without sisterhood.

'I took your model of the glass mountains,' Sadie snapped. 'Yes, you left it lying around, you weren't bothered with it then.'

The theft of Ria's model symbolised to her the depth of Sadie's long held resentment of her. And Ria could not help responding. It was cruel, but it had to come out — all of it.

'And the women he had on the side. Everybody knows. They talked about it in my restaurant. One of the girls who'd been with him had pictures on her phone—' Ria regretted saying it as soon as the words were out. She did not want to fight, and was surprised at the feelings of rage and revenge that boiled in her.

'Your dad never gave me a piece, so I took it,' Sadie glared at her, ignoring Ria's words.

Years of resentment between them reared and they could not stop it now. 'You think Ijay wanted this place to grow mangoes?' Ria carried on. 'Where have you been? He was a dealer. We don't even know what really happened to him—'

Sadie tightened her lips. Ria regretted going so deeply into her sister's secrets, especially in front of the family, and bit her tongue. She had been nasty and cruel. Ria asked herself why nobody else had told her about Ijay's double life — the stupid girls at her old restaurant. It had to be Ria. Sadie was tough but fragile and Ria had found a breaking point.

'You always hated him,' Sadie's defences were still up and strong at the moment, but Ria could see past them.

'I want it back.' Ria was determined not to be involved anymore and was about to go upstairs and pack ready for home when Bijal came down the path.

Padma looked up in tears at her husband as he passed her without comment and went in the kitchen, followed by Daya and Madhu.

All was quiet for a time, Sadie holding back tears as she took Krish upstairs. Ria watched her go, guilty a moment for telling her the truth.

The silence that followed was broken by Padma as she dashed outside. 'The contract.'

Daya followed her, with Madhu behind.

'Daddy-ji. He's lost it. The contract. He's lost the contract,' Daya said. 'The hotel. He didn't turn up. How can you do this to us, Daddy-ji?'

'It's gone to another tailor,' Madhu shouted.

*****

239

'Why are you here?' Dickie sat on the edge of her bed, a torn red shawl around her shoulders. The same shaft of light beamed through a hole in the plastic roof. Mickie was sweeping the floor with a switch-broom causing motes to rise in the beam and turn sparkling.

They gave Ria a cup of orange juice and pulled up the rickety chair for her. A couple of pakoras were placed for her on a plate, but she was not ready for them.

Nobody back at Padma's needed to know what she was doing, it was better that way, she might work out a solution. Having struggled sleeplessly through the night she had got up and walked out into the dark. She had pulled covers round her to ward out the cold but it was not enough, although she was so moved by what she had seen, the icy drafts around her had seemed to melt away. The night sky, untouched by neon below, shone as a unity of stars. So many pin points of light were discernible as a whole they became a night brightness. And then, a star falling across space like a dying rocket, plunged into nothingness. She decided then that she could not leave them to it, she had to do something.

'Are you coming with something new,' Dickie said. 'If you are bringing the same words take them away with you, but if you are bringing new words—'

'You have to go,' Ria spoke quietly while Mickie brushed the floor, hearing all that was said.

'The same words.'

'I know your dream, Dickie. It's a good dream. I understand it, I know it. It's a good thing you want to do.' Ria wanted to touch her, but drew back. 'But you have to take it somewhere else. You will finish the family.'

Dickie shifted and leaning towards the plate on the bed picked up a pakora and took a bite. 'The old teachings talk of Dharma — the thing we have to do in life. Nice pakora, Mickie. Not too spicy—'

The sweeper beamed, her heavy body lumbering the brush in corners and under chairs.

'Does it tell you where to do it, this Dharma?' Ria said.

Dickie laughed. 'To achieve it is a great struggle for some. Dharma is finding your place in life, in society, what you have to do, and who you are.' Ria nodded. 'Nobody said it was going to be easy. As a hijra you can't set out to be liked, but you must like yourself. Imagine the struggle Gandhi-ji went through to achieve his Dharma. Even when the world is against us, we have to do it. If we do not, we will never find our true selves and our tiny cog in the mass of the universe.'

'You are like — a poet, or prophet, or something,' Ria pulled a roll of twenty pound notes from her pocket. 'I can give you money.'

Dickie smiled, did not move, but shrugged. 'Around five hundred?'

'Pounds are worth more than rupees. You can get loads.' Ria watched him shrug his shoulders in a non-plussed way. 'You know a lot, you're clever with words. Where did you learn that? Your English is so good. The things you say — they're too good for the streets.'

Dickie ignored her question. 'You think that would fix your family's problems? And Bijal?'

'Take it and go.'

Mickie stopped brushing and looked over.

'This place seems right,' Dickie looked her in the eye and Mickie satisfied, carried on brushing.

'Why?'

'Where I belong, under the glass mountains. It feels like home, like when I first knew I was a hijra.'

'People will accept you if you go.' The dust motes rising in the shaft of light reminded Ria of the stars she had seen the night before.

'If I run? Get paid off?'

Ria was getting accustomed to the darkness of the room and could now see how well Dickie's bruises were healing. The patch on her cheek and over her eye were purple, the cuts had gone from red to bloody-black. Ria remembered Madhu's ideas about how to solve the problem and wondered who was really behind the attack.

'It's just like when I was in England,' said Dickie.

'You were in England? When? You learned English there?' Ria found herself getting more interested in her, wanting to know more about her background, why she had gone to England and why she had come back. And was she a hijra in England?

Dickie left her questions unanswered. 'You've all got too much money. You throw it around and think you can buy people's souls. And you can. Not mine.'

'At what cost?'

'Of everything. That's how much it costs to be yourself.'

'All that hurt you cause to other people by being yourself.'

'We have to be who we are despite the world. You think change comes without it? That's it, isn't it? Change is painful for people — they have to look at their beliefs, their prejudices —'

Ria could not stop herself from admiring her. 'Maybe you will be a leader one day. Take it.' She held out the bundle of cash again.

'Have you found yourself, Ria? I don't think you have yet.'

Ria was unnerved. 'I know who I am.'

'Bijal changed. He knows what love is.'

'Knowing yourself is knowing what love is?' Ria said.

'Yes.' Mickie had one hand on the broom, the other on her hip.

Dickie was quiet a moment then said, 'Just because it is a love that the world does not accept does not make it wrong.'

Mickie nodded.

'Bijal has a family. They will go under and get hurt. Can't you see that? God knows what will happen. He's lost the contract, there's no money—' Ria pleaded. 'They'll be out on the streets—'

'Give the money to them.'

'Then what changes?'

'There has to be another way,' Dickie said.

'What way?'

Dickie lowered her head, 'I don't know.'

'Just go, Dickie,' Ria was firm.

It seemed they had come to an impasse and Ria was about to leave, feeling she had failed, but Mickie came and sat with them.

'We need village,' Mickie said. 'Make good friend in village. Every place hijra go, make friend, get respect. We need village. Need village.' Mickie nodded.

'I had a sister like you once.' Dickie picked up a woollen bag with red and yellow string pulls, rummaged and came out with a small model and placing it on his open palm held it out to her. The quartz lump was a tiny range of peaks in Dickie's hand.

'Hah,' Dickie laughed, 'if only your name was not Ria. Parvati was my sister. Headstrong, just like you. Our dad gave us both a little model of the glass mountains—'

The words 'glass mountains' echoed through her. And 'Parvati' — her sister. Full of fear and apprehension, she could not fully grasp what Dickie had said.

'I've always kept it,' Dickie ran a finger over the tiny peaks. 'I've lost all my other possessions on the way but this — this always stays with me. The glass mountains. Beautiful don't you think?'

Ria struggled to understand what was happening. She felt dizzy. It was hard to take in, but Dickie did have part of the model. It must be Hari.

'You can touch it. I keep it so I can remember her, what I was and what I became.'

'Hari,' Ria said to her, 'Hari—'

Dickie was startled. 'My old name? How do you know that? I never use it, it was another world.'

'Hari. It is you, isn't it?' Ria reached her hand out to one of Dickie's and held on. 'I'm Parvati, your sister. I changed my name — like you — I always hated it, remember? At least yours sounded English — Hari,' she laughed through tears.

Mickie stowed the broom in a corner and slipped out through the torn curtain.

'I can't believe it's you,' Dickie stared at her. 'You really are Parvati?'

They held each other's hands for a long time and hugged in the beam of sunlight from the tiny hole in the plastic roof.

They sat in silence for a moment. Ria put her arm round Dickie and she put her head on Ria's breast as she sobbed.

'I wanted you so much, you were the one who knew me,' Dickie choked through tears. 'It is you? You found me—'

'Why did you go? You left no messages, nothing—'

'Dad took me. I didn't want to go. I bawled and kicked. He made me. I never forgot you, never.'

She pulled back and stroked the wounds on his face. 'All this—'

'I wanted to phone you, tell you, Ria but he wouldn't let me. Said they would kill us.'

'Why didn't he take me? All my life, I thought—'

'I never thought it would be possible to find you again. I don't know much.'

She rocked Dickie's head on her breast. 'I thought you both left because of me.'

'You don't know any of it? 'Dickie said. 'Nothing? He wasn't a good father, Ria. You know he kept going off to Manchester. He said he was doing business up there for days, weeks even, you remember? Dad had deals up north with some big Indian guy. There were territory wars going on, mafia-like gangs, drugs, prostitution, the lot. Then it all crashed one day — there was even a murder, life got very hot for dad. I don't know how deep in he was but he had to run, I was too young to know. I was in the car with him one day when he's doing courier work in London and he gets a call — lots of shouting and dad saying: "I can't. I can't." They made dad come to India to shut him up, I think. There was no time, we had to go right away. What could he do with me? He had to take me.' He paused a moment and smiled. 'But that brought me to the hijra.'

'Mum was in bits.' Ria was still shaking with emotion, trying to take it all in.

'He couldn't contact. Too risky. You'd have had the police round your house. Stuff was hidden in your house, and stacks of cash. Big stashes. He had to vanish.'

'So where is he?' Ria said. Dickie shrugged her shoulders. 'You didn't keep contact?'

'He got into things over here, that was part of the deal about getting him out. They weren't going to let him go, he was too important and knew too much. He had to work for Red Hand, the secret security arm of Shiva Sect, the criminal network. I was a kid, but they wanted me in it. Beat me, threatened me. I ran away. My Nayak found me wandering in a market.'

'It's been terrible for both of us.' Ria squeezed her again.

'I disappeared from my dad for months, but he found out and came to where I lived. When he saw I was a hijra he spat in my face. They threw him out. I haven't seen him since — years ago.'

'And now you're a hijra — you are happy? You have found yourself, Dickie?'

'It is not easy. No one is pure hijra without going through with it — all the way. To become full hijra—' Dickie looked up at her.

Ria could not stop looking in her eyes. 'You will go that far? You have to pay? Lots of money?'

'I am saving. One day it will happen and I will be a full hijra, nothing about a man will be with me anymore. Hijra save for years for it. Just for that. We live in poverty for it.'

Ria sighed, smiling at her. 'You will still be my brother. I will say: "I have found my brother at last — she's wonderful."'

They laughed again.

'A special Nayak does it, someone trained,' Dickie spoke quietly. 'You fast, you're kept in a dark cell away from anyone. It's a test, I suppose, that you really want it. Other hijra look after you. We do prayers, puja and burn incense, and the special Nayak midwife comes with a knife and takes it away quickly. Then you hang between life and death, blood pouring from you, and have visions of Shiva-ji in his androgynous body — Shiva encompasses male and female.'

'Dickie, the pain?' Ria shuddered.

'Then you are whole, true, hijra. Change is pain, Ria. But if it is the change your heart craves for the pain is nothing. I am nobody until then. Everything will fall into place, it is my Dharma — a different gender, a new individuality, a third gender to be discovered by the world and recognised. As a full and complete hijra other hijra respect me and will come and join our co-operative.'

She stroked Dickie's hair. 'We will help you find that recognition,' Ria told him.

'There is another sister who stands in the way, Ria.'

'I've got to get my glass mountains back from her,' Ria said.

10

Daya was sitting in the early morning sun reading her book on birds of India as Madhu came out of the house with a basket of clothes to hang on the line and banged them down.

'I'm sure Ria went up there,' Madhu complained to her sister. 'She must have slipped out in the dark. I said she shouldn't go anywhere on her own. I don't know what's up with that girl. Why isn't she on her sister's side? Why isn't Daddy-ji doing anything?'

Smoke was rising down the valley from a couple of distant fires and mixing in with slips of distant misty cloud. Madhu began throwing wet clothes up on the line and ramming pegs on them.

'I was up early this morning — the best time,' Daya said dreamily, trying to hold back her own feelings of distress and anxiety around her father. 'That shimmering light from the glass mountains while people are getting up and things are not too busy yet, and the snows glow with purples and oranges, and the sky rushes past.' Daya watched her sister's movements, the jerking backwards and forwards, up and down as she hung the washing. 'This has all been too much for you,' she closed her book. 'What Daddy-ji has done.'

Madhu snapped a peg on.

'We'll sort this out,' Daya said, 'I'll go to another hotel, get new contracts. You won't have to leave college, I promise.'

'How could he do this to us?'

'We have to accept him, Madhu. We have to keep loving him.'

'No we don't,' Madhu handled the sopping wet shirt Ria had given to Bijal, twisted it into a roll and strangled the last drops out of it. 'We have to be here, but we don't have to do that,' She shook it out and hung it.

'We do Madhu.'

'I want to get married,' Madhu was holding back tears.

'You will. You will.'

'You think — after this—'

The washing swung in the breeze.

Realising Madhu's anxieties about her future, Daya went to her. 'Prem?'

'He's gone. What do you care?'

'He was never going to marry you, his family are rich.'

Madhu shook her head. 'He's gone to Goa to work, his friend said. Gone. He never told me. To find out who he is.'

'Men are always trying to do that.'

'He promised, but he never told me. All his promises — what do they mean?'

Daya took a breath. 'We will talk to Mummy and Daddy and they will find someone.'

Madhu slapped Bijal's shirt on the line. 'Everyone knows about Daddy. You think anyone will want me. They talk and talk. I'll be lucky to get a Dalit.'

'We'll find somebody—'

'You're stupid if you think that.' Madhu smacked Bijal's wet shirt with her fists.

Watching Madhu slapping about Bija's shirt, her anger and anxiety triggered an insight for Daya. 'What then? Madhu? Madhu?' Madhu ran to the house. 'What has Prem done, Madhu? Madhu? No Madhu, you can't be? Madhu? Tell me you're not—'

Daya pushed her way through flapping washing, chasing her sister but was halted by the entrance of Dickie and Ria on the veranda. Daya stared at the hijra, then at Ria, and Ria felt the accusations of her gaze.

'Why have you come here?' Daya confronted Dickie.

Ria went forward to Daya. 'She's my brother, Daya, my lost brother, Hari. It's so exciting. I'm over the moon.' She expected Daya to share her excitement but was perplexed by her reaction.

'I have to go to Madhu,' Daya looked worried as she waved at the kitchen door. 'She needs me—'

'We have to celebrate,' Ria went on. 'It's amazing. She's got the other bit to my model. You remember?'

'You must think of Mummy-ji,' Daya said. 'And Madhu—'

'Show her, Dickie,' Ria smiled at Dickie as she pulled the piece from her bag and handed it to Daya, but she waved her away. 'It's all right. We can work this out,' Ria continued, 'You're always telling me to believe.'

'I don't know anymore. I need to be with Madhu.'

Perturbed by Daya's cold response, she said, 'Get her, get Mummy, Daddy, Sadie — quickly — it's good news.'

Daya was still holding back. 'Not Mummy-ji.'

'We can change things Daya. For the better.'

'Everyone is so upset. And you bring her here—'

Dickie waited.

'We can help Madhu,' Ria said. 'I promise.'

Sadie stepped down from the upstairs bedroom with Krish in her arms and Ria went to her. 'Sadie, Sadie. This is what we've always wanted. Dickie. She's our brother. It's Hari, Sadie. Dickie is Hari.' For a moment Ria believed Sadie would share her joy, but Sadie looked over blankly at the couple. 'She's your brother too. Hari.'

'He's not my brother,' Sadie looked down at Krish in her arms.

'But—' Ria began.

'Madhu—' Daya nodded urgently to the house. 'I've got to look after her.'

Ria stopped her. 'We can work this out. Dickie has ideas. We need your help, Daya.'

'There is only one idea that works,' Sadie raised her head to Dickie. 'Give me back my land.'

'Dickie wants to build a community. We can help.'

Sadie glared at Ria. 'Are you on his side?'

'I want it to be right. It can be.'

'He's ruined everything. Taken everything. Broken the family.'

'We can fix that,' Ria said confidently.

'Yes. Give it back. Now.'

Padma came out from the house unsteadily. The tiredness in her eyes made her look older now to Ria. Daya hugged her mother and was about to go back in to find Madhu as Bijal followed his wife.

'Daya,' Ria called, 'Help us. Tell them.'

The family looked in silence to the eldest sister.

'Dickie is my brother,' Ria told Padma and Bijal. 'It's Hari. It's true, it's Hari. We've got to celebrate.'

Padma and Bijal looked at each other. Padma said, 'Your brother Hari? How can this be?'

'That can't be.' Bijal shook his head. 'Dickie?' And Dickie nodded to him. Ria watched them looking on in disbelief.

'What will you do?' said Daya.

'Dickie wants to set up a business.'

'It's not happening, not on my land,' Sadie insisted. 'Bijal, you've got to do something, it's all up to you.' Bijal shrugged his shoulders. 'Make it right again.'

Ria went to Sadie. 'You want to buy and sell Indian fabrics and goods. You can do it — with Dickie.' Sadie laughed, but Ria ignored it. 'I've got money, Sadie. Some here and stacks back home. My dad's hidden stash from way back. Dickie told me dad must have left it there. It's ours, we deserve it. Let him pay for it. I'll give you money for the land, it sets you up in business and it pays what you're owed for the land. Dickie stays and sets up a commune. Daya and Madhu manage the buying and selling, so everyone gets something — everyone survives. Sadie? Sadie?' Sadie stared at her coldly. 'It can work.' Sadie shook her head. 'You don't want the land, you just want the money. You need it, you and Krish. You can have it. We share out some for Padma's family. We can do it, Sadie. Tell me yes.' Sadie pursed her lips. 'Daya?' Ria appealed.

'And Daddy-ji?' Daya said.

'He has to decide.'

'So he can keep getting the best of both worlds then,' said Sadie. 'With Auntie and with Dickie. Someone should tell him.'

Daya looked at her mother, then at Ria. 'And Mummy-ji. Do you really know what it is like for women in India, Ria?'

'We will make sure she has enough to live well. In time people will accept it.' Ria kept going, feeling more certain of herself. It felt good having her twin with her, it gave her confidence to see events through. 'They will come round, people always do — they'll warm to Dickie's plans. What else is there for her? To be on the road? Now that I've found her? Do we want her hurt and beaten? Or do we want something better for her? We can make it better.' She turned to her brother.

Dickie stepped forward in her long gold and white sari, her gold earrings twinkling in the morning sun, the bruises disguised by make-up. 'I want to build a self supporting community of hijra — a co-operative, but not one that is alone on top of a hill away from people. It must reach out to the families and villages. To do that we must change. Hijra have the same talents as everyone. They can create and build and buy and sell. Then everyone can see what we have got to offer. They can find themselves, go out in the world and be business people, teachers, artists, accountants — politicians even. A day will come when I can walk down the street in my best sari and hold my head up and people will respect me as an entrepreneur who they can approach and work with, someone who can make things happen.'

'Daya?' Ria held her hand.

'Madhu,' Daya pulled away, remembering her sister. 'Where is Madhu?'

'This changes everything. Sadie?' Ria turned to her.

Daya rushed inside, shouting, 'Madhu. Madhu.'

'We must do this,' Ria gesticulated to Sadie. 'Before it's too late. Can't you see?'

Dickie had Ria's hand: 'We must go.'

Padma and Bijal turned to go back inside but were halted by the sound of Daya's call from the house. 'Madhu, what have you done?'

11

A few clouds were hanging around the snowy peaks when Ria came downstairs two days later. A bank of cloud out over the foothills to the east was blocking the sun. Covered in mists and without sunbeams the glossy tips of the glass mountains were hidden.

In the background she could hear the faint noise of a woman slapping washing on a rock down at the stream and the sounds of bus and taxi horns along the road to the village.

Madhu's wrists and inner arms were bandaged and she looked pale next to her sister.

'You can do this, Madhu,' Daya was telling her as Ria watched.

'I'm not going. No.'

'I'll come with you.'

'No, not there.'

Ria had never got on with Madhu, but she felt sympathy now seeing the events had driven her to self harming.

'It's the only way. I will be with you all the way. In Delhi we can get everything sorted for you. Everything.' Daya made her look in her eyes. 'Everything, you understand. They will fix it.'

Hesitating a moment, Ria went over, sat next to Madhu and held her hand. Daya had told her about the pregnancy and the plans to help her in Delhi.

'I'm not staying with them.'

'When things are right — they will find someone for you.'

'I'm not getting married, I'm not going there. Not the cousins in Delhi.'

Still holding her, Ria said to Madhu, 'You want to stay here in the village and face it all? People shunning you, talking behind their hands. You can go away now, and everything will be all right. How will you survive?'

Madhu stared at Daya. 'Don't tell me: "I told you so."'

'I will be there. We will look after you,' Daya said.

'They will make me—'

'Make you?' Ria wondered how they would deal with the pregnancy in Delhi.

'You can't keep it, Madhu—' Daya rubbed her thighs. 'What else is there for a woman? What else can we do?'

'My studies—'

'You can do it in Delhi,' Ria took her hand and rubbed it.

'You think so? That mob think I'm some street girl. They'll get me married quick then—' Madhu continued, 'They'll tell me what to do all the time.'

'You do it for the family, Madhu,' Daya said. 'Not just yourself.'

Dickie entered the veranda with a necklace of saffron flowers, stepped over to Madhu, who did not resist, and put them round her neck.

Daya addressed her sister again, 'Madhu?'

Madhu lowered her head. Sadie came downstairs with Krish and coming over held out the baby for Madhu who turned her away. Sadie took a step forward with Krish and held him to her again, but she shook her head and tightened her hands in a ball.

'Hold him, Madhu—' Ria said, taking her hands and unfolding them. 'It's just a baby.'

'I don't want a baby—'

'Krish wants to go to you,' Sadie nodded. 'Take him.'

Ria and Daya guided Madhu's hands up to the child and she took him tearfully.

Krish smiled up to Madhu, making her smile back while Ria and Daya had their arms around her.

Sadie pulled out an object from a knitted bag, came to Ria and handed it to her. 'Yours.'

Ria unfolded the leaves surrounding it, finding inside a little piece of quartz shaped like a miniature part of a line of mountains. Holding back a yelp of joy, she smiled at her sister.

'Sadie.' She explored it with her fingers. 'The other bit. The glass mountains. Thank you. Dickie. We can put it together.' Ria stood and hugged her sister who held on embarrassed. She kissed her on the cheek and left her, leading Dickie to the wall at the edge of the veranda.

'Sadie, thank you,' Dickie took out his piece and they sat on the wall and put them together, chatting and laughing.

Sadie followed them. 'For a moment the other day I thought we had lost her — Madhu. I realised how much they all mean to me.' Sadie looked abandoned and tired without the baby in her arms. She was pale and had bags under her eyes. She stood watching them and they watched her silently. 'Ria,' Sadie said. 'Give Dickie the land.'

'Sadie?'

'Give it to her.' Sadie's shoulders were slumped, she leaned heavily on one leg. 'Dickie. You have it. The land.'

Ria smiled at her. 'Sadie, that's wonderful, really good of you, you won't regret it. When we get home I'll make sure you get the money.'

Dickie stepped forward to hold Sadie's hands. 'We're together again. You were the girl who stood up for me at school once. I was different, everyone saw that, even when I was little. I was an easy target. You saved me from beatings so much that one day I heard a boy say: "Don't hit him, Sadie will get you." I want to do business with someone like that.'

'You should learn Hindi, Ria,' Daya came over to them. 'It can be so poetic. I should teach you. And a sari for you, or Punjabi Suit.'

'Can we really do this together?' Ria said.

Daya shook Dickie's hand, then she said, 'We can have lots of contracts. We can build up a good business.'

'Without me,' Madhu brought Krish back and handed him over to his mother.

'You'll always be part of us,' Daya assured her.

'In deepest Delhi — with a stupid husband.'

Ria spent the morning on the roof talking with Dickie, Sadie and Daya until they got thirsty and sent Ria down to get some juice.

Bijal was sitting on the opposite end of the bench as Madhu, with Padma standing over her.

Madhu looked over at her father. 'It's you who have to go. Everything you have done to this family, to Mummy-ji.' And turning to her mother said, 'You are a fool if you let him stay. You are not going to give in. He can't keep having the best of both worlds and pulling the family apart. Mummy-ji?'

'Stop that now,' Bijal shouted.

'Listen to your daughter,' Padma said. 'You have found a new life, it's not the one where we are swimming in a waterfall anymore. We loved then, but you have a new love now.'

'I'm still here, still your young Bijal.'

'He has gone now. He lives up a hill on a piece of land, that's where his happiness is. You must go there, that's where you belong now.'

'This is my home.'

'It was, Bijal,' Padma said with tones of sadness. 'But that has gone and our lives go different ways.'

He shook his head.

'You will go, Daddy. If you love us,' said Madhu, 'You will not keep wounding the family. Nobody wants you here anymore.'

He stood, shaking. 'You don't speak like that. Not to me. You have brought shame on us. I am the father of this house.'

'Those days are gone, Daddy-ji,' Madhu spoke quietly.

'I built this house. My wife and daughters do what I tell them.'

Madhu looked up at him. 'The shame is yours.'

Daya had heard her father shouting, and coming down the stairs watched him shaking with rage. 'No Daddy. You leave Madhu. And you leave Mummy-ji.'

Scowling at his eldest daughter, the sides of his mouth down, he bunched his fists. 'You are dividing the family, Daddy-ji,' she said. 'You cannot have both. What about poor Mummy-ji. You will live here and go up there and keep her suffering? That is not right. I love you, but you must go. Yes, I will carry on with the shop, I am still your daughter, but you don't belong here anymore.'

'You tell me to leave my own house, you—' he shouted.

Daya looked him in the eyes. 'If you stay, I cannot help you in the shop.'

'You Daya, my daughter, and you threaten me?'

'No more contracts,' Daya was firm.

'And you will not be part of our new business,' Padma added.

Bijal fumed. 'You don't tell me—' He shook his fist, pushed past Ria and strode off.

Padma smiled. 'I will not cook for him and clean for him, that will make him go.'

They laughed.

Madhu said, 'You told him, Mummy-ji — at last. After all these years, the way he treated you—'

'He put food on the table,' Padma still sitting, clasped her hands. 'He sent you to college. He loved you all. He is still your father. I loved him—' She was in tears. 'He took me to waterfalls—'

'It was hard, Mummy-ji,' Daya said. 'But we are with you.'

'And you are going, Madhu,' Padma was still tearful. 'Like your father, you don't belong here now, you have another world to go to. It will be better in Delhi, a big city with lots to do and people to see. Your auntie there will sort things out and find you a nice boy.' Padma smiled, patting her arm.

Daya led Ria along the path by the side of the house. Clouds had evaporated round the peaks. It was too late for the early morning splendour of the reflected light, but the mountains stood snow tipped and rugged. Below, buildings trailed along the road and houses were dotted up the lower slopes. Above, the sky seemed to move the peaks with its motion of high cloud.

'She will be all right? Madhu?' Ria said as they watched.

'A girl without a husband can't be pregnant, not in the village. How can she survive?'

Ria sighted a couple of buzzards high up, rising on air currents, their wings still as they swayed. 'There's other ways then?'

'If you have money there's always other ways. In the city money can buy you out of all sorts of trouble and shame, money can keep you quiet. Money and career can buy you a husband, money can end a life. A woman in poverty is the lowest form of life. Madhu knows it is impossible for her to stay.'

'I have the money—'

'And we can't repay your generosity, Ria.'

'It's your Dharma,' Ria shrugged, 'Who you become.' Ria watched Daya as she stared up at the swirling birds. 'You're not happy with this?'

'It's already arranged—'

'I know, it's all working out for everyone.'

Daya shook her head.

'Did I do wrong, should have I talked to you first before telling the whole family?' Ria mistook Daya's meaning.

She shook her head again, turning to Ria.

Then Ria realised. 'Madesh? You can't do it.'

'The marriage is set, everything.'

'But you don't love him.'

'Love doesn't have anything to do with marriage for us. Not at the beginning. As a woman you have to learn to love,' Daya walked a few steps and looked back at her.

'And serve — a man. Don't do it, Daya.'

'I have to, to save the family. You don't understand, Ria. What is there for me without that? I have had little education and I can't get work as a woman on her own. Who will support me, what will I do?' She sighed. 'His family know about what's happened with Daddy-ji and they want to go ahead anyway. Many women still don't have choices in India — not like for you in England.'

Ria came to her and touched her arm. 'Did you always know yourself? Like Dickie, from young?'

'Marriage is the only way for a woman here.'

'So you hide it,' Ria suspected Daya was in conflict about her sexuality, but it was for Daya to bring that into the open if she wished, not for Ria to push it.

'India is not ready.'

'You showed me how to change, to know myself.'

'Women have to follow the rules. One step out — and shame.'

'You showed me to be strong,' Ria could hear the repeated slap of women washing clothes at the river again and became confused about her feelings for Daya.

Daya said, 'The business with Dickie will take years to get going, to break the way people see her. I have to hold the family together, help Daddy-ji through his feelings when he lives with Dickie, help Mummy-ji find herself. It's what's expected, it's all about the family's money. We haven't got so much we can live forever. I'm marrying the son of a hotel owner. I can get lots of tailoring contracts. We have to survive. Us poor women are not free. Not even as free as Dickie.'

'Love only exists in Bollywood movies then?'

'It takes a long time for the wheel of India to turn, for women to find their way,' Daya kissed Ria's forehead, causing Ria to tremble a little with emotions for her. Daya smiled at her, 'Perhaps a day will come when this will change —'

Ria held her for a long time and drawing away said to her, 'Let's go and watch the women.' Daya looked at her puzzled. 'The women washing clothes at the stream. The way they slap them on the rock. And chat with them —'

'The same rock — perhaps for thousands of years,' Daya said.

They were about to go when Madhu ran up to them, holding them back. 'I want it — the baby —'

'Madhu?' Daya couldn't hide the shock in her expression. 'On your own?'

'I could see it in Krish's eyes when I held him,' Madhu was excited. 'I'll go to the cousins. But I want this baby —'

'A woman on her own with a child?' Ria said.

'They will help me in Delhi. I will study, get work.'

Daya looked in her sister's eyes. 'You're brave if you do. Is it what you want?'

Madhu nodded and Daya held her hand and led her to the path with Ria. 'We will help you — and the new little one,' Daya smiled and they all laughed.

As they began their descent along the rocky path they could hear Dickie banging her drum and singing on the veranda.

Shiva rules the skies of our intent,

In the morning he rises in the east

And brings us the confusion of daylight,

Trips our ego with his enlightenments,

Throws chaos, hurt and hate,

Falls and dies in the west,

Destruction, death and resurrection,

Shiva brings change,
The certainty of the change the Buddha sent.
Lie down with your love in gardens with fountains,
The world bangs his drum of anger and hate
But nothing will shake us:
Love can move all things — even glass mountains —'

About Neil Beardmore

Leaving school early to work in a factory and buy an electric piano, Neil joined a band, and that paid off as today he still enjoys playing the Blues. He continued to get pleasure from writing as it initially grew from writing songs, poetry, then plays. Later on teacher training opened up the world of literature.

He went on to win the Sussex Playwriting competition and the Richard Burton Poetry Prize. An MA in Creative Writing followed and as a poet published in magazines from Orbis, Cannon's Mouth, and Erbacce to The French Literary Review, he performs regularly.

Pristine in Blue was staged as part of the Milton Keynes Fringe (2014). A stage version of *A View of Glass Mountains* was performed at Questors Theatre, London (2019), along with *The Garden of Izzat Baig* as part of a fund raiser for the Globe Theatre. (Fractured Time Productions 2020)

His wife and best friend Ashra gives him much support, inspiration and laughter. She has opened the doors of India, her country of birth which continues to intrigue, fascinate and mesmerise him. His first novel, *Lemon Seas* (Pneuma Springs 2016) was set there and received much acclaim. He follows that now with further explorations of the country through the eyes of several characters in *Painted Ghosts*.

He and Ashra enjoy painting together.

For more information see his website: neilbeardmore.com

Other Book(s) By Neil Beardmore

Lemon Seas ISBN 9781782284239

Goa – this was the break Rich had looked forward to after a broken marriage and his mother's death. At last he could breathe again on a beach lined with palm trees. The discovery of the body of an Indian dancing girl as he arrives shatters his expectations and he's quick not to get involved. Nina, the wild young singer in a band provides romantic distractions. Dinesh and Frank befriend him and all is going well. Until his world is turned upside down when interrogated by Lakshya, the local Police Chief, a clever, well-educated man who's strong on accusations.

When other dancing girls go missing and another body is found, Rich is prime suspect. The heat is on and proving his innocence is not going to be easy – there's only one thing for it: follow the trail through a tropical paradise of forests and beaches to find the truth. But can he trust those around him? Who can he count on when he goes on the run through the shadows of the underworld? The conflicts of death, a fiery romance and trying to chill become intertwined. Will he be able to stay alive long enough to expose the deceit and cover ups and enjoy this place of paradise?